THE GOVERNOR II

Lynda La Plante was born in Liverpool in 1946. She trained for the stage at RADA, and work with the National Theatre and RSC led to a career as a television actress. She turned to writing – and made her break-through with the phenomenally successful TV series *Widows*. Her four subsequent novels, *The Legacy, Bella Mafia, Entwined* and *Cold Shoulder*, were all international bestsellers and her original script for the much acclaimed *Prime Suspect* won a BAFTA award, British Broadcasting award, Royal Television Society Writers award and the 1993 Edgar Allan Poe Writers award. Lynda La Plante also received the Contribution to the Media award by Women in Films, and most recently, a BAFTA award and Emmy for the drama serial *Prime Suspect 3*.

THE
GOVERNOR
II

LYNDA LA PLANTE

PAN BOOKS

First published 1996 by Pan Books
an imprint of Macmillan General Books
25 Eccleston Place, London SW1W 9NF
and Basingstoke

Associated companies throughout the world

ISBN 0 330 34864 7

1 3 5 7 9 8 6 4 2

A CIP catalogue record for this book is available from
the British Library

Typeset by CentraCet Limited, Cambridge
Printed and bound in Great Britain

The Governor II is dedicated to Governor Vincent McPherson. My special thanks to PJ for his patience and support, and my gratitude to all staff and officers of Wheatfield Prison, Dublin.

ACKNOWLEDGEMENTS

Special thanks to the Prison Service whose co-operation and assistance throughout the series made it possible to be filmed, Derek Lewis, Roy Webster, Deborah Hermer, Audrey Nelson and Patrick Harrison. I would also like to thank the many inmates from various prisons whose lives are depicted in the series, especially 'Charlie Bronson'.

I would like to thank the talented writer Robin Blake, without whom this book of the series *The Governor II* could not have been written.

My object all sublime
I shall achieve in time,
To make the punishment fit the crime
The punishment fit the crime . . .

CHAPTER 1

Wednesday, 22 November

'HELP ME, HELP ME,' screams Helen Hewitt, as she is dragged into a cell by a powerful, hooded man.

As the heavy steel door slams shut behind them, her terrible, rasping shrieks can be heard echoing round the wing. 'Help! Ow! That hurts, you bastard! He-elp! Aaah!'

'Shut up, bitch. Shut your fucking mouth!'

His breath comes in surging, hyper-adrenalized gulps. His eyes are hidden, but Helen can just see his pulsing jugular vein on his flushed red neck. He has her hair tightly bunched in his fist, and is pulling her head back into his chest. He holds a highly polished, razor-sharp knife to her bare neck. He seems to be turned on by her screams. She is terrified, and thinks this time she might really die. Where are the prison officers? Why are they taking so long to make their presence felt?

Suddenly she hears a tentative male voice from outside the cell, and sees a pair of eyes appear at the flap in the prison door.

'Miss Hewitt, can you hear me? Are you all right?'

The prisoner violently pushes Helen aside, and yells at the officer, 'Oi, you! What's your name?'

1

The officer hesitates for a second, and then answers shakily, 'Officer Smedley.'

'Your first name, shithead. What's your first name?'

'Peter. It's Peter Smedley.'

The prisoner's smile is twisted and evil. He momentarily releases Helen, but only to take a new and more painful grip. 'Right, Peter. I want you to get me ten grand. Cash. Used notes. And I want a car. STAY WHERE YOU ARE!'

Smedley has looked round, as if about to move back. To his left stands Jumbo Jackson, bouncing up and down on the balls of his feet. He's itching to get in on this. Just behind him on the other side is Maureen Stapleton.

'Anybody moves and I'll fucking cut her throat. OK. You know my name, do you? You know my name?'

Again Smedley is too slow.

The prisoner almost whispers, 'Johnny Franks.'

Then he roars: 'FRANKS!'

Suddenly Smedley's tongue is loosened. He's looking desperate now. 'All right, Johnny. Just don't hurt her. Don't— Come on, Johnny.'

Franks snarls at him, '*Don't* "Johnny" me, you two-faced piece of shit. Now, you got fifteen minutes. Go on. GET ME WHAT I WANT!' He takes a shuffling step back, dragging his writhing victim with him.

Smedley makes a convulsive movement with his hand. 'I'm sorry. But I can't get that much – that much money, in fifteen minutes – Mr Franks.'

The prisoner and Helen make another clumsy lurch sideways as Franks's strangulated voice bellows: 'For every five minutes' delay – EVERY FIVE MINUTES – she loses a finger. You hear me?'

He kicks the door violently. As Helen screams again,

a long, sobbing shriek, Smedley reaches forward to lift the flap.

Frank's yellow eye is there, anticipating his move. 'What you waiting for? You got fifteen minutes to do what I want. I mean it. I'll cut off her fingers, then her hand.'

Smedley releases the spyhole flap and draws Jumbo and Maureen away from the cell door. Bangs and thumps can still be heard from inside the cell.

'Let's get on the blower,' says Jumbo. His great six-foot-six frame heaves as he draws breath. 'We got to talk to Bronze Command. We need back-up.'

Maureen is shaking with nerves, flicking her eyes between the cell and her colleagues. 'Is that the best thing to do? Shouldn't we keep talking?'

'Don't talk bloody daft,' says Smedley. 'He's going ape in there. Listen to that.'

'But if he does something awful—'

'He's doing something awful now!'

'And he's got to be stopped.' This is Jackson, with all the authority of his ten years on the Wings. 'We got to go in. Do we need the armed-response team? Shoot him?'

Smedley clicks his fingers.

'What about gas? We can gas him out?'

Another terrible, choking scream sounds. Jumbo winces, fiddling with his walkie-talkie, his large fingers clumsy on the buttons. At last he gets it working.

'Hello, Bronze? Negotiating team. We need armed back-up. Repeat. We need armed back-up. There is severe danger to the hostage. Our assessment is to go in.'

*

It took all of the fifteen minutes for Bronze Command to pass the request up to Silver. Silver then had to get the OK from Gold Command. At length the answer came back: permission is given. Weapons to be issued. Hostage cell to be forced if necessary.

The armed team assembled with amazing speed. They were crouched in various strategic places around the corridor, their arms at full extension as you are taught when aiming weapons.

But now, suddenly, Franks was pounding on the inside of the door once more, with new threats this time. He seemed to be laughing. 'Time's up, you bastards. And I'll rape her next – you hear me? I'm gonna rape the bitch.'

There were more bumps and crashes, and a series of whimpering moans from Helen. Suddenly it went quiet. Smedley was about to say something, to give the order, when Franks's voice was heard again, a savage, urgent yell.

'I'm coming out! I'm coming out!'

They saw the steel door move, jerking open just a crack at first, then inching wider. Then, all in one movement, it swung wide and the tall slim masked figure stood there, framed by the aperture.

Curtis 'Jumbo' Jackson, who appeared to have lost all inhibition in the excitement of the moment, jumped in the air and screamed the order.

'Shoot! SHOOT!'

The armed team twitched their trigger fingers. There was a moment of complete silence, then Helen casually raised hand to head, picked off the hood and shook out her long brown hair.

'Well, congratulations, Mr Jackson,' she said crisply.

'Congratulations all round. You've just shot the hostage. You've just killed the Governor.'

'Miss Hewitt!'

Jumbo's face was blank, gobsmacked, unable to take it in. Then with a rich laugh, Dr Williams, senior psychologist at Barfield Prison, appeared behind his 'hostage', Helen Hewitt, erstwhile Governor of Barfield herself. 'You've been had, Mr Jackson,' he observed simply.

Helen looked at her wristwatch. 'OK, everybody, coffee break, then we'll meet back in classroom 4B.'

When they had all filed off she turned on Williams, laughing. 'Cameron! I could have sworn you were enjoying yourself in there.'

'I rather was, Helen. And so were you, if I'm not much mistaken.'

'Well, it's nice to be able to make a drama out of a crisis just once in a while. Have a good strong scream, very therapeutic. And all in a good cause, too.'

'Who is she, Jumbo? How d'you know her?'

The students on the officer's crisis-handling training course were clustered round Jackson, the man with the best information about the woman they'd just collectively 'shot'. He was enjoying being the centre of attention.

'She ran Barfield for a few months,' he boomed. 'During the refurbishments. Then she got the—' He moved the air with his elbow. 'I was told she went to the States to do some research.' He snorted, his eyes rolling around in his head. 'And she needed it, an' all.'

Maureen Stapleton, determined to be a governor herself before long, couldn't hear enough of this. She

5

could never now become the first woman running a major prison. That was Helen Hewitt's achievement and no one could take it away from her. Maureen could always chip away at it, though. 'She wasn't good enough to run Barfield once it was fully operational again after the riot – that's right, isn't it, Curtis? Prison Service gave her a cushy research job travelling round America instead. Sacked her from Barfield because she—'

Someone tapped Maureen urgently on the shoulder. There was a gasp from another female officer on the course. They all turned round to find Helen Hewitt standing in the door, holding a briefcase.

'Hello,' she said firmly. 'My name is Helen Hewitt, I am a Governor 2.'

She moved to the lecturer's table and laid down her briefcase as the students dispersed to their places in class. Jackson crammed himself laboriously into a small desk at the back.

'I've been working in the United States for almost two years, studying their Category A regime, and their hostage and siege procedures. And, for your information . . .' Helen walked smartly across to where Maureen Stapleton sat and took a close look at her lapel name-badge. '. . . Ms Stapleton, I was not sacked from Barfield. I was a Governor 3 at the time and, as I am sure you're aware, to run a Cat A prison you need to be a Governor 2. I applied for the job, of course, but . . .' She shrugged and smiled. The sarcastic edge evaporated from her voice. 'Well, there was someone else better placed, so . . .'

A knock on the door and Dr Williams came in, grinning broadly. He wore a sheepskin coat over his tracksuit. 'Sorry about this. I knew it was touch and go whether I'd get this course finished. But I've got to go

6

almost before we've started. My wife's just gone into the delivery room.'

Helen waved and smiled. 'Go on, then, Cameron. I can cope. And I hope you're feeling strong. Labour's such hard work for fathers, so I'm told.'

'Oh, don't worry about me.'

He left to a chorus of catcalls and cheers, which Helen allowed to die away. Then she moved round to the front of her table and sat on it.

'OK. Let's just discuss a few things about the exercise we had earlier this morning. See what we can recall. Miss Stapleton, start with you, shall we? What was the prisoner's name?'

Maureen sat up, straightening her spine defiantly. 'Er, Johnny Franks.'

'Do you all agree with that?'

Helen's eyes swept the room as murmurs of agreement were heard. Jumbo Jackson well remembered that look from countless briefings and adjudications back in the days when Barfield was rebuilding and she was on the bridge. He remembered her face that morning after the whole of D Wing got pissed on tea laced with industrial alcohol. That *was* a morning-after, Jesus. Set in granite, her expression was. And that other time, when she had to face down the psycho Victor Braithwaite in the security tunnel, with gates locked both ends. Jackson had thought Braithwaite might just rip her head from her shoulders before an officer could get to her. Braithwaite lost his bottle, but, Christ, she looked like a schoolkid lost in a war zone. That was Miss Hewitt: half bulldog, half schoolkid.

'OK. Let's see. Was it a one-man or a two-man cell?'

'One-man,' said Maureen Stapleton.

'No, two-man,' said another student.

The class seemed evenly divided about whether it had been a one- or two-man cell.

'And how many hostages?'

'One,' said Maureen Stapleton.

'Only two persons in the cell, then?'

'Yes. Two.'

'Thank you, Miss Stapleton. You all believe it was Mr Franks's cell because he *told* you that was who he was. But you never saw his face because he wore a mask at all times. The cell door also clearly listed the cell as being occupied by *two* inmates.'

She looked at Maureen Stapleton, whose face was wearing a puzzled frown. 'Yes, not one – two!'

Jackson felt a twinge of hollowness in his stomach, a message which said: 'Feed me.' He had a tube of Opal Fruits somewhere. His hand slid into the pocket of his tunic, which was slung over the back of his chair. No luck. He tried the other side. Where were the cursed sweets? He turned round and unslung the tunic, to give the pockets a proper going-through. Then he heard Helen calling his name.

'Mr Jackson!'

He swung round. That fierce look again. 'I'm listening, Miss Hewitt.'

'I sincerely hope you are because if it had been a real situation you – *you*, Mr Jackson, because I heard you, did I not?, give that order – you would have killed the hostage.' She turned her eyes back to include the class as a whole. 'Let's just talk about guns for a moment, shall we?'

A barely noticeable ripple of movement, of raised attention, ran through the group. Quite a few officers, a

8

minority but significant nonetheless, are fascinated by the subject of firearms.

'The use of guns would only be a last resort. Those of you operating the Command Suites seemed to have no ideas at all beyond firearms.'

'We thought of gas,' volunteered Smedley. 'You know, gassing him out.'

Helen shook her head. 'No. Gas is *never* used. It's too much trouble evacuating prisoners and once you've done it you have a whole area of the prison – might be a whole Wing – out of action through contamination.'

She moved across to the blackboard, stooped to pick up a piece of chalk from the floor and used it to write her bullet points.

'Three basic rules apply to all hostage situations. One: protection of life. Two: negotiation. Three: no concessions.'

She drew a chalk line under the 'no' and swung round to face the students, most of whom were scribbling in their notebooks.

'During the past five years how many hostage incidents do you think there have been in British prisons?' She cocked her head to one side. No one raised a hand or spoke. 'Well, I'll tell you. Eighty. Rather a lot, wouldn't you agree? In sixty of those incidents it was another prisoner taken hostage. The rest were prison staff, as in our simulation just now. Seventy-five per cent of the hostage-takers used barricades.'

'What about weapons?' asked an officer.

'Eighty per cent had weapons present, mostly knives or blades of some kind. To date, we have no record of firearms being used, thank God. Only two of the incidents resulted in serious injury to the hostage – that's pretty good going when you think about it. A high proportion of all hostage-taking is resolved with no injuries to either party. Luckily none of them had Officer Jackson on duty.' She looked at Jackson with a smile.

He would not meet her eyes. Bloody cow.

One of the trainees raised his hand. 'Were there any fatalities?'

'In the past five years, none. But there's always a first time. Never ever believe a hostage situation cannot spiral into tragedy. So let's just look once again at the Golden Rules . . .'

She tapped the blackboard with a scarlet-polished fingernail.

'Rule number one – protection of life.'

CHAPTER 2

SENIOR OFFICER Russell Morgan sat in the 'bubble' and looked out on the Wing. With him was the new boy Hully on his first day – twenty-eight, just. He was showing young Jason how they called lights out.

'OK, we've locked up, we've done the roll call. Everyone's present and correct. So now we can kill the lights – there's the master light switch. Go on.'

Hully threw the switch into the off position. The main lights in the Wing immediately went down, and those in the bubble and around the Wing security gate dimmed.

'What do you notice, Jason?'

Hully looked out. 'Some of the prisoners' cell lights are still on. I can see the light coming through the cracks.'

Morgan nodded. 'Prisoners have switches in their cells. They control their own lighting.'

'What if they're switched off and we want to see in?'

'We can override, of course. There's a switch outside each door. But there's nothing to say they have to sleep in the dark if they don't want to.' Morgan stretched his arms up and yawned. 'Give it twenty minutes, then we'll

11

do a round. I'll give you a run-down on who's to be monitored throughout the night.'

They fell silent. Jason Hully obviously wasn't much of a talker, but his presence reminded Morgan of when he himself was new to the place. Jason was more diffident than the Morgan of ten years ago. He had been cocky, really, with all the swagger you get from a few years in other prisons, not to mention previous years in the Parachute Regiment. But, of course, Barfield had been new then, too. There were none of the old greybeards you get at places like the Moor or the Scrubs (some of them prisoners!) lecturing you on the traditions of the place. HMP Barfield had to make up its own traditions as and when the need arose.

It was built in the 1970s as a showpiece Category B dispersal prison, a forty-seven-acre 'five-star nick' for the South Midlands. It had been an easy-going place from the first. The Prison Officers' Association – in the past a force for severity in the treatment of inmates – was weak, and the Education Department and Psychology Unit had all the real power. They used it, in the opinion of a lot of officers, to mollycoddle the cons. As a result the place got a name for itself as a model liberal gaol, a 'Butlins', where 'rehabilitation' was a buzz word and 'punishment' was one you rarely heard.

Then, two years ago, the dream was abruptly terminated. Put simply, the place was trashed. Amazing how little time it took. After a mere twelve-hour spree of riot, arson and destruction, the inmates were able to wreak awe-inspiring damage: the entire recreational area, the workshops, educational units and three Wings either completely burnt-out or derelict. Not one of the 432 prisoners was unaffected. Most had to be shipped out, their accommodation either unfit or insecure. The rump – eighty-odd men – were the hard cases, the ones no other prison governor would look at. They stayed on in the two remaining serviceable Wings, though with limited and, in most cases, improvised work, exercise and recreational areas. The officers who stayed, with their own canteen and club put to the torch, made do with a Nissen hut for their dinners and snooker.

Russell Morgan had been one of those: he'd been there through the aftermath of the riot, through the rebuilding under the extraordinary but – it turned out – temporary leadership of a thirty-three-year-old Joan of Arc called Helen Hewitt, and now through the reopening of the prison as a spanking new Cat A unit under Governor Keller.

Morgan was one of those stalwarts of humanity without whom the great institutions of the British state – schools, prisons, police, armed forces – would soon fall into anarchy and brutality. But all his life he had been used to men's worlds being run by men. He thought having a woman governor was like giving 2 Para a female brigadier. All the more respect to Helen Hewitt, then. She'd won them over, all the way up to the Deputy Governor himself, Gary Marshall, Morgan's great mate on the staff. Actually, Marshall had been the woman's worst enemy at the start. But then, when she'd failed to get the upgraded job after the rebuild, it was he who'd shaken his head one evening over a fourth pint at the club and first given her billing as St Joan.

'A Joan of Arc, Russell, that's what that woman's been in this prison. Joan of bloody Arc.'

'Yeah, she was good news. But she was too much of a handful for HQ, so the story goes. Now if they'd really wanted her to run the new Barfield, she could have got bumped up to Governor 2, no problem. But they didn't, did they?'

'Seems they wanted to drag her down, Russell. Bastards. Just like the original St Joan.'

'I forget – what did happen to her?'

'They called her a witch and burnt her at the sodding stake, mate. That's what.'

Morgan smiled, remembering the long face of his friend in despair at the permanent wrong-headedness of all deskmen. And then the Wing gate opened and in walked the man himself.

Morgan rose. 'Evening, Gary. You off now? You've not met our new lad. Jason, this is the Dep, Gary Marshall. Jason Hully.'

Marshall nodded at Hully. 'Nice to know you, son. Settling in all right? A minute, Russell.' He drew Morgan aside. 'Got a problem in the morning. Udding's got flu, as well as Michaels and Norton. Leaves us short-staffed in Health Care.'

Morgan rocked back on his heels and lifted his hands as if to push away this threat to his plans for the next day.

'The hospital? Have a bloody heart, Gary.'

'Eh, eh, come on! I got to have an SO on duty. They got three new arrivals coming in early.'

Morgan sighed, shut his eyes, then opened them again. 'All right, I'll do it. Thousands would tell you to stuff it.'

'Thanks, Russell mate.'

'And I've got to be away by lunchtime, Gary. I'm taking Nora to Homecare – we're starting decorating.'

Marshall opened his arms wide. 'What can I say? You're a pal.'

Morgan tapped his friend good-humouredly in the

chest. 'You owe me after this, and don't forget it. If I go straight from here to the hospital it means I've done eighteen hours straight.'

Marshall grinned and, making a fist, jabbed Morgan lightly on the shoulder. 'That's all right, you'll earn enough to hire a decorator, won't you? Oh yeah, there's something else. It's going to be our turn to get the jungle man. He's being transferred back to us.'

Morgan reeled back in mock horror. 'You bastard! Is he one of the new admittances tomorrow?'

'No way. Not to Health Care. We'll have to get the cage ready for him.' Marshall gave one of his graveyard laughs and moved towards the gate. He nodded again to the new recruit. 'Night, son.'

'Night, sir.'

Hully snapped a smart salute and watched Marshall off the Wing. Then he turned back to the Senior Officer, who was already moving out into the Wing, carrying a clipboard.

'Who's the jungle man, then?'

'A right psycho who used to go by the name of Victor Braithwaite. But he changed his name by deed poll. Now he calls himself Tarzan.'

'Tarzan? You're joking.'

'No, son, believe me. I know this bastard. He stayed on here during the rebuilding and he's a bloody nightmare. And look at us – we're already bulging at the seams.'

They were approaching a cell from which reggae boomed out at club strength. Morgan looked through the flap, then hammered on the steel with his fist. 'OK, Snoopy, lower the sounds down, will you?'

Hully had gone ahead of Morgan, stopping to look into one or two of the cells, feeling a little more proud of himself with every lift of a flap. Look at me! A prison officer, doing his rounds. This felt good.

He opened the flap of a cell in which the light had been doused. He put his eye to it and was startled to see, dimly, the inmate's eye looking back at him. He let the flap fall. And then, as the reggae faded down five doors away he heard a sing-song voice, calling his name out of the darkened cell.

'Yoo-hoo, Jaay-son. Jaay-son.'

Hully glanced at the name card alongside the cell door. It told him this particular inmate was remand prisoner Keith Smith. He moved on up the Wing, feeling vaguely uneasy. He could still hear that thin, mocking voice following behind him: 'Jaay-son. Jaay-son.'

And suddenly he didn't feel so good after all.

Unlike yesterday there was to be no simulation at Newgate House this morning. Just chalk and talk. Helen had a lot of material to cover.

'We've looked in some detail at hostage situations. Today I want to talk about the art of negotiation. But first, I will mention what may seem to you a surprising form of hostage-taking: when the perpetrator takes *him-self* hostage. When he goes on a . . .?' She cupped her hand expectantly behind her ear. No? No. It was too early in the morning. 'On a *hunger* strike, all right? Can you see it? OK. Well this is an important subject because, though some of you might be foolish enough to suppose hunger strikes are quite a rare event in our prisons, statistics in fact show this to be far from the case.'

At the back of the room, Jackson's eyes never left the lecturer, though on his lap he was silently pulling open a packet of crisps and easing two huge fingers into it. It was like one of those NASA docking operations: a blind, precision-controlled pick-up. The guys in the group had taken the piss remorselessly over the last week about his eating habits. He didn't want to advertise that he was at the trough yet again.

Helen went to the blackboard and wrote the word WEAPON. 'The thing to remember about the hunger strike is that this is a weapon we're talking about. Remember the way you used to refuse to eat things as a child? You were using food as a big stick with which to conk your parents on the head. Well, surprise, surprise. Adults use this trick too, and for the same reason. To assert themselves. To refuse to eat is a threat. Look at me, you're saying. I can hurt myself and there's nothing you can do about it. For a prisoner to say that is often a tremendously powerful feeling. What does a prisoner want most in the world? Well?'

The class muttered their replies and Helen walked back to the board and wrote: FREEDOM.

'Exactly. And the idea that this is his – or her – only way of feeling free can grow and grow until it becomes an obsession. Then something very odd can happen, something completely paradoxical. The difference between being powerful and weak – between being alive and dead – can completely dissolve. The subject literally doesn't know how to tell them apart.'

Delicately Jackson closed his fingers scissorwise on two or three of the greasy, misshapen wafers and began to withdraw them. Imagining the food already in his mouth, he could feel the saliva trickling around the string of his tongue. Cheese 'n' onion.

It was bloody stupid, all this, to his mind. They were just like a bunch of bloody Sunday-school kids, sitting in their uniforms in rows, listening to an over-educated prat giving them the benefit of her limited experience of life. Life? It was the Book, that was all most of them knew. Jackson had ten years behind him in the Prison Service, four years at Barfield where he'd gone through the trauma of a major riot. Actually, he had to admit Hewitt hadn't done a bad job, and ended by making some good noises about prison being a question of loss of freedom and its purpose was punishment. But Jackson still couldn't quite accept the idea of a woman Governor. Prison to him was a hard man's world, a float-or-go-under school. You learned by the knocks you took. So, with all his experience behind him, what was there some woman could tell him that he didn't already know?

Helen continued to try, nevertheless. 'So how do you distinguish the real do-or-die kind of hunger strike from some local protest about suppers having too much Hole and not enough Toad? Well, I'll tell you a trade secret. After a while, abstaining from food kills the appetite. So if, after five days, the individual is still hungry, then I have to tell you he's not for real. In fact, he's almost certainly getting sustenance from somewhere or other.'

Jackson looked across at Maureen Stapleton. Only yesterday she'd said something about the cons being victims too. Talk about naïve. Often as not they *had* been victims, of course – child abuse, broken homes, taken into care. But Jackson knew better than to play mummies and daddies with the cons. They didn't thank you, they just took advantage. Most of them wouldn't know an act of kindness from a four-seasons pizza. On the other hand they always recognized a soft touch when they saw one. Not a bad-looking bint, that Stapleton.

By now the crisps were safely in his massive palm. He only had to raise the hand as if to stifle a yawn and they would be in there, mission accomplished. Pity he had no

18

Cadbury's bar. He was particularly fond of eating crisps with a few chunks of Dairy Milk, the sweet to vie with the salt, the tang of onion to be luxuriantly smothered under a fat, satisfying mulch of chocolate. Casually his semi-clenched hand negotiated his button-straining stomach. As it floated upwards towards his mouth he simulated a yawn, which instantly turned into a real one. And then, with his crisp-laden palm about to touch down on the pad of his lips, the violent impact of an elbow on his arm forced it to jerk up, the hand opening, the crisps flying away into the air.

'Christ's sake, Jackson,' whispered Pete Smedley, sitting immediately next to him. It was Smedley's elbow that had done the damage, and he was grinning with cruel glee. 'Don't you ever stop bloody feeding your face?'

Helen, interrupted by the disturbance, paused, her eyebrows raised. The rest of the group turned round to get an eyeful. As they did so the half-consumed packet of Walker's slid between Jumbo's thighs and plopped onto the parquet.

'There are always some people, of course, who might *benefit* from going on hunger strike – am I right, Mr Jackson?'

Senior Officer Morgan had come off the night shift on C Wing at 6 a.m. Within thirty minutes he'd had a hot shower, shaken out a clean white shirt from his locker and packed away a fry-up breakfast in the canteen. Now he'd been back on duty for more than two hours. His eyes were scratchy from lack of sleep, but he was ready to admit the three new patients to Health Care.

Old-style prison-hospital wings never bore much

resemblance to a hospital. Many were more like Salvation Army doss-houses, tricked out with drip-stands and crank-up beds. Nowadays they're called Health Care Centres and, at a place like the new Barfield, they come bright, airy and primary-coloured with an atmosphere of brisk, almost friendly efficiency. The up-to-date facilities they can offer mean that sick men from less well-favoured prisons are constantly coming in for treatment.

Officers Brent and Chiswick were standing on the landing beside a row of cubicles – so-called, but cells in reality – arguing mildly over the footballing merits of Paul Gascoigne versus John Barnes. An orderly was wielding his mop in and out of the cells. Morgan, a rugby man himself, appeared and sharply broke up the debate. 'Come on, now. Bloody football can wait, they're coming over from reception. A bit late, but anyway. Have we got their reports handy?'

Brent looked blank. Chiswick twisted his body and scanned the area. All he could see was the orderly's mop-bucket.

'I think the doc had them. Oi, clear that bucket away, please. Prisoners coming in!'

The orderly humped the bucket away to slop it out. Chiswick turned back to Morgan. 'I don't know where the doc is right now.'

A plump, balding man popped his head out of one of the occupied cells and waved a small bundle of reports. 'I'm here. These are the new inmates' medical histories but I've not had time to check them yet. Oh, God, here they come.'

Dr Davyd Harris, posted to Barfield after it was rebuilt and up-rated, was a popular guy, but not the greatest time-and-motion man. Now he bustled up to the convoy of three wheelchairs, each occupied by a man holding a bulging pillowcase on his knees. As if to emphasize the extraordinary demands this job placed on a man, Harris flapped the air with both hands towards the cells. 'One of the cubicles on the far side can be used for my examination. I'll take the first man in five minutes.'

Morgan suppressed a yawn and checked his watch. Five to nine. 'Where d'you want them in the meantime, Doc?'

'Well, in these cells here, of course, Mr Morgan. I believe they've just been made clean and ready.'

The new men were shunted into their respective bays, decanted from their chairs and left to make themselves at home, while Morgan went round checking them off against the list on his clipboard and recording their names on the cards outside their cells. The last one he came to was moving in an almost deliberate parody of slow motion, unpacking a small collection of books and medicines from his pillowcase, refolding a pair of pyjamas, unwrapping a toothbrush from a face-cloth, placing a small Roberts radio on the table. He was a thick-set type, but his face was white as paper and his mouth set in a grim scowl, whether from pain or anger Morgan could not tell.

'Come on, hurry it up, Mr Falla. The doc'll be ready for you in a minute.'

Falla looked round slowly at Morgan and stared hard. But he made no comment. Then he removed a vacuum flask from the pillowcase and began to turn the cap.

Morgan clicked his tongue. 'Start making up your bunk now. You're not that sick.'

He glanced round the cell. Something was wrong. What was it? Hang on, what the hell was that mop doing propped under the window? Must have been left by the orderly. Stupid prat.

'That shouldn't be in here,' he muttered, moving towards the offending item. He knew nothing at all about Falla and even this innocent-seeming mop might present a temptation. Morgan stretched out his hand to grasp the smooth wooden mop handle.

Falla, with his back to Morgan, had the top off the flask. He opened his left hand and began to tip the flask, as if pouring its contents out into his palm. There was no tea in it, though Morgan, intent on recovering the mop, didn't see what the real contents were: a five-inch home-made blade, which looked as if it had been fashioned from a baked-bean tin. It slid out and glinted maliciously in its maker's hand.

There came a point in Morgan's progress across the cell when Falla sensed the officer was further from the door than he himself was. Then he snapped out of tortoise mode and moved like a whiplash, pouncing at the doorway, reaching round and pulling it to in a single movement. Morgan, reflexes dulled by lack of sleep, didn't even twitch until he heard the door go boom. Then his heartbeat went heavy, like a stone. It is what every prison officer waits for. It is what he has been trained, and trained again, to avoid. It is what he always believes can never happen to him because he's too well trained.

But he isn't and it can and now it had.

Falla let Morgan see the blade, holding it up proudly like a kid with a new box of Lego. He jabbed the air a couple of times to show how he'd use the knife if provoked. Morgan eyed the cell's alarm-button, just beside Falla's shoulder. Falla registered the glance.

'*Don't* even think about it, feller. Get over to the bed. No. First drop the mop and kick it over here to me.'

Russell Morgan did as he was told. A blade over a mop was superior force. There was no weapon he could use now except his tongue. He moved slowly, reached the bed, his shins touching the frame.

'And don't look at me. Look at the wall.'

He looked at the wall. A line of graffiti had been written there, in pencil. It said, *Paranoia is a Conspiracy of the Unafraid.*

It was the last thing he knew before a thudding blow struck him exactly where the back of his skull connected with his neck. A fork of scarlet lightning gashed his brain and then velvet blackness descended.

In his office Gary Marshall, Barfield's Deputy Governor, was sipping coffee and wondering when the Governor would put in an appearance. He'd muttered something about an 'outside appointment' yesterday, which usually meant the golf course. The man was besotted by the ridiculous game. Marshall picked up a fax that had just come in about Victor 'Tarzan' Braithwaite and was inserting it on his clipboard just as Len Syons – Wing Governor of C Wing – knocked and walked in.

Marshall waved a hand at the coffee machine. 'Hi, Len. Help yourself. Seen Keller?'

'Bit early yet, ain't it?'

'I wanted to fill him in on Tarzan, our jungle bunny.'

Syons grinned as he helped himself to a cup. 'White but not too fluffy that one, eh, Gary?'

Marshall ran his eye over the fax. 'He's due today, God help us. Since leaving us in 1994 he's been in Wakefield, Strangeways, Walton, Highdown, Belmarsh, Lincoln, the Scrubs, Winson Green, Lincoln again,

Bullingdon, Full Sutton, Frankland. The guy's been in more nicks than Lord bloody Longford. Unbelievable. Only lasted ten days in Bullingdon – eight in Frankland.'

'Well, we know what'll happen,' added Syons, as the phone on Marshall's desk started to chirrup. 'He'll go straight on the Block. Not going to take no chances there, are we?'

Marshall picked up the phone. 'No way. Yeah? Speaking.'

The voice on the other end squawked urgently, and Marshall's face changed. It went rigid for a second, and he stood up as if activated by a spring. When he spoke he was practically bawling into the phone.

'Where's Dr Williams? What? Newgate House? Shit. OK, we'll have to – OK, I'll have to find someone else.'

He cradled the phone and scrubbed his face with his open hands. 'Jesus!'

'What's happened?' asked Syons. 'Tarzan here already?'

'No, worse even than that, Len. Come on.'

Marshall led the way out of the room. Mrs Gill, the Governor's secretary, was standing at her filing cabinet. With a supreme effort Marshall managed not to shout. 'Somebody find the Governor, a.s.a.p. And contact Dr Cameron Williams. Get him back here.'

Mrs Gill preferred to project an unflappable manner, suggesting superior knowledge of such important questions as the Governor's unspoken wishes, the veiled policies of HQ, the mind of God. She thought Marshall was coarse, an over-promoted NCO to be handled with coolness bordering on disdain. But now his agitated appearance startled her. 'What's going on?'

'And I want the records of a new inmate, arrived today. George Falla. I'll contact HQ, press office, police.

There's a hostage been taken in Health Care, and it's Russell Morgan. WHERE'S THE GOVERNOR?'

Mrs Gill smiled innocently.

'Oh, he's around somewhere.'

'Where?'

She shook her head. It meant she knew but she wasn't going to tell him.

As Gary Marshall made his way along the endless corridors of Barfield, forcing himself to walk as fast as he could, he was shaking his head in disbelief. That Gill woman hadn't been able to come up with Falla's records. Stupid cow probably misfiled them. That was why he was on his way to see for himself.

Mentally he was reviewing the procedures to be followed. The idea was for a hierarchical chain of command centres to be set up, connecting the negotiator who was actually speaking to the hostage-taker via a series of links all the way up to the Prison Service HQ. The names of these centres are coded on the metals used for Olympic medals. 'Bronze' Command Suite is sited nearby to the incident controlling movement around the area and relaying information to and from the negotiator. The Governor – Keller if he ever turned up – heads a 'Silver' Command, which can make tactical decisions but not authorize major operations such as the use of firearms or an assault on the hostage cell. All such moves needed a thumbs-up from the Area Manager, John Bunny, at 'Gold' Command sited at Prison Service HQ and linked to the incident prison by radio, telephone, fax and computer links. Gold Command would naturally be in touch with the Director General and the Home Secretary.

These procedures are part of a national plan and, of course, Marshall was breaching them already: he shouldn't go up to Health Care at all. With Keller on the missing list, he was the responsible Governor at Barfield and ought to be in the comms room, a dedicated communications suite stuffed with listening equipment, faxes and video links of a kind with which all modern nicks are equipped. That was where their Silver Command Suite would be set up, providing the necessary links as well as working space for prison officials, police, 'watchdogs' and, ideally, medical and psychological back-up teams.

One problem Marshall could foresee was lack of psychological support. These days every prison has a psychological department, which in Barfield's case was headed by Cameron Williams. His deputy, Annette Bullock, was on leave, which meant right now that there was only young Mullins, fresh out of college. He was hoping someone would tell him what kind of a nutcase they were dealing with, but he didn't fancy Mullins to know. The kid had a first-class degree, yet he didn't strike Marshall as a particularly bright lad.

The shrinks also provided negotiation skills, and they'd certainly need a good negotiator. That ought to mean Williams, who was such an expert that he spent most of his time at Newgate House, teaching others how to do it. He wouldn't be here immediately and so, lacking both Williams and Bullock, it would have to be Mullins.

Marshall's first task was to get Bronze Command up and running, get the cells round the incident cleared and the area isolated sharpish. Probably screen it off in some way. No way should other inmates be too well informed about something explosive like this going on.

The police were on their way. Marshall hadn't even thought whether he was going to need a control-and-restraint team. Maybe Falla would come out on his own. Maybe he wouldn't do Morgan any damage. Maybe he would turn into Santa Claus.

Senior Officer Chiswick was waiting for him at the door of Health Care.

'What's going on, what's he want?'

'He wants the Governor, his mother and – you're not going to believe this – a life-size blow-up rubber dolly.'

Marshall snarled, showing his teeth. 'Is this a frigging leg-pull, Chiswick?'

'We don't know. In fact, we don't know much. Every time we try to see in the cell, he jabs at us with a broken bottle he's stuck on a broom handle or something.'

'How the hell did he get a bottle? How did he get a sodding broom handle?'

At that moment, Dr Harris appeared behind Chiswick, carrying an armful of files. 'I'm just getting these away from here.' He giggled. 'Be a bit sensitive if this man started a fire and they all got burned.'

Marshall shut his eyes. He saw in his mind's eye Barfield ablaze again. Dear God, not that. Not again. 'Look, Doc, apparently Falla's broken a bottle and made a weapon. D'you know how he got his bottle?'

'He had some medication with him.'

Marshall couldn't believe what he was hearing. 'In a *glass* bottle?'

Harris shrugged. 'Well, he didn't get it from me.'

'So what's wrong with him?'

'Inflammation of the bowels. Here's his notes.'

He extracted a card from the pile of folders. Marshall took it and tried to read the medical jargon: 'Enteric

27

inflamm. (pre-ulcerative?). Hyperchlor.? Neg. pyrexia. Treatmt: sod. carb. 1.2 g/2hrly.'

He handed it back. 'Greek to me. What's it mean?'

'He's got gut-ache, heartburn, odd spasms. Convinced it's cancer but more likely there's an ulcer on the way. He's been taking baking soda and a painkiller.'

'Baking soda? Nice to know we're at the cutting edge of medical technology, anyway. Anyone know what the bastard's in prison for? They haven't got his records in the office.'

As Harris and Chiswick shook their heads, a pair of orderlies and an officer entered the corridor. Marshall swung round when he heard them. 'Hey, clear everybody out of the corridors, get them all out. Come on, guys, we got a procedure to follow. We vacated the cells either side of Falla and Russell Morgan yet? Good. And, by the way, anyone spoken to Russell?'

Chiswick shook his head. 'Like I said, Mr Marshall, we can't get near.'

Inside the cell an amateur Gestapo interrogation appeared to be under way. Morgan was on a chair, gagged and bound, his back against the wall. Immediately above him was the grille of the air vent, to which was tied a rope made of torn strips of bedsheet. This rope had been run down tautly to Morgan's neck, wrapped several times around it, taken across the cell to a radiator, wrapped around a pipe and finally extended to the cell door, where it was firmly attached. Sweat dripped from Morgan's forehead.

With the officer immobilized except for his bulging eyeballs, a change had come over George Falla. His pallor had gone and he was flushed with excitement, jigging up and down like a man on methedrine, jabbing the air with the weapon he'd made by sticking a medicine bottle onto the mop handle and breaking the bottom of it.

'How's it feel, Morgan? Let's call this valuable professional experience. Now you know what it's like bein' a prisoner. And it ain't such a lot of fun, eh? Eh?' Suddenly he was shouting at the door, his voice already hoarse.

'Lemme tell you. Just open that door a fraction and he hangs. I got a rope tight round his neck, turned round a pipe and attached to the door. You push on that door and he'll be strangled. You will *hang* him! Got that?'

'Just tell us what you want, George. Tell us why you're doing this.'

It was Brent's voice, pleading with him. Oh, yes. Falla liked the sound of that – a screw pleading.

'I won't talk to anyone but the Governor. And I want my mother. And I want that blow-up rubber doll and . . . yesss!' He gave a screeching laugh and jumped in the air, ecstatic at the idea he'd just formed. 'Yes, that's right. I want to see the Governor blow up the dolly. Got that, shitface? Nobody listens to me. Nobody pays any attention to me. WELL, NOW THEY WILL! Because I can keep this up for weeks, you know. I got food, I got supplies, I got smokes, I got everything I need in here. I got weapons and I want my mother and I want to talk to the Governor about visitation rights.'

Falla's word-flow was running out of control, he was gabbling and spitting.

'I want him to blow up that rubber dolly. I am sick and tired of being treated like an animal. *Sick and tired*! They were poisoning me, I know that. They tried to give me drugs but I'm *not* sick in the head. I AM NOT!'

Outside the hostage cell, Brent grimaced. He was not

qualified for this and it showed because he was getting nowhere. It scared him shitless. Too much was at stake – an officer's life – and Falla held all the aces. So what was holding up that negotiator, what's-his-face, Mullins?

Meanwhile down in Silver Command, Gary Marshall bit his fingernails, preoccupied with a similar question. Where, in God's name, was Governor Keller?

There was a symmetry about the whereabouts of these two men, though neither Brent nor Marshall would have been in any condition to appreciate it, had they known. In the mornings, Barfield's brand new squash court was reserved for the use of staff and, by ten a.m., Howard Mullins had played five close games off the reel with Tom Harbourne from Education, winning the last, the decider, after sixteen deuces. When he returned to the locker room, his pager was bleeping. He didn't even look at it. Bloody thing could wait till after he'd had a shower.

And there was another piece of electronic equipment that should have been bleeping: Gordon Keller's mobile phone. But while negotiating the particularly tricky seventh hole, a narrow dog-leg fairway at the end of which lurked three ferocious sand-traps, he'd turned the damnable device off. After that, so absorbed was he in the game, he entirely forgot to switch it back on again.

CHAPTER 3

BY TWELVE THIRTY Helen's blackboard was a chaos of diagrams, pictograms and bullet points. The trainees were writing furiously. Helen knew she had a tendency to talk too fast, indeed to talk faster and faster towards the end of a session because there was always so much to communicate. But she lacked the patience to proceed, as one probably should, at the pace of the thickest student.

She had now reached the question of how to deal with a hostage-taker's demands.

'As the negotiator,' she was telling them, 'it is imperative you *never* give in to the prisoner's demands. The aim is to keep him talking, keep his attention drawn to you, listening to you, arguing with you. You talk *to* him, not *at* him, and if a hostage screams that she's being raped . . .' She looked purposefully at Jumbo Jackson. '. . . *don't* dismiss the idea.'

Jackson shifted his massive frame uncomfortably in the too-small desk. 'But, Miss Hewitt, if he's also cutting off fingers, how can he . . .?'

'Very easily, Mr Jackson. Men are beasts, didn't you know?'

The class, predominantly male, laughed. It was a

release of tension. This Hewitt woman seemed like a class act, all right.

'Anyway, saying he'll do something doesn't mean he'll carry through. It's a threat, a *real* threat, but one which you have to assess. Get all the information about the perpetrator, keep it on hand. What is his crime? Has he a history of violence or mental illness? Is he on medication? A psychologist will be monitoring your interactions. He will feed you insights until you, the negotiator, know this perpetrator like he was your own brother.'

One of the students had a hand raised.

'Yes?'

'Should food be provided for the perpetrator?'

'No. No concessions.'

Now Jackson was waving his paw in the air. 'But if the guy asks for food, you could drug it, couldn't you? Drug him up. When he keels over, you walk in.'

'Sounds like a nice idea, doesn't it? But remember, some of these men are fantastically cunning. Obviously they're going to be very careful even if they're not raging paranoiacs. So they'd probably make the hostage eat or drink first, and then wait to see if he or she nods off. And if the guy knows you tried to drug him, you've lost him. He becomes very angry, he won't trust you. There's *got* to be trust between you.'

She flicked a look at her watch. 'Right, lunch everybody, then straight back and we'll pick up from here.'

The duty officer put his head round the door. 'Miss Hewitt, I got an urgent call for Dr Williams. Any idea where he is?'

'He's already left. Probably having a baby by now.'

*

Keller sank his final putt around twelve and motored in a leisurely way back to Barfield, looking forward to his lunch. Cook knew it was impossible for him, with his digestion, to eat the basic prison food, so he usually had a nice mushroom omelette or plate of *pasta e pesto*. Keller realized he should do his share of daily tasting the inmates' meals, but somehow it was easier to let Gary Marshall and the other Governor-grades get on with it. And, besides, his food was prepared by the same chef and it was fine, so . . .

When he arrived at his office it was bedlam. Mrs Gill looked as if she had a wasp up her nostril. Marshall was shouting the odds – God, that man could shout! – from the incident room, a few paces down the corridor. People were milling around like Calcutta railway station.

'What in God's name is going on, Mrs Gill?'

'Senior Office Morgan's been taken hostage.'

Keller had been striding purposefully towards his office door. He stopped like a freeze-frame. 'What? Hostage? How?'

'A prisoner in the Health Care Centre's threatening to kill him with a knife unless we get him a – well, a rather unappealing toy, Mr Keller.'

'And you didn't call me? Oh, God, that's right. I remember, I turned the bloody mobile off. Look, you'd better come into my office, Mrs Gill. Tell me everything you know before I face Gary Marshall.'

Five minutes later, he was in conference with Marshall where, thanks to his secretary, he made an appearance at least of knowing the facts.

'He's been in there since nine o'clock, right?'

'Yes,' said Marshall, speaking extra crisply. 'Mullins is the only negotiator to hand, and he's wet behind the ears. We need Dr Williams.'

'Well, he's been called, Gary. On his way, no doubt.' Keller opened a file on his desk.

Marshall gaped. 'That Falla's papers? I been trying to get those all morning.'

'Well, we only just got them.'

'How come we only just got them?'

'I don't know, Gary. But someone's going to get a bollocking because – ' he lowered his voice, 'because it turns out this bugger's done it before, not once but twice. Just did it at Frankland. And before that at Parkhurst, when he actually did it in the Health Care Centre, held an officer at knife-point, broke a table and two chairs to make weapons, the lot, just like here. And we didn't know! Unbelievable.'

'Christ! So what's he in for?'

Keller ran his fingers through his hair as he scanned the file. 'Robbery, GBH. And fourteen offences of assault, property damage et cetera *inside* prison. I mean, this is a very, very violent man. Why they bloody sent him to us, God knows! Now look, Gary, I can't leave the command post. Please will you go and check at reception for that nutter calling himself Tarzan. He's scheduled any minute.'

'OK. I'll sort it.' Marshall heaved a sigh and headed for the door. Half-way to it, he turned. 'I contacted Russell's wife. She's sitting tight at home. He wasn't even supposed to be on duty this morning, you know. They was papering the hall today. When I phoned she had the pasting table all set up. Jesus!'

Five minutes later, Marshall was in reception. He had Victor 'Tarzan' Braithwaite's file in his hand and was watching the closed-circuit television screens showing the prison approaches and reception yard. A police car heralded the coming of Tarzan, followed by a Category A prison van and two more squad cars to shepherd them in. The first car and the A van came through while the shepherds parked outside the gate. On parade in the delivery zone a team of three officers in control-and-restraint gear stood ready to escort the wild man to reception. A blanket had been asked for, as the protocol on transporting Victor Braithwaite was that he was virtually naked throughout the trip.

The A van opened and Tarzan was brought out. From the moment he breathed the fresh air he was twisting this way and that, irked by the grip of the two officers on each side of him and the body-restraint belt which pinioned his arms to his waist. Apart from the belt he wore only shorts.

'Bloody chaos over in Health Care,' Marshall was saying as he watched. 'Williams isn't here, we've got Mullins and the doctor having kittens trying to talk one nutter down, and now here comes the biggest nutter of all time.' He flicked the file with his fingers. 'And according to what it says here, this one's a sane nutter. We've got it on file, so it must be true.'

What it all amounted to was a mystery to Marshall. Years in the Prison Service, and he'd seen time and again how helplessly at sea they could be with real animals like this one. The money it cost shuffling Tarzan around could have built him his own private mental home – or zoo.

The reception officer spoke into the radio. 'Ready when you are, guys.'

On screen they saw one of the helmeted C-and-R officers raise his own radio. 'We're taking over custody now. He's got a new gig, by the way. He spits like a llama.'

Marshall turned and snapped his fingers. 'You got that blanket? Give it here!'

He bustled out into the open air with it. Tarzan was still making life difficult. He had to be pulled along and was mouthing insults and obscenities. Marshall could see he had chosen his alias well, for his huge body was gym-built on monumental lines. Several nasty scars could be seen on the skin, but the most spectacular was a deeply gouged ravine running up his neck.

Marshall thrust the blanket towards a C-and-R man. 'Get that over his head and stop wasting time.'

But the words brought a change like a magic charm. Tarzan suddenly stopped struggling and raised his head. He smiled in recognition, then his lips curled back and a jet of saliva spurted out. It caught Marshall on the right cheek. The Barfield Deputy Governor knew better than to show anger. He merely took a handkerchief from his pocket, wiped his face and pointed at the blanket. 'Wrap him in that and drag him inside. Move.'

Then Tarzan laughed, showing faultless teeth. 'No need for that, pal.'

He looked around, sniffing the air, his nostrils dilating. 'Block all nice and ready for me, I hope. Well, the show's over, so let's go. And nice to see you too, Mr Marshall.'

After the reception formalities were over, Tarzan was taken direct to the Punishment Block. He held his fantastic body as upright as possible, the shoulders set square, and wore a proud look on the face. With the body-belt holding him in restraint and the woollen blanket thrown over his shoulders like a cape, he was thinking of Kirk Douglas in *Spartacus* on his way to be crucified – which, of course, was itself a reference to Jesus Christ, on his last walk up the hill. Mocked, abused, unbowed, that was the style. And as far as Tarzan was concerned they were three of a kind.

The journey involved a passage through open air, not far from C Wing's exercise area. As soon as the small detail appeared in view, a knot of prisoners raced to the corner of the yard, cramming into the angle of wire mesh to get a good gawp. Two cell-mates, Brian Samora and Eugene Buffy, were at the forefront, jiggling the wire, almost climbing it. Samora was even more excited than the rest.

'Eugene, it's him. I was right, see? It's him, like I told you.'

Keith Smith, the remand prisoner, was trying to barge into the space between them.

Buffy did not like Smith. 'Gerroff me, Smith,' he growled. 'Stop pushing.'

'Is that the bloke holding Morgan hostage?' shouted Smith, ignoring the warning.

'Like fuck it is,' said another man behind him. 'That's Tarzan.'

The noise from the group in the exercise yard, directed at the officers around Tarzan, began to rise to a crescendo of whistles and yells of abuse. Prisoners react like a pack of dogs when they see a man being paraded around in a body-belt. Someone started a chant.

'TARZAN! TARZAN! TARZAN!'

In seconds they had all taken up the cry. Now walking away from them, the prisoner half turned and they could see his face. As far as the belt would allow him, he gave them a thumbs-up.

'Yes, it's Tarzan,' shouted Samora. 'It's the King, he's back! Victor bloody Braithwaite's *back*! See that thumbs-up, Eugene? That was for me. I told you I knew him. He's my mate.'

Trying to leap up to see better, bespectacled Eugene Buffy received another dig in the small of his back from Keith Smith.

'I hate being pushed, you bastard. I'm trying to see.'

Smith snatched Buffy's glasses and tossed them up in the air, over the top of the crowd.

'Can't see nothing now, can yer?' he jeered, retreating backwards out of the mob. Buffy started to claw his way through the crowd in pursuit.

Smith got no further than the fringe of the crowd when he felt a tap on the shoulder. He turned and Buffy's fist exploded with crude force into his nose. He spun into clear space, Buffy following. He grabbed Smith by the arm, leaned back and began to spin, hurling his tormentor into the mesh fence.

An officer saw what was happening. He blew his whistle and now he and several of his colleagues were running towards the disturbance. The mob of inmates dispersed fast, except for Buffy and Smith, the one with unfinished business, the other unable to escape because Buffy's punches were mashing repeatedly into the soft tissue of his face. Samora, too, stuck about, dancing around the shindig, trying to place stylish but ineffectual kung-fu kicks on the back of Smith's neck.

When the officers connected with the fight they wasted no time. Three of them moved immediately between Buffy and Smith. The fourth caught Samora's foot in mid-kick and twisted it. The martial artist teetered for a moment and with a gurgling cry went down. In between his head and the tarmac lay his friend's glasses. They smashed like a nut under a stone.

*

In Health Care, young Mullins had retired for a smoke and now Dr Harris was sitting on a stool beneath the flap of the hostage cell. 'Come on, George, this has gone on long enough. Can't we just see if Mr Morgan's all right? It's the doctor here, George. Won't you let me just see him?'

He held a rubber-encased gripper in his hand, a device that would allow him to open the flap without putting his hand on it.

'I'm opening the flap, George. I just want to talk to Mr Morgan. I want to make sure he's all right.'

He pushed the gripper up to the flap and closed its jaws. But as soon as the flap moved, it was crashed into by a broken bottle fixed to the end of the mop handle. The makeshift weapon poked wickedly out through the flap, jabbing back and forth. Suddenly Harris had had enough of patience and reason. He reached up and grabbed the shaft of the mop handle. He stood up and with all his strength he yanked it outwards. He heard a satisfying thump on the door as Falla, trying to hold onto the other end, lost his balance and cannoned into it. Then the home-made spear came away and flew across the corridor before clattering to the ground. Several officers, standing as if mesmerized, had to jump out of its path.

Morgan had now sat gagged, immobile and noosed for five hours. He watched with jacked-open eyes as his captor catapulted forward and slammed his face against the door. Falla froze for moments in this position, then deliberately levered himself away from the door and turned to Morgan.

'You saw that! That could've broken my fucking nose, that could. Well, it gave me a headache instead. BAS-TARDS! *I got a headache now!*'

He looked around the cell. What to do? He picked up a Lucozade bottle, but it was plastic and useless. Things ain't what they used to be. He reached for his knife and examined it. Never been used in action. Took him a week to make it but it was nearly as sharp as a cut-throat razor. He looked at Morgan, considering. What part should he start by cutting off?

Under Morgan's chair was a damp pool. 'Here, you pissed yourself.' He moved closer. 'You know, if they do open that door, it'll pull you off your chair and then your neck'll break. You do know what happens when you get strangled, don't you? All your bodily functions happen, just like that. One last time, you might say.'

He lost interest in cutting bits off his hostage. Instead he went across to the table, where the radio stood. He switched it on. 'Bit of music, eh? Bit of nice country and western.' He got a golf commentary instead. 'Shit! I want the local radio. I want the news. Oi! You lot. Where's the local radio on this dial?'

Harris's voice came shakily from outside. 'I don't know, George. Do you want me to find out for you?'

'Course I do. Why d'you think I asked?'

'Well, you know, George, you'll have to give us something. I mean, we're doing everything for you, everything we can to help you. You do want medical attention, don't you?'

Falla kicked the door, and turned to Morgan, waving the blade in front of his eyes. He edged it near the gag and slit it, releasing Morgan's mouth. 'You know it?' The blade was against Morgan's cheek now, pressing in, the blood seeping up on either side of it. Then Falla pulled it back. 'Oh, sorry about that. You *do* know how to get local radio on this thing, don't you?'

Morgan's voice was hoarse, barely audible. 'Just

move the dial a bit to the right of this. That's what I do.'

Falla picked up the radio and tried it, finding country and western music. He scrutinized the dial. 'This it? 1-5-4-8.'

'I don't know. I don't know the exact numbers.'

Falla turned up the volume until Kenny Rogers filled the cell. 'What *do* you know, *Mister* Morgan? What do you know about men like me? About why I'm doing this to you? OK, I'll tell you why. BECAUSE NO ONE PAYS ME ANY ATTENTION!'

Morgan squirmed in his chair. He cleared his throat and tried to clear his head, still throbbing from the blow he'd received. Falla was dangerously unpredictable. It was time to start working to save himself.

'I'll pay you attention, I'll listen. You got *me* here, George. I'll listen to you.'

When it reassembled, Helen's afternoon class was depleted by one.

'Mr Jackson had enough of me, has he? Not rejoining us?'

'No, Miss Hewitt,' said Officer Smedley. 'He was recalled to Barfield during lunch.'

'Oh? Something must be up. Pity.'

She resumed her teaching position, sitting on the table. 'Now, the security of our modern prison cells has made it impossible to get out via a window. Can't even see out. Same with doors. Paradoxically, that helps the hostage-taker because what you can't do from inside to out is also true the other way.'

A student shook his head. 'But we've perfected removal of doors. It can be done in under a minute.'

'I've seen it done in the States in three seconds, actually. But the problem is, you can't see inside the cell – you can't see if it's booby-trapped in some way. So it's always highly risky to go blast in through a door. Any other suggestions?'

At this moment a uniformed officer, whom Helen recognized from reception, appeared outside the classroom door. He tapped on the window pane. 'Miss Hewitt? You're wanted on the phone, HQ. They say it's very urgent.'

Five minutes after that Helen was in her coat, running across the car park. An unfastened briefcase, threatening to spill all its papers, was in one hand, the key of her Range Rover was in the other and a large smile was decorating her face.

She could cover the distance in an hour. It was fifty miles to Barfield.

CHAPTER 4

JUMBO JACKSON had walked into the Silver Command Suite and found a scene of hubbub and confusion. Two fax machines buzzed and beeped. Keller sat hunched with a CID officer over a PC console, going over Falla's file. Next to them a second computer, this one dedicated to e-mail, was attended by a uniformed officer while a detective sergeant took the statements of officers Chiswick and Brent, witnesses to the events earlier that morning in the Health Care Centre. There were at least three phone lines. Len Syons was on one to John Bunny's PA at Headquarters and the press liaison officer was using another. A third bleated in vain while Mrs Gill stood with a sheaf of letters, hoping to intercept Governor Keller and get his signature.

Jackson, having just arrived from Newgate House, reported his availability as a negotiator to the Governor and was told to stand by. He spotted Gary Marshall, wearing headphones and sitting with negotiator Mullins, trying to listen to the live relay from the hostage cell, where, at last, a microphone had been brought into use. Jackson moved across to join them, almost bumping into a prison officer as she hurried in from the kitchen with an enormous platter of sandwiches.

The speaker was mounted on a trolley, along with a two-deck tape-recorder and other audio equipment. Jackson leaned over and pressed his ear to the speaker. The quality of the bug was not very good. Falla had been coming through best when he was on form, shouting the odds about not being listened to and nobody respecting him: the softer talk was indistinct, to say the least. Much of the time Falla was apparently muttering to himself. In the background music could be heard and nasal disc-jockey prattle. There was also much banging and calling out as noise spilled in from activities outside the cell door.

'What's going down, Gary?'

'I don't know. Been a change. I think the gag's off Russell. I reckon him and Falla are talking.'

Mullins chipped in. 'That's a good sign, I think. Falla's beginning to feel isolated, lonely. Morgan's a very experienced officer. He might be able to play on that.'

'OK, Russell's not an idiot,' said Marshall. 'But he's very, very tired. And tired men can't always think straight, that's what's worrying me.'

He turned back to the audio feed, trying to visualize the inside of the cell, Falla's body language, Russell Morgan's face. Every now and then the thought broke through of Nora Morgan in suspense at home, with the cordless on one side of her and the pasting table on the other. He'd call her again in five minutes.

On C Wing the telephone was placed in a barred pen to which prisoners with phonecards had access only under the eye of an officer and strictly one at a time. Keith Smith had to wait until the rastaman, Oswald Snooper, had finished an interminable conversation with his wife.

Then at last he got to it, ramming the card into the slot and keying the number he'd memorized from the radio.

He heard a Barbie-doll voice answering: 'Thank you for calling Fifteen Forty-eight. Your call is being held in a queue . . .'

He danced up and down impatiently and transferred the earpiece to his other ear. Ouch! Mistake. The ear was puffy and tender. It had taken a nasty rap from the knuckles of that bastard Eugene Buffy.

'Hello, you're through to Fifteen Forty-eight. How may I help you?'

'I got some information for you. News story.'

'Will you hold, please? I'm putting you through to the newsroom.'

There was a pause, then a hoarse-voiced guy came on. 'Yes, newsroom.'

'I don't want to give my name, mate. I'm calling from Barfield Prison. I got a big story.'

'I see. What sort of story?'

'All I want is a record request. For my wife.'

'Well, I don't deal with record requests, friend. Let me just talk to someone.'

'Can you hurry it up? My phonecard's going to run out.'

A queue of prisoners waiting to get on had formed beside the steel grille. Some of them were tapping the bars with the edges of their phonecards.

'Come on, come on,' whispered Smith. 'Oh, hello? Yes, I want it played three times, yes, three times, please. For Sandra Smith – yes, San-dra Smith. Roy Orbison, "It's Over". Got that?'

'OK – what's the news story?'

'There's an officer, a prison officer, being held hostage

45

– since nine o'clock this morning. He's a Senior Officer called Russell Morgan.'

'And who is holding him hostage?'

'I don't know. New inmate, that's all. But he's armed and very dangerous. He's got the officer's neck in a noose and – SHIT!'

The time remaining on Smith's card expired and the line shut down. He held his position for a moment, then replaced the receiver and grinned. Oh, well, he'd got the message across, and the request. Sandra would be well wound up about that. Bitch.

In Silver Command, Officer Jackson was giving anyone who'd listen the benefit of his truncated training course. 'They got to just keep him talking. Try and get him to discuss his case. Exactly why he's doing this, make him explain it. Mr Keller, can't I get up there and have a go, sir? What with just being at Newgate, it's all fresh in my mind, like.'

'Thanks, Jackson, we may be needing your skills in a little while. But Dr Harris is on it right now and HQ's sending in an experienced negotiator to stand in for Dr Williams, to be with us in . . .' he looked at his watch, 'half an hour, if all goes well.'

Marshall turned sharply when he heard this. 'Half an hour? That's great, that is. In the meantime Falla's screaming blue murder about being fed arsenic or something. He thinks someone poisoned him.'

'Let me have a go,' urged Jackson.

Marshall stuck out his lower lip defiantly. 'Anyone goes down on the Wing it'll be me.'

'I been doing the training course. That's what I been *doing*!'

Keller broke in, placing a hand on Marshall's sleeve. 'As Deputy Governor, Gary, you go in and it's a complete breach of rules.'

'There's been more than a few breaches already, Governor. All right if I take my break now?'

Keller nodded. 'Go on. But for Christ's sake be back in an hour.'

Morgan was screaming. It was the kind of screaming most grown men only ever do in their nightmares, but this was no dream. Falla had the knife blade on his throat, the point pushed just a millimetre into the skin, and was moving it down from the angle of the jaw. He was drawing a thread of blood – thin, red and wet – towards his Adam's apple.

'I told you, Morgan. Don't try talking to *them*. Next time you talk to *them* you're dead. One word! You can only talk to *me*. OK?'

In spite of the knife in his skin, Morgan nodded fractionally. At the same moment Falla's face changed. It creased into a hideous grimace, showing the man's long uneven teeth, edged with nicotine stains. He staggered back and held his stomach. 'Jeee-sus! See? I've been poisoned. I *know*! And I know who's been doing it but they refused to listen. It's arsenic. I read up on the symptoms and I've got them.'

Morgan shut his eyes and tried to rest his head. If he let it fall back a little to the left, it leaned against the rope coming down from the air-vent grille.

'You've got inflammation of the bowels. That's all, George.'

Falla's face distorted in a sudden tantrum of rage. 'I *have not*! I know all about that. That's what they said my dad had. Infla-bloody-mation of the bowel. He died in agony, Morgan. It wasn't no inflammation of the bowel. It was cancer.'

He sank to his haunches, head bowed, mumbling as he tapped the point of the knife against the floor. 'I can't die like him. I'll kill myself first. It's arsenic. I'm sure of it. The bloke in the cell next to me, that's what he was in for. He did a whole factory of people, arsenicked them.'

Morgan roused himself. *Keep the bastard talking.* 'But how would he get arsenic in prison, George?'

'One of his visitors could have brought it in. Passed it over like they do with the heroin. He didn't like me, that prat . . .'

Morgan kept his next thought to himself as he watched his captor endure another spasm of gut pain. He was bent almost double, leaning against the wall, his eyelids screwed shut, his lips stretched white, and Morgan thought the sight of George Falla hurting was not unpleasant.

When he spoke again, Falla's voice was thin and wheezy. 'Know something, Morgan? I – haven't – had – a – woman – in *eight* years!'

Suddenly he threw himself at the steel door, hammering on it, screaming, 'WHERE'S MY RUBBER DOLLY? OI! YOU OUT THERE. I WANT MY RUBBER DOLLY, NOW!'

With the Range Rover's sound system tuned to the local rock 'n' roll station, Helen drove fast, relishing the size and power of the machine. The car wasn't hers, which gave her even more of a buzz. For Simon Lennox to let her have unlimited access was a real act of faith. He adored these wheels, called them 'My Pet Monster'.

48

Maybe it meant he adored her even more. Now *there* was a thought.

She'd had no car since selling her beloved Jag when the Service sent her to America for five months – money she'd used over there to buy an old sixties Chevy, which took her on a Cook's tour of every type of correctional facility, from the huge state-of-the-art Federal institutions like Oak Park Heights, Minnesota, to state penal colonies in the Deep South where they were re-introducing chain gangs and gas chambers.

That trip had gone a hell of a distance towards compensating her for losing Barfield. Because that's how she'd felt about the way Gordon Keller got that job. OK, they'd upgraded it, made it the site of one of the Special Secure Units and upped its category from B to A. But Barfield had been *hers*. She'd not only overseen the plant's rebuilding, she'd rebuilt the morale of the staff too. And there'd been rough times, no doubt about it. To have gone through all that and not reaped the benefit was a bitter mouthful. But now! Now she was on her way back to Barfield, on a special mission. To talk down a maniac. Suddenly her confidence was turbo-charged. She felt great. She was on her way back!

Purposefully she changed down and surged into a long bend. Beyond it was a stretch of Roman road, straight as a ruler. Helen switched on the carphone, punched John Bunny's number and turned down the radio.

'Hello, Mr Bunny? I'm on my way to Barfield now. I'll need this guy's family history, his entire prison and medical records. And, at all costs, whoever's negotiating with the perpetrator at Barfield must not in any way give in to his demands.'

Bunny started to tell her what he had in place at the

prison, but now Helen was not listening. Something on the radio had caught her attention. She said, 'Can you just hold a moment?'

The music had ended and the DJ was talking.

'. . . just heard that this very minute, as I am speaking to you, a prison officer is being held hostage by a raving madman at Barfield Prison. We hope, we pray, it will soon be all over. And now a request from the inside – Roy Orbison: just for you, Sandra Smith.'

She turned the volume down and went back to Bunny. 'Does Governor Keller know there's a broadcast going out live and the guy's going on about a hostage situation at Barfield? . . . I'm listening to it, right now.'

CHAPTER 5

T HE LAST TIME Helen had felt Gordon Keller's icy handshake was when he'd toured Barfield with the Home Office top brass two years earlier. That day their roles had been reversed – she the Governor of Barfield, he the visitor with the critical eye – and she'd known then there wasn't any love lost. Who cared? It sounded like Keller wasn't quite as flash as he thought and his team had got themselves into a hell of a dither over this hostage. Knowing he didn't like her would make Helen's task all the more of a pleasure.

As they stood face to face in his office, his eyes clearly betrayed him. Helen Hewitt was the last person Keller had expected or wanted coming in to set his house in order. His 'Nice to see you' had that 'I'd rather spit on your shoes' ring to it.

'HQ's given me most of the details about Falla,' she said briskly, dispensing with the niceties. 'But who's the hostage?'

'Senior Officer Morgan. Russell Morgan. You may remember him as he was here when you—'

'Did my caretaking job? Yes, of course I do. Poor Mr Morgan, a good officer.'

She glanced around. The office was much larger than

when she'd had it. Keller had knocked through into the next-door conference room, redecorated in approved big-wig fashion, established a bonsai rain-forest in one corner, built a huge wall of bookshelves and stuffed them full of legal and criminological tomes.

'Good heavens, you *have* had this place made over. Very impressive.'

Keller cleared his throat and walked round to the other side of his large desk. He pointed to a scaled-down model of the Health Care Centre, which lay on the polished mahogany.

'He's being held in this cell, right at the end. Falla says – but we can't be sure – that the door is rigged to hang Morgan if opened.'

'Hmm. Well, the door opens inwards, which suggests that might be difficult to achieve. But we have to take his word on it.'

A file lay beside the plan. Helen picked it up and opened it. An incident log – a minute-by-minute account of everything that had happened in the Health Care Suite since nine a.m. It wasn't as detailed as she would have liked.

'What's this? Where on earth did he get a "possible half of broom"?'

'Mop handle, actually. Left in cell. We're really short-staffed after—'

'Does Falla have a radio with him?' Helen was not going to stand there listening to Keller's whining excuses. 'Because you *do* know they're talking about the hostage on air?'

Keller stood rooted, staring at her. 'You're joking. Nobody even knows about this situation for the simple reason that it's contained in Health Care.'

Helen smiled. She *was* enjoying this. 'Well, they

obviously do know. And the last thing we want is the local-radio wide-boy making a meal of this with Falla listening in. Better contact them.'

Keller was on the point of reminding this bloody woman of their relative positions. But he sensed that to argue the toss with her might be disastrous. He kept his temper. 'If you're ready, we should go down. The negotiator will need a break.'

Helen was still reading. 'Go down? Oh, no. I won't be interacting personally with Falla. I'm just here to give my advice on how to handle the negotiation.'

Keller frowned and looked at his watch. 'You see the thing is, his demands . . . I mean, they're bloody ridiculous. He wants us to send in a blow-up rubber doll!'

Helen favoured him with an ice-queen's smile. 'After he's watched you blow it up for him, I gather.'

She opened the file, put the incident report with the other papers and snapped it shut. 'Well, all right, then. Let's see what I can do.'

Keller was already at the door. Now he opened it and made an ushering gesture. 'After you, Miss Hewitt.'

Yes, thought Helen. You were *after me*.

The first person she saw when she walked into the Health Care Centre was Gary Marshall. Helen had been looking forward to seeing him again, a man of intense loyalty to what he believed was right. Her arrival as Governor at Barfield three years ago had been a great shock to him, because it was a job he'd expected to fall into his own lap. Marshall and the other more traditional members of staff had felt that she would be bound to injure the system unless they protected it against her. Yet it turned out that Helen had only to prove herself and she automatically won Marshall to her side. He didn't harbour resentment for being shown to be wrong and she liked him for that.

Off the Health Care Centre's waiting area was an office that had been converted to the Bronze Command suite. When she walked in Helen could hear the noise of telephones, faxes, argument. She didn't expect to see Gary Marshall there and, in fact, she knew he shouldn't be there. Quite apart from his personal involvement – as Russell Morgan's best friend – it was against the letter and spirit of the procedure officially laid down for hostage situations if a Deputy Governor was anywhere near such an incident.

But apart from that, coming in from the corridor where his mate 'was being tortured by a borderline psychopath, the man looked completely done in.

'Sit down with me a minute, Gary.' She gestured to a seat.

Marshall tried to smile a greeting: it was more a weary twitch of the lips. 'He's been in there since nine o'clock this morning, Miss Hewitt. Don't you think we—'

She put a hand on his arm. 'That's why I'm here, Gary – to do the thinking. So let's just sit down a moment.'

He sat down heavily, but didn't relax. He was ready to leap up again at the slightest alarm. 'I knew from Dr Williams you were at Newgate. We was wondering if they'd send you to help us out.'

Helen moved a pile of magazines from a low table and sat on it, balancing the file on her knee. 'You shouldn't be in here, Gary.'

'I'm not on duty. I'm on my break.'

Helen sighed and let it go. 'How's Morgan?'

'He's taken the gag off of him.'

54

'Is the doctor the main person Falla's been interacting with?'

'He was. But he's exhausted and the prison negotiator didn't do too well. Falla became very hysterical, saying he'd been poisoned. So now Governor Keller's let another officer have a go.'

Helen blinked. Have a *go*? She looked at the incident report to see how long this new negotiator had been on the case. It hadn't been logged – must be a recent changeover.

Marshall didn't wish to see her reading a file. He wanted action. 'Can you get Russell out of there or not?'

'That's what I'm here for.'

'Oh, bloody marvellous.'

'Gary, you obviously find that hard to take, but you'll just have to trust me.'

As she said it, the words were echoed by a booming voice coming from the incident corridor, cutting through all the noise from Bronze Command.

'WE WANT TO BLOODY TRUST YOU. WE GOT TO GET SOME TRUST GOING HERE, MATE!'

Helen looked up, alerted. The voice was angry, familiar. 'Who's that?'

'Officer doing the negotiating.'

She moved swiftly to the door connecting with the hostage corridor. The immediate surroundings of the cell door had been screened off with tarpaulin and the furious voice was coming from behind it. '*One* minute you say you won't harm Officer Morgan. Next you're going to bloody *kill* him. Well, how d'you think that makes *us* feel, out here?'

Helen turned to Marshall and pointed down towards the screens. 'Is that . . .?'

Marshall nodded. 'He's taken over from the doctor. Curtis Jackson. You remember him, he—'

At this moment Officer Jackson could be heard giving voice to a fluent stream of obscene expletives. Helen tapped Marshall's shoulder. 'I suggest we get Officer Jackson away from the perpetrator. Right now!'

Inside the cell, the air was thick with bodily odours induced by fear. Falla was sitting on the bed, his face a mask of sweat, rocking back and forth as he tried to ease the pain in his gut. The trussed-up Morgan sat in an unchanged position. For the last hour, he had felt his bowels churning and he desperately wanted a shit. He even toyed with the idea of using his need to have the rope untied. Maybe then he could tackle Falla, overpower him.

Once during the Malayan Emergency, when his platoon was ambushed on patrol, he'd seen an insurgent killed by a British squaddie using only the thumb and index finger of his right hand. They'd all been taught various techniques, but Morgan had never had occasion to try any of them and as he'd never believed he could really make them work this seemed a stupidly risky moment to experiment. The Paras were a long, long time ago. And right now he suspected his legs would buckle under him when he tried to get up. He couldn't even be sure he could use them to save himself from being hanged if Falla should suddenly kick out the chair from under him.

Falla had the radio on his lap. As the pain receded again, he started to fiddle with the controls. 'I won't die in agony,' he muttered. 'No way. I'd rather be shot. I'm *not* going to go through all that— Aaah!' His line of thought disintegrated as the pain clutched again.

'Give in, George,' pleaded Morgan. 'You need help and you can get it. They know how to take the pain away, make you well again. George?'

But scant notice was taken of this and, as soon as he was able, Falla started to play with the radio again, listening intently to a station for ten, fifteen seconds before moving restlessly on to the next. Then suddenly he heard a name he recognized.

'. . . in Barfield Prison a senior officer is being held hostage at knife-point by a mad, bad and dangerous prisoner. And for the second time tonight, this is just for you, Sandra.'

When he heard the doomy, quasi-military drumbeat opening of the Roy Orbison song, he jumped to his feet, pointing back at the radio, which had fallen onto the mattress. 'It's a sign! *That is a sign!*'

Falla shook his head. 'Over? Is it? *Is* it?'

He looked consideringly at Morgan for a long time. Then he bent and, rather laboriously and meaningfully, picked up his blade.

'No! You listen to me,' Keller was shouting into the telephone, 'I'm asking you to make no further broadcast.'

Surrounded by the uproar in the Silver Command suite he was straining to hear the programme director of the local radio station putting his case.

'No! I do not want to go on air. What I want is co-operation . . . Yes, yes, I know. But a man's life is at risk, an officer of the prison.'

A few feet away, wearing headphones, Helen had been listening to the tapes of Falla talking to Howard Mullins and Dr Harris earlier in the day. They hadn't done exactly well, but they hadn't done too badly under the circumstances. Jumbo Jackson, on the other hand ... Well, he'd just lost his rag which, on a scale of usefulness, was roughly on a par with taking a claw hammer to the door and dropping lighted Vestas through the peephole.

'Thank you,' Keller was saying, 'thank you very much.' He hurled the phone down. 'Bloody radio people. They think they're God Almighty.'

Not the only ones, Helen was tempted to remark. But she had more pressing considerations. Gary Marshall was on his way back up to the hostage scene. All right, he was exhausted. All right, sending a Deputy Governor in was contrary to every established procedure. But Marshall was the safest pair of hands she knew in Barfield, the best man for the job by far. But it was still a risk. She'd fought hard to have him do it, going over Keller's head to get clearance from John Bunny at Gold Command, and putting her prestige on the line.

'*Please!*' she shouted, waving her arms in the air. The noise dwindled to a murmur. 'Let's cut the noise down. Mr Marshall's on his way up there and I do want him to be able to hear me talking about what he should do next, not you lot shouting about sandwiches.'

She switched her receiver over to the live voice-channel, and pressed the key of her talk-back console, with its little mike sticking up like a chrome cobra. The cell door had had a steel bug, the width of a fingernail, Blu-tacked onto it, which picked up the sounds from within the cell and would also relay the negotiator, standing by the door. So she'd hear everything Marshall,

Falla and, perhaps, Officer Morgan said. Meanwhile, Marshall was earphoned up to her talk-back channel, ready to do her bidding. She was mission control.

'Gary,' she said, into her mike, 'it's important he doesn't twig about the line down to us. As far as he knows, you're up there on your own dealing one-to-one. When you get there, start straight in. What we rehearsed.'

She could hear a certain amount of scuffling and radio music breaking through on her headphones. Then Gary Marshall's breathing, a little laboured after he'd climbed the stairs.

'George! Will you talk to me, George? Turn the radio off and listen to what I have to tell you. You see, I've got the medical reports here. From the tests you had done at Frankland Prison.'

The music's volume was suddenly lower. Falla's voice, when it was heard, was aggressive. 'I've got cancer, right? I knew it.'

'No, you haven't got cancer. With the right treatment you'll be fit and well within a couple of weeks. OK?'

Helen broke in, whispering to Marshall in case breakthrough made her voice audible to Falla. 'Really play this one, Gary. Tell him no *way* does he have the same thing as his father. Keep him steady. He does not have the same disease as his father. Give him the whole story.'

She heard Marshall clear his throat.

'George, there's scientific proof you don't have the same thing as your dad. I'm telling you. I got it here.'

'What d'you know about my dad?'

'He was wrongly diagnosed. He had a tumour, yes, but not in his intestines. He had it in his stomach.'

'He told me different. Shouldn't he know where his own sodding cancer was?'

'We've talked to your mum, George. She was told by

59

the hospital, but she didn't want your dad to know how ill he was. And the point is – the point is, George, it's not hereditary—'

'WHY DIDN'T SHE TELL ME?'

Helen looked at her notes. His mother, his mother . . . Ah! Here it was. She leaned towards her mike and held down the key. 'Her name is Stella. Use her name as much as as you can.'

She released the key, stood up and stretched. It felt like the middle of the night. She looked at her watch. Christ! It would be, soon. The noise level in the room had crept up again. 'Hey! Can we please have quiet? Mr Marshall's very tired. I'm very tired. And I'd like some more water, please.'

How many cell doors had Gary Marshall stood outside? Thousands, could be millions. But he was looking at this with an almost hypnotic intensity. If the sheer force of his desire could work magic, he would be able to see through it by now.

'Now, Stella,' he was saying, 'Stella will explain it all to you – why she didn't want you to know. We've talked to Stella, George, and Stella will *explain* it to you.'

'*You were young, scared.*' It was Miss Hewitt's voice, whispering in his ear. Marshall was close to the edge himself. He suddenly saw a picture of his own mother at home, throwing a ball at him across the tiny patch of scrub they called a garden. '*She protected you, she loved you. Heavy on the protect, Gary. Make him feel special.*'

The ball was red. Somewhere behind him as he ran to catch it, his dad was there, mending the fence . . . He shook his head, forcing himself back to the present.

'The point is, George, she didn't want to frighten you.

60

She wanted to protect you. And now Stella's all upset about this situation. I think we can get her to talk all this over with you. But you've got to agree to releasing Mr Morgan first . . . George?'

'*Give him his symptoms again, Gary. Tell him about the prisoner in the next-door cell.*'

Marshall's mind went blank. There wasn't a prisoner in the next-door cell. The Wing had been cleared except for this one. He looked at both adjoining cells. Doors were open.

'Eh? You there?' Falla's voice. 'You still there, Mr Marshall?'

Then Marshall remembered. They'd rehearsed this: that he was to introduce the subject of the poisoner Falla had seemingly met in some other nick. 'Yes, I'm here. Don't worry, George. You know that prisoner you thought was poisoning you? We've had his cell stripped and we couldn't find anything, truly. He swears he never put nothing in your food. Says he wouldn't do that to you.'

'Wouldn't he?'

'No, George, he respected you, he did. That's what he told us.'

'*Gary. He's nibbling the hook. And you're getting on brilliantly with him, so tell him it'll be just you there if he decides to come out. You and one other officer of his choice. No one else.*'

Morgan sat helplessly and listened. He was glad Marshall was out there – better him than anyone. Morgan had a fair idea of the huge commotion this event would be causing up and down the prison and beyond. There'd be officers called in for special duty, psychologists and police and Home Office watchdogs. But it was right that his best mate in the Prison Service should be the one haggling for him.

When they'd played 'It's Over', an hour ago, he thought for sure Falla was going to kill him. Now, since Marshall's arrival, things had begun to get a bit more rational.

'Hey, Morgan.'

Falla was talking to him. He blinked and tried to concentrate.

'Yes, George, what?'

'You think it's true, about my mother and that? About Stella?'

'Well, you were only young, weren't you? And it makes sense not wanting to scare you. Nobody wants their dad to die, George.'

Ask my kids, he thought, but didn't say it.

Falla was pacing, thinking. 'You reckon I'll be OK?' He slumped on the bed, frowning. 'All I needed was somebody to explain all this. This is what I've been asking for . . .'

He began rocking back and forth, not in physical pain this time but from the realization that he was now in serious trouble. He covered his face with his hands. 'Oh, shit,' he said. 'Oh, shit. What'll they do to me now?'

'You can trust Gary Marshall, George. You can trust him.'

Falla raised his head and looked pleadingly at the door, his psychotic nature momentarily diverted.

'Don't go away, Gary. Eh, Mr Marshall?'

'Yes, George?' came Marshall's calm voice through the flap. 'I'm still here.'

'Just a minute, just a . . . I'm tired out. What'll they do – to – me? If I come out?'

Marshall had had a chair brought and was sitting on it, his forehead resting against the cool steel. He was drained. But Helen's voice in his ear was goading him on.

'*Keep him steady. Ask what he wants if he does come out. And if it's a bloody rubber dolly, we're back to square one.*'

He couldn't help smiling. Everything's a stupid joke, if you can learn to look at it that way. He lifted his head and attended to Falla, whose voice, suddenly quavering, was coming from immediately behind the flap.

'Did you hear me? What will they do to me if I come out?'

'*He's taken the hook, Gary. He's on the line. Reel him in, gently, don't unnerve him. He's worried about what'll happen to him when he comes out, so be nice. Lots of flannel, Gary.*'

Marshall tried – he thought he failed, but he tried – to sound concerned. 'You're not a well man, George. Until you got this problem you were a good prisoner and that'll all be taken into consideration. You'll be put on report but on the other side you haven't hurt Officer Morgan. You took care of him, didn't you?'

'Yes, I did. I gave him some Lucozade.'

'Well, like I say. All this was a kind of a . . . protest, right?'

'*You come out, I'll be here.*' Helen's voice echoed in his ear.

'You come out and I'll be here.'

'*And if you want to name anyone else.*'

'And if you want to name anyone else that'll be fine.'

'No! Just you, Gary. I don't want anybody else. You and the doctor.'

'OK, George. That's all that'll be out here. Me and

the doc. But I'll need a couple of minutes to arrange it. All right?'

Marshall left his chair and walked unsteadily out towards Bronze Command suite. A knot of officers mimed applause but he merely shook his head and wagged his hands at them, telling them to come silently forward. He got them all lined up behind the tarpaulin, then he beckoned to Dr Harris, who was sitting with a coffee in the waiting area.

The door sprang open a fraction, then began to swing. Falla stood there, wearily, looking exactly like the victim he imagined himself to be. Behind him was Morgan, still not daring to move.

'You'll take care of me, right, Gary?'

'Right. Just me and the doc out here. Take a look. It's all yours, George. Come on, look.'

Falla took a step, then another. They were dragging, unwilling steps, but he knew he had no choice now.

Marshall smiled, using all his reserves of will-power to give the appearance of goodwill towards this maniac. 'And I'll personally see you get to discuss this with the Governor. Be all right, you'll see.'

Falla teetered towards him, another step . . . another. And now Marshall could touch him.

'Good lad, George. Just put your hands up so I can say we did this by the book.'

Falla nodded. He had walked a fraction past Marshall now, two, three, four feet away from the cell.

'It was all a protest, Gary, that was all it was.'

Helen left the Silver Command suite to a rousing cheer. She'd looked for Keller but he was talking on the phone so she decided to go down to the Health Care Centre at once and pat Gary Marshall personally on the back. She also wanted to see how Russell Morgan had come through.

As he knew they would, Morgan's legs completely failed him when he tried to stand to acknowledge Helen's arrival. Marshall was standing beside him.

'No, don't try to get up just yet,' she said.

'Legs are numb.'

Marshall went down on one knee and massaged Morgan's calf.

'Would you like the doctor, Mr Morgan?' she asked.

'Hell, no. I'm fine. Just a bit stiff. Like the drink I could do with right now. But, my God, you bastards took your bloody time. I was getting worried around lunch-time, you know.' His face broke into a grin. There was genuine relief there, but that was only half of it. The rest was performance.

Helen smiled and withdrew outside the cell. Officer Morgan would prefer her not to be around should his bravado crack. Now, from where she stood, she heard him ask: 'My head's a bit muzzy. But was that who I think it was?'

'Yup,' said Marshall, without further comment.

'Oh. Did you call Nora? She'll have been worried.'

'Yes. More than once.'

Helen started to make her way through the knot of prison staff, including Gordon Keller, waiting to greet the ex-hostage as he came out. Everyone was quiet, out of respect for a colleague's suffering but also straining to hear what Marshall was saying.

'Now, you sure about all this, old son? Why don't I ask Doc Harris to give you the once-over?'

Morgan's reply was louder now and they all heard it clearly. 'I don't want the bloody doctor. But if I don't take a leak I'll have a burst bladder.'

Tottering and smiling weakly, Morgan emerged from the cell to the sound of his colleagues' applause.

It was another ninety minutes before Helen climbed into the Range Rover in the almost empty car park, and accelerated towards the main gate. There had been the debriefing to attend to, and then a session with Keller that had been electric with his suspicions and resentment.

Suddenly Helen saw Gary Marshall swept by her headlights. She pulled up and lowered the window. 'You were very good, Gary. You deserve congratulations. Why don't you have a few days off? These negotiations take a lot out of you – even more so if you've been in on them right from the start.'

Marshall leaned on the window-sill. Something told her he wouldn't respond to the suggestion. After all, he didn't work for her, did he?

'You working at the training college full time, are you?'

'Yes.'

'After you and the Governor left the debriefing there was a lot of bad feeling among the officers about how things were run today. Not by you. Some of us have grave doubts about the way Keller handled the situation. After this . . .' He stood back and shrugged. 'Well, Barfield just could be up for grabs.'

Helen smiled, shaking her head. 'A lot of water under the bridge since I was here, Gary. Don't think I'd want to come back. Besides, I doubt if they'd even consider me.'

Marshall patted the roof of the car with the flat of his hand. 'Who knows, eh? Good night, Miss Hewitt.'

Driving back through the night, the image that stayed with Helen was of a weak and unsteady Russell Morgan in his white officer's shirt, stained with blood, standing outside the hostage cell, as his colleagues clapped and cheered. Men like him were a credit to the Prison Service.

CHAPTER 6

Tuesday, 5 December

'HEY, WAKE UP, beautiful. Here's your prize cup of tea,' said Simon Lennox.

Helen had not been sleeping, just lying with her eyes closed, roughing out the shape of the day ahead. She opened them and looked up at Simon, who was sitting on the side of the bed, already dressed in his junior partner's uniform: double-breasted suit in grey flannel, woollen tie, Oxford shirt. Nothing too conservative, thank God. But serious, which was all right by Helen. She didn't really like frivolous men.

'Prize for what?'

'For being pretty damn pretty.'

'I'm not. Don't say that. Makes me into some babe.'

'Oh, no, you're not a babe. I just happen to find dragons appealing. Maybe it's the fiery breath.'

'Or the scales. It certainly can't be the hoard of gold. You going already?'

'Yes, soon. Aren't you teaching today?'

'No. I'm due at Barfield, but not till eleven. John Bunny's convened a meeting to look at the hostage incident the week before last.'

'Bit late for a debriefing, isn't it?'

'We debriefed the same evening, that's what you have

to do. This is a sort of extra post-mortem. Talk to the victim, see how procedures can be tightened. The trouble with having the debrief as soon as the incident's over is that everyone's shattered.'

'You going to stick the boot in on Keller?'

Her smile made Simon chuckle.

'I know that smile. It's pure mischief. You still fancy Barfield, don't you?'

Helen's smile broadened as she nodded her head slowly up and down.

'More than you fancy me?'

'Well, you're both wonderfully well built and exceptionally secure.'

He kissed her. 'I used to be insecure till I met you. But do you really want Barfield back? More to the point, is it a goer?'

She shrugged, lifting herself and settling back against the headboard. She reached for her tea. 'Well, I'm a Governor. But Barfield's got a Governor, his name's Gordon Keller. On the other hand . . .' She paused to sip the tea, looking with laughing eyes across the mug's brim at her lover.

Simon tipped his head towards the clock. 'Come on, no time to play games.'

'You mean your presence is required at the offices of Rippoff, de Gully, Bull & Leggit, Solicitors-at-Law?'

Simon laughed. 'I've got an early case conference. On the other hand, what?'

'On the other hand, Keller's incompetent, and I think I can prove it.'

Gordon Keller sat in the silent boardroom and looked apprehensively from face to face. John Bunny was humming to himself and tapping a biro on the tabletop, the Hewitt woman was buried in a file and Dr Harris had his head tilted back, looking abstractedly through the window at the grey December sky. Next to him was Marshall's empty chair. The others were either HQ suits or Barfield prison officers: people who couldn't really hurt him.

The discussion had paused while they waited for Marshall to come back. He had gone out to chase the whereabouts of Senior Officer Russell Morgan, whose attendance had been requested. In the wake of the hostage incident Morgan had refused to concede he was in any way affected, taking the mandatory three days off before insisting on returning to work. He had been asked to attend the meeting but it seemed there was a problem: Senior Office Morgan couldn't be found.

Bunny cleared his throat. 'I think we'd better start. Afraid I have to be back in London by three. Gordon – the incident on 22 November. Do you feel that anything was not done which, in retrospect, you perhaps wish had been done?'

'No.' He began counting off the items on the fingers of his spread hand. 'I instructed prison routine to continue as normal, staff to go about their duties except for the trained negotiators. Doctor to be in attendance. Door jack to be in the area in case we needed to force it. All inmates cleared from around the hostage cell, area screened off. I asked the Works Governor to be brought in to advise if necessary on cell construction . . . Under the circumstances, I don't think there was anything else that I could have instigated. Barfield's psychologist was at Newgate House with Miss Hewitt and subsequently had to go to the maternity hospital to witness his wife giving birth.' He glared at Helen, as if she had been personally responsible for Mrs Williams going into labour at that inconvenient moment.

John Bunny held up a placatory hand. 'Please, Mr Keller, this is not an inquiry.'

Keller continued to glare, then put his elbow on the table, pressing his cupped hand into his chin.

'Damn well feels like it,' he muttered.

'Well, we would just like all the facts. Any observations, Miss Hewitt?'

Helen straightened her back. 'Yes. My main one is that there were too many people in Silver Command – trying to be helpful, no doubt. But nevertheless an unnecessary presence. Then I would say that—'

'Excuse me, Miss Hewitt,' broke in Bunny. 'One moment.'

Gary Marshall was back. He walked round and stood by the Area Manager's side, saying in a quiet voice, which they all could hear, 'SO Russell Morgan hasn't come on for duty yet. I double-checked the roster and he should have been here an hour ago. We've called his home but there's no reply.'

Bunny sighed. 'Check up where the hell he is. We need him here. This is the entire point of the meeting.'

'I'll see if I can find him.'

Marshall strode out again, and in the slight pause which ensued, Dr Harris leaned forward. 'Can I put in a word here? It was just that being unfamiliar with this kind of situation meant I was dependent on being given instructions. And at times it was very confusing as to who was doing exactly what.'

Howard Mullins raised a finger. 'I kind of agree with the doctor. I was receiving duplicate information from two different offices in the Health Care Centre. So it would have, erm, been helpful if, erm—'

71

Helen grew quickly impatient with Mullins tentativeness. She decided to go for the jugular. 'Mr Keller, are you aware of the new procedures HQ have instigated? Barfield appears to be short of trained negotiation officers and, in a prison this size with this mix of inmates, that should have been a priority.'

Keller looked like he might explode. 'I did what I could as soon as I was informed we had a hostage situation. And that was not until—'

'Mr Keller! We are not here to apportion blame.'

Bunny had seen the danger. A quiet, exploratory meeting was going to turn into a kangaroo court, if he wasn't careful. 'Miss Hewitt has very kindly joined us as she was present at the incident and also because she is very familiar with siege and hostage training.'

Keller scowled, pointing a finger at Helen. When he spoke his voice was icy. 'I am sure, Miss Hewitt, that *you* have a hidden agenda. And, Mr Bunny, you *were* made aware that, at the time this hostage situation arose, we had a flu epidemic, which meant that we—'

There came a tap on the door and a prison officer appeared with coffee. Bunny was quick to seize the respite. 'Ah! Coffee. Good. Then, I think, we will adjourn to the Health Care Centre to view the actual scene – yes?'

Helen was already at the trolley, lifting the coffee jug, almost brandishing it while smiling towards Keller. Yes! She knew it now. If he was reduced to dragging in a few cases of flu as justification, she had him.

'Shall I be mother?' she asked, sweetly.

Russell Morgan had risen that morning with a sense of oppression he could neither shake nor understand. He sat down heavy-hearted to Nora's breakfast. She tried to cheer him up with stories from the *Daily Mail* and managed a tweak of a smile for WOOF OF SCANDAL AT DOG CYCLING EVENT but could see nothing funny about POLICE TO TEST GLOW-IN-THE-DARK TRUNCHEON and finally snapped altogether when she began to fill in the details of a story headlined: CORDON BENNETT! PRISON FOOD GETS THUMBS-UP FROM DELIA SMITH.

'*For God's sake, woman!* If I had my way, it'd be back to gruel and black bread for every one of those bastards.'

He climbed laboriously onto his motorbike and puttered off along the road towards Barfield, a three-mile ride. He felt pent-up, frustrated, his stomach taut with nerves. This was not like him. Calm and reason had always been his way. And snapping at his old girl like that. What was the matter?

The grass verges and bare trees were white, dusted with a hard, glittering frost. In the past the almost snowlike landscape would have given him a lift. Today its bleakness matched his mood. He reached half-way in his journey when a delivery truck approached fast from a spur road and swept out just in front of him. Morgan, preoccupied, had seen the truck a little late and, hit by the backdraught, wobbled and swerved, almost coming off. He looked after the truck, now accelerating away from him. They'd never seen him at all. The vermin. Morgan set his teeth, changed down and twisted the grip to the maximum. He'd catch those pricks and give them a piece of his mind. They wouldn't be allowed to get away with this.

At the next set of traffic lights, he swept up alongside on the driver's side. Loud heavy-metal sounds throbbed from the vehicle's stereo system and the men in the cab were singing along and furiously throwing their heads around. Morgan flipped up the visor of his helmet and pounded on the driver's door.

'Hey! You should look where you're going, pal. *Hey!* You hear me? You cut me up back there!'

The driver looked out in surprise. Some old chap on a bike. He couldn't hear the words but saw that the bloke's face was distorted with anger. The driver grinned, slowly raising his middle finger in front of his face and, as the lights changed, juddered away. As he picked up speed he again began throwing his head of long greasy hair around in time to the music. Morgan stuck to his tail.

A mile later they came to a T-junction, with the truck indicating right while Barfield was to the left. But Morgan had not finished with this guy. Oh, no. He roared off to the right in hot pursuit, gaining advantage on a short uphill stretch where he was able to draw level and then get ahead, weaving in and out of the oncoming traffic, which hooted at him angrily as they swept by. But Morgan was thinking only of teaching the young ruffian truck driver a sharp lesson. He sat right in front of him, then began to slow down, forcing the guy's front bumper almost on top of his rear wheel. The truck driver hit his horn. Morgan took no notice, speeding up, only to slow again, then doing it all over again. Every time he did it, he got a blast from the truck's two-tone horn. They went along like this until, coming to a built-up area, a red light forced both to stop. Meaningfully the driver opened his door and jumped from his cab; Morgan climbed off his bike and propped it on its hinged side-stand. They confronted each other, snarling like dogs.

'You stupid old git! What's your problem?'

'You! You think you can just ride over people, do you

son? Well, let me tell you, you picked the wrong bloke this time.'

He lunged forward to grab the driver's bomber jacket, but was pushed away by the heel of the man's hand in his face. Morgan rushed at him with a roar, bunching his fist and aiming a swing that connected ineffectively with his opponent's shoulder. At the same time he received a kick on the thigh and another on the side of the knee from the driver's heavy boot. Other cars were already lined up behind, their drivers leaning out to get an eyeful of this interesting moment of road-rage. One or two pipped their horns, either from impatience or encouragement.

'*You'll pay for that!*' yelled Morgan, panting. He was just about to charge in again when he suddenly felt hot all over and his heartbeat seemed to be going at double the usual rate. His attention wandered away from the present and he saw Falla's face superimposed on that of the truck driver. He shook his head in disbelief as the truck driver abruptly turned away.

'Just shut it, you stupid old prat. Get back in the rest home where you came from.'

He was striding over to where the bike was propped on its support. Morgan, disorientated now, watched as the driver raised his boot and kicked over his precious Suzuki. Then the man climbed back into his cab, fired the engine, spun the wheel and took off, avoiding the fallen bike by inches.

'Oi, you fucking—'

Morgan leaped towards the truck, grabbing the driver's door handle. For a moment he hung on as the truck continued to accelerate, but he was being dragged along now and was no way in control. After a few yards his grip was unsustainable and he fell, rolling several times on the tarmac, and narrowly missing being crushed by the turning wheels.

He lay there, listening to the roar of the departing truck. Then, dimly, he heard an anxious voice. 'You all right?'

Morgan rolled over again and got up into a crouch. Blood seeped from a graze on his cheek and he was dribbling from the mouth. 'Get *away* from me. *Get away from me!*'

The car driver shrugged and, in a single movement, turned and marched back to his car. Before sliding back into his seat he paused and pointed. 'Then move your bloody bike.'

The column of cars began to file past, each deviating to avoid the bike under which a pool of spilled fuel was beginning to form. Ignoring them, Morgan walked unsteadily towards the pavement and sat heavily on a municipal bench. He didn't see anything or, if he did, notice it. He was staring into nothingness as he felt the physical reactions of anxiety and incipient panic taking over. He flushed hot and cold, he shook uncontrollably. He wrapped his arms around himself in a vain attempt to control the shakes.

Within twenty minutes he found himself sitting in a bay at the local hospital's A and E department, receiving a tranquillizer by injection, with no idea of where he should be.

Police tape barred access to the hostage cell in Barfield's Health Care Centre. Standing in the corridor, Helen was asking about George Falla's prison record.

'The normal routine paperwork that accompanies a

transferral prisoner was not available to SO Morgan, am I right?'

Keller sighed and checked his watch. His voice registered a weariness that shaded into boredom.

'The nominal index card, the prisoner's long-term allocation report, his re-allocation report, and his security sheet were all—'

'Apparently stuck in reception. Did you see them, Dr Harris?'

Harris shook his head. 'I wasn't given any details whatsoever. Just his medical notes.'

'So at no time were you or any of the staff on duty here told that the inmate George Falla was extremely dangerous?'

Keller clicked his tongue. 'It didn't take us long to find out, Miss Hewitt.'

'No – not once Mr Falla was making threats to kill a hostage. And there was, according to the incident report, a belief that Mr Falla would carry out his threats. So don't you think that—'

Gary Marshall joined them. 'I'm sorry. Can't find SO Morgan.' He shrugged.

Helen turned to the doctor. 'When you examined Morgan after it was over, did he appear to be in good shape?'

Harris considered. 'Mr Morgan had a bad nick at the side of his neck, which was also bruised from the noose that had been tied around it. Also both wrists had severe burn-type bruising.'

'I really meant his mental state.'

'Fine. Appeared to be fine. Look, is this going to take much longer? I haven't finished my morning round.'

Bunny, who had been standing as if mesmerized by Helen's almost forensic questioning, suddenly snapped back into action. 'Quite. And I think that's all we need to see. No need to delay you any longer, Doctor.'

Harris nodded and went away to his office. At the same time, Keller spun on his heel and made for the door. Bunny stepped in front of him. 'I meant Dr Harris. Do you mind if we take up just another half-hour or so, Mr Keller?'

Keller's face showed the strain of Helen's assault on his competence. 'I'm beginning to mind. If I'm to be subjected to this kind of scrutiny, you'll get my resignation.'

Bunny coloured. 'Now look, Gordon, no talk of that, please. This is merely a fact-finding process.'

'Well, I don't know of anything more I could have done.'

'Let's go back to your office, shall we?'

Five minutes later, Keller was sitting at his office's small conference table, holding the edge so tightly that his fingers were white.

Helen was pursuing the question of Morgan's state of mind. 'After an incident such as this it is normal procedure to set up a so-called "Care Bear" support team to help anyone affected to cope. Did you do this, Mr Keller?'

'Senior Officer Morgan returned to duties and without any ill-effects. That's all there was to it. Now, I'm sorry but I have three adjudications so, if there *is* anything else, please could we leave it to another time?'

Bunny gathered his papers and returned them to the file. 'Well, it was most unfortunate that Officer Morgan was not present this morning. Anyway . . . Thank you for your co-operation, Mr Keller.'

But Helen had not quite finished. The *coup de grâce* had yet to be administered.

'There is just one more thing, Mr Keller. According to the log book, there was almost an hour's delay before you actually instigated the Gold, Silver and Bronze teams. Was there a reason for this? You *were* here at Barfield at the time, weren't you?'

Keller's face visibly tightened. 'Yes, Miss Hewitt. I was.'

'I see. Well, thank you. Now I have to report to HQ but could I speak to the prison chaplain before I leave?'

Bunny picked up his file and walked towards the door. 'I think we should leave Mr Keller to get on with his adjudications, Miss Hewitt. May I help you track down the chaplain?'

The dust-up in the C Wing exercise yard and attempted redesign of Keith Smith's face two weeks previously had earned Eugene Buffy and Brian Samora a spell on the Punishment Block. As they were locked away in individual cells, the normally inseparable Liverpudlian duo had blamed each other.

'This is your fault, Eugene,' yelled Samora, as he was restrained by Officer Chiswick.

'Bollocks,' replied Buffy, even louder, as he was bundled into his cell by another officer. 'I'll get you for this!'

'What about me edeecation?' whined Samora, in his most injured tones. 'I'm due for a one-on-one tomorrow.'

'You just lost it,' answered Chiswick, shutting the door in his face.

The two lads were out, however, inside ten days, and Samora was able to resume his study of reading and mathematics. His release from Barfield was imminent, its date only marginally put back by Governor Keller's adjudication. But he had also put his name down for prison psychologist Annette Bullock's grand production of *The Mikado*, which meant special privileges for prisoners involved. Now, on the day Helen returned to Barfield for the post-mortem on the hostage incident, both prisoners were at the first casting session, held in the chapel. This was the only room in the prison able to accommodate a play and its audience.

With the help of Chaplain Fuller and inmate Kevin Watts, Annette pushed a piano into position, then moved to the front of the large dais which would serve as a stage. She was a pleasant-looking woman in her early thirties, who had been working at Barfield for the past couple of years and who loved her job.

'Quiet! Quiet, please! Eric, Roddy, would you pass round those music sheets? All I shall do today is start to audition for named roles and the chorus.'

The seated rows of prisoners began whooping as their imaginations pictured fishnet stockings and high-kicking legs. Chaplain Fuller took a seat at the back of the hall and settled down to enjoy the fun. Something told him this was shaping up as a very promising shambles.

'Now those chosen – quiet, *please*! – those chosen to be in the show with leading roles will get special privileges for rehearsal periods three times a week and will be excused from workshop. So—'

'Please, Miss Bollock, I'm—'

'Just wait a moment, Brian. First, I should make it clear to you all—'

'But I'm going out on—'

Samora received a sharp dig in the ribs from Eugene Buffy's elbow as Annette ploughed on with her briefing.

'Don't tell her!' Buffy hissed.

'But I'm going out in two weeks, Eugene!' whispered Samora. 'I won't be here for the first night.'

'So?' Buffy cocked his head at the tall rastaman sitting next to him. 'Nor will Snoopy. But if we're in the play we won't have to do workshop, savvy?'

Buffy suddenly noticed that Miss Bullock had fallen silent again and was standing, hands on hips, looking at him. 'Oh, sorry, Miss Bullock. We was just wondering who's going to be the soprano.'

Annette crooked a finger at Samora. 'Come up on stage, please, Brian.'

'But I ain't done nothing, Miss.'

'I know. Bring your sheet music. I just want to hear you sing. Don't worry, I'm not thinking of casting you as Yum-Yum. We're going to be joined nearer the time by a group of men *and* women from the local amateur dramatic society.'

A ripple of excitement ran along the row of prisoners as they savoured the prospect of women coming into the production.

'Kevin! "A Wandering Minstrel, I",' said Annette with an air of command.

Kevin Watts, sitting at the piano, squinted myopically at the music in front of him. This was the moment he'd been dreading. Strumming the joanna down at the Pig and Whistle was one thing. Making sense of all these printed tadpoles jumping around on the page was something else again. He was beginning to wish he'd never claimed he was the local Richard Clayderman.

He fumbled a few notes, then launched into a bit of boogie-woogie he once learned from a jazz player. The audience cheered and started jiving around.

Annette shut her eyes. 'Kevin!'

'Need to get some practice in, Miss Bullock.'

'But that's nothing like the tune. It goes like this.'

She hummed the first phrase of 'A Wandering Minstrel' and Kevin, whose ear was sharp enough, picked it out with one finger. Then he tried a two-handed version.

'No, no, Kevin. That's all wrong.'

'If you'd hum it again, I can usually pick it up in the end.'

'You mean you can't sight-read at all?'

'Read? Course I can read.'

'Music, Kevin. Can you read music?'

By the time John Bunny and Helen Hewitt walked into the chapel, Annette had had enough and signalled to the escorting officers that the session was over.

'Mr Bunny, I did hear right?' Helen asked, as they stood aside watching the prisoners filing out on their way back to C Wing for lunch. 'Governor Keller did say he was here at Barfield at the time the hostage situation started, didn't he?'

'Er, yes, he did,' admitted Bunny.

'Well, I think you'll find he wasn't even in the building.'

Before Bunny could respond to this unwelcome news, the chaplain had come up to greet them. 'Ah!' said Bunny, with relief. 'Here's the man you want to see. Mr Fuller, this is Helen Hewitt from the Prison Service.'

Fuller stuck out a hand and shook Helen's vigorously. 'Hi. Nice to meet you.'

'I was wondering if we could have a chat,' said Helen.

'Of course.'

'Well, look, I want a word with Gary Marshall,' said John Bunny, glad to hand the difficult Miss Hewitt on to someone else, if only temporarily. 'Mr Fuller, would you escort Miss Hewitt back to me in his office later?'

'I do know the way,' Helen said, with a trace of annoyance.

'I dare say you do, but it's a question of security.'

Helen smiled at the chaplain. 'Well, can we go into your office, Mr Fuller?'

'Yes, of course, it's this way.'

Helen walked past his gesturing arm. 'Yes, I know. I used to work here.'

'Really?' said Fuller, glancing at Bunny. Helen's confident manner was a little puzzling. 'As what, exactly?'

'Oh, as Governor,' said Helen, lightly.

The chaplain's office showed little evidence of religion beyond a plain crucifix on the wall and a framed photograph of a young, pleased-looking and surpliced Mr Fuller taken on the day of his ordination. The chaplain quickly organized coffee while he told Helen how he had gone straight down to the Morgans' house when Russell's ordeal was only a few hours old.

'How long did you stay with Mrs Morgan?'

'Until very late at night. Well, until her husband was released, actually.'

'Have you seen her since?'

'No. I said she could call me if she needed to.'

'And have you spoken to SO Morgan since the incident?'

'I haven't, actually.' Fuller's tone was guarded. Was this woman here to take scalps? 'He's a very experienced officer. I doubt if there's anything to get unduly worried about.'

'I try never to get unduly worried, Mr Fuller. But you know there should be a hostage-support scheme here. There isn't one, is there?'

Fuller frowned. He was beginning to see where this was going. An ex-Governor of Barfield sticking one on the man who had taken her place. But secretly, below that insulating layer of Christian charity, he himself had never much liked Governor Keller.

'Well, no, I don't think there is. I do agree that a support scheme should have been instigated by Mr Keller but, you know, I don't have much to do with him. And . . .' Was this the right thing to do? A tremor of guilt flickered across Fuller's conscience. Where ought his loyalty to lie? With the Governor? No. With Barfield itself, with the prison and its inmates. The guilt was dismissed and Chaplain Fuller made the decision to speak his mind. 'Well, to tell the truth, he has not instilled much confidence here. There's been a lot of ill-feeling about his delay in getting to grips with this hostage thing. A *lot*, I would say.'

Helen put down her coffee cup and stood up. Her voice oozed satisfaction. 'Well, thanks for the coffee, Mr Fuller. Thanks very much.'

In Gary Marshall's office, John Bunny was alone and finishing a phone call as Helen returned. He looked up as she closed the door.

'On the day of the hostage incident, Governor Keller was at a management conference.'

'Really?'

Now she knew she had Keller on toast. Bunny wouldn't like it, of course – he'd been one of those who'd appointed Gordon Keller in the first place – but this seemed as good a moment as any to take a trial bite.

'They usually take place on the ninth hole of a golf course, do they?'

'According to all the reports the doctor, even without much experience, proved an able negotiator. At one point he almost got Falla to leave the cell. So I'm satisfied—'

'Almost?' interrupted Helen, seizing the file from in front of the Area Manager and opening it. 'According to the control-room log, Falla refused to speak to anyone on the negotiating team. Said he didn't trust any of them. If I hadn't arrived, they might even have provided him with the blow-up rubber doll he demanded. How can you be satisfied?'

Bunny's face reddened. He got up and walked to the window. He could see a group of prisoners playing basketball behind some wire mesh.

'I'm only here to ensure that, if such an incident should occur again, any mistakes that were made will not be repeated. If you have anything further to add . . .'

'You could start by making all prison staff aware of the hostage and siege procedures. Perhaps even encourage the Acting Governor to have a refresher course.'

Bunny turned from the window. '*Acting* governor?'

That slightly mocking smile twitched on Helen's mouth as the door flew open. Gary Marshall stood there, out of breath, holding the door frame. He was very upset. 'You two want to know where SO Morgan is? He's in the emergency psychiatric ward of the local fucking hospital.' He held up his index finger and shook it at Bunny. 'You better take my accusation seriously or I'll have every officer inside Barfield prison sign a petition and vote him out.'

'*Your* accusation?'

'That Keller cocked up the hostage incident. That he put an officer's life in danger.'

'Just calm down, Mr Marshall. Do you realize what you're talking about? Your contract—'

Marshall's face was bright red, his eyes popping. He was making no effort to control his rage. 'To hell with my contract. This is not going to be brushed under the carpet. HQ try it and you'll have a riot – only not from the inmates.'

The door crashed again as he left. For a few seconds Helen and Bunny looked at it, swinging ajar, as if expecting it to drop from its hinges. Then, quietly, Helen wound the tension a little bit tighter. 'Just routine enquiries, Mr Bunny? I'd say a vote of no confidence among the staff would spark something a bit more serious than that. That is what Mr Marshall was implying, isn't it?'

A petition of no confidence by officers was a rare event in the Prison Service. But it was even rarer for a Governor to survive one.

'Perhaps you have a personal motive for welcoming such a move, Miss Hewitt?'

She shook her head. 'No, this isn't personal, it's professional. It's my professional opinion. Just as *you* had no personal motive – I presume – when you felt I was too inexperienced to continue running Barfield.'

Helen snapped open her briefcase and dropped in the file. In the open doorway behind her, Keller appeared. Bunny saw him and Helen didn't. She saw the Area Manager's eyes flicker wider open and she read it as fear. It made her take a huge risk. She decided to threaten John Bunny.

'I hope you will not retain any personal grudge against me, Mr Bunny. Your own inexperienced handling of a siege situation could also, possibly, come under scrutiny.'

Helen spun on her heel and came face-to-face with Gordon Keller. The man's face looked drawn and white, which was hardly surprising, she thought. After all, he was a man awaiting summary execution.

'Both you gentleman will get copies of my report. In the meanwhile, good morning, Mr Bunny, Mr Keller.'

And she was gone.

Keller scowled and crossed to the window. 'Full of herself, isn't she?'

Bunny fiddled with a pen on the desk top. 'There's a vote of no confidence.'

Keller swung round. 'A *what*?'

'Petition to be got up by Marshall, or at least supported by him, saying you handled the hostage incident incompetently. And I don't think I can stop it. Or *her*.'

CHAPTER 7

Thursday, 7 December

T HE INVITATION to the office of Royston
Andrews, Operational Director for Midlands and
East Anglian Prisons, had been expected but it
came with almost indecent haste. True, Helen had sat up
most of that Wednesday night, her word-processor crackling as she hammered out her report on HMP Barfield.
Reading it over, she congratulated herself on the sen-
sational findings: a prison that had failed even to prepare
itself for – let alone follow – emergency procedures; an
incompetent Governor who had lied to cover up his
inadequacies; a demoralized staff on the edge of revolt.
She knew Royston Andrews would be the first to read it
and she knew he would want to see her. But she had
reckoned on a week, at least, of conferring and delibera-
tion before the summons arrived.

She hadn't encountered the smooth Mr Andrews since
before America. Ushered into his presence, she felt a
surge of adrenaline as they shook hands. Was this it? Was
she going to get Barfield back? The next few minutes
would tell.

'It's been a long time,' said Andrews, smiling. Turned
out, as ever, in the peak of pin-striped elegance, he
seemed, nevertheless, strangely keyed up and held him-

self oddly, as if afraid he might suddenly give out a loud involuntary fart. And that smile might have been cut out in cardboard and sellotaped on, for all she believed in it. 'Can I offer you coffee or tea?'

'Nothing, thank you.'

They sat down, the Director lowering himself cautiously into the comfortable armchair behind his desk. He tweaked the smile, as if he, too, was unsure whether it carried conviction.

'Did you enjoy your time in the United States?'

'I think "enjoy" is not quite the way I would describe it. But it was very informative. I've been back almost six months now.'

'Yes – and you're now in London?'

'I'm staying with a – with friends at the moment.'

Andrews glanced down at a typewritten memo on his desk, and then peered at Helen over the top of his reading glasses.

'You must be aware of why you're here?'

Helen smiled. *To be offered the bloody job at Barfield, I hope.* 'My report on Barfield?'

Andrews referred again to the memo, shifting it minutely with his fingertips. Beneath it lay something that looked like Helen's report.

'In his two years, Governor Keller has implemented a number of changes, some not as successful as others. In the meantime, Barfield is one of several prisons being considered for privatization. It is also earmarked as a potential first ever "supermax" prison, on the American pattern.'

Helen had, of course, heard these rumours and was concerned about the idea of Barfield getting this new 'supermax' tag. The American term referred to a string of hyper-modern units being built across the States. They were subdivided throughout by computer-controlled gates that could instantly seal off an area of any size within the prison. They had central control rooms that resembled Mission Control at NASA.

Did this make sense for Barfield, which was already very high-tech with the £60 million that had just been spent? And if they thought it did, surely they wouldn't give it to her, a mere Governor Grade 2 in her mid-thirties. Not to mention being female. Her mouth felt dry. She swallowed hard. 'But under Governor Keller, Barfield has been re-rolling,' she said.

'That's correct. Barfield has been changing from a purely high-security prison to become a multi-functional local prison, with prisoners on remand, sentenced prisoners, lifers and a special wing for young offenders.'

'Has it incorporated all the different categories yet?'

'Not as yet. Now, er, this is not yet public knowledge but Governor Keller has resigned and—'

'Resigned? Already?'

'Resigned. And until we have had time to replace him permanently, the position of Governor would be a transitory posting.'

Helen was thinking: Here we go. And then, *No! Why should I let them drag me through this again?* She broke in. 'Mr Andrews, I am obviously grateful for the research opportunities in America. And teaching at the training college has been very satisfactory. But I am *not* interested in any transitory posting.'

Andrews shook his head and held up a hand. 'Miss Hewitt, I—'

'I am more than aware of how much dedication a job like this would entail and I am prepared to put in all the—'

'I think we're at cross purposes, Miss Hewitt. I am

90

not offering you a transitory post. With your experience and interest, particularly in the psychology of serious offenders, together with your training in the US, I want to ask you to take over the Psychology Department at Barfield.'

Helen sat and looked at him in disbelief. She was gobsmacked. Psychology Department? What the hell was the man gibbering about? Barfield already had a magnificent chief psychologist in Cameron Williams, and she was a Governor, wasn't she? She shook her head. 'I'm sorry, I was confused. I thought—'

Suddenly her head cleared. She realized what Andrews was trying to do. The report on Keller was dynamite, which was why he'd been fired so rapidly. The whole thing *was* going to be shuffled under the carpet and they'd ensure her silence by tucking her into this job at Barfield.

She stood up. 'I've learned a lot in the two years since I was Governor in charge. I would have been most grateful if you could have given me the chance of putting that into practice.'

'Look, I'm sure that at some point in the future you will—'

'Let me make this clear, Mr Andrews. I don't want to head any Psychology Department. I would have liked to return to Barfield, yes, but only as the Governor. And not on any transitory contract but with a guarantee that I'd be there for a minimum of three years.'

Andrews looked acutely embarrassed, as if he'd let out that smell after all. 'A short list is being drawn up and I—'

'I'm sorry, but your offer clearly indicates how you feel my experience should be employed.' She turned and walked to the door, spinning round as she got there.

'And we're going to have to disagree on that because its not what I envisage for my future. Therefore I have no alternative but to resign from the Prison Service.'

It had been a shade theatrical, perhaps, but it got the message across. Andrews was incredulous. His mouth had dropped open.

There seemed nothing else to do but make a smart exit. After she had shut the door she found she needed to steady herself against the wall. She blinked. *Jesus! What had she done?*

Barfield's local trust hospital was, like Barfield itself, intended to be a monument to modern standards of market-driven efficiency. That didn't make it any easier for Gary Marshall to find where they were keeping Russell Morgan. Within a couple of hours of Morgan's arrival the accident and emergency people had shot him full of Valium and posted him across to the psychiatric ward. Two day's later, he was still there, but the directions from the front desk had taken Marshall, with his flowers and a bunch of grapes, on a tour of Haematology, Radiology, Paediatrics and what he took to be the clap clinic before he finally located the emergency psychiatric ward, housed in a detached building at some distance from the main block.

He was appalled by what he found. The patients seemed to be roaming largely unsupervised in their pyjamas and dressing gowns. An elderly man was carrying out an elaborate mime of winding an endless cord or ribbon around his head. Another man stood facing a corner and called out in a querulous voice to be released. From all around came the sound of moans, cries and sobs.

Then a distraught Nora Morgan was coming towards him. 'Gary. Thank God. A normal face.'

'How is he, Nora?'

'He wants to come home. I don't know what to do. I'd have to take even more time off work.' She looked at Marshall, a short, thin woman, trembling from the shock of it all. 'I knew something like this was going to happen,' she said. 'I *knew* it, the way he was going on.'

'What do the doctors say?'

'Oh, you know Russell. They walk in to see him and he's putting on a great act. But as soon as they walk out the bravery disappears completely and he doesn't seem to be able to stop crying. They gave him something for depression today. Pro-something.'

She grabbed Marshall's arm. 'He's not himself! He won't talk to me. He keeps going over and over what happened.'

Marshall put an arm protectively around Nora's shoulder. 'Why didn't you call me? I would have been here earlier.'

'Oh, he doesn't want anyone to know. He's ashamed to admit anything's wrong. And when he does talk to me . . .' She sniffed, on the edge of tears. 'Well, he can get really nasty, as if it was all *my* fault! I'm a bit scared of him, Gary. I don't know what to do.' Still held in Marshall's arm she fished out a Kleenex and blew her nose.

He patted her shoulder. 'Let me have a chat. You want to wait down in the coffee bar?'

He found Russell Morgan in bed staring ahead of him. He looked in a trance, as if he'd been sitting propped up like this for hours.

'Hello, mate,' said Marshall. 'All right for some, laying

around in bed while the rest of the world has to go to work.'

Morgan registered his friend's arrival with his eyes. He seemed neither surprised nor put out: simply distant. He said, 'I'm not lying here by choice, as you well know.'

'Oh, yeah, of course.' Marshall unpacked the grapes and balanced the bunch of flowers on the small bedside table. 'It's just a delayed reaction, that's all. I mean, they've not found anything serious, have they?'

Morgan could do no more than shake his head. Marshall ploughed on, telling Morgan about the odd thing that had been happening at Barfield. Not Keller's resignation, though. The Deputy Governor had an inkling of it, but it wasn't official yet. So he talked about the stir caused by the arrival of Victor Braithwaite, and the uncertain start young Jason Hully had had on the staff at C Wing. It was an uphill struggle: Morgan could hardly have been less interested.

'I just need a good night's sleep that's all. Can't sleep at all at the moment.'

Marshall touched Morgan's pillow, thinking he might fluff it up, make it more comfortable, like a good nurse would. He felt daft, though. 'Come on, lie back properly now. Get your head down. I'll come in again tomorrow. I put your grapes there. And ask one of the nurses about a vase – hey, Russell!'

Morgan had hurled the bedclothes angrily aside and suddenly he was shouting with an explosion of anger that shook him out of his lethargy. 'I've *never* let them down – not once, in fifteen years! I'll be back on the Wing this afternoon. I will. *You* tell them. *You* tell them I never let them down and I never will.'

'Yeah, yeah. They already know, Russell. Your record's better than anyone's. Now, why not get some kip, eh?'

Morgan's spasm of energy had already dissipated. He sank back into his pillows and closed his eyes.

'See you, Russell.'

When Gary Marshall left his friend in that psychiatric bed, he was hurting too.

By mid afternoon, Helen was back at Newgate House, where she was surprised to find Cameron Williams coming in as she was readying her classroom for the next session.

'Oh! You're here. We have a session after coffee break – you can join us. How's Susan?'

'Cries if I look at her but the baby's fine.'

Helen started to arrange furniture for the simulation she wanted to set up. Williams helped her. 'Cameron? You going back to Barfield?'

'Oh, yes, of course. I'm only on a sort of extended paternity leave. We mere males get that now.'

'Well, it may be more extended than you think.'

'What's that supposed to mean?'

'It means I've just been offered your job.'

'Helen! *My* job?'

'Oh, it's all right. I turned it down.'

'It is not all right!' Williams was angry and concerned. 'I had a completely legitimate reason for not being at Barfield on the day of the hostage incident. I'm not going to be used as a scapegoat for Gordon Keller's cock-ups. Did he offer you my position?'

'No, Andrews at HQ. I turned it down and resigned from the Service. I thought he was going to offer me Barfield as Governor.'

'Do you mind if I take this up with him?'

'Not at all. And if I were you, Cameron, I'd make him

fully aware of what you know about everything else that's wrong at Barfield.'

'Don't worry. I'll tell him, all right. Do you mind if I *don't* join your session today?'

'You going to see Andrews?'

'You bet I am. Will you cover for me?'

'Sure – if you put in a good word for me.'

'I'm trying to hang on to my job. Didn't you just say you resigned?'

'Well, I'm hoping that was a ploy. I'm not after your job. I'm after Keller's. Know what I'd do?'

'Something extreme?'

'Threaten to go to the press. That's the last thing they want. Do it, Cameron.'

Williams sighed and considered. Then he shrugged. 'What have I got to lose?'

CHAPTER 8

AT BARFIELD Annette's production of *The Mikado* had progressed to a second casting session in the chapel. She had been forced to give up on Kevin Watts and a tremulous spinster, Miss Purvis, had been drafted in from the local community to play the piano. More used to accompanying the amateur choral society, Miss Purvis had decided that her best bet would be to treat Barfield as a similar gig and she was now sitting at the keyboard while an elderly inmate, Wilfred Samuels, solicitously turned the pages for her.

'Mr Samuels, if you'd be so *very* kind, please wait for my nod before you change the page. You're doing it awfully well, but it's just a little bit too fast.'

'Oh, Miss Purvis, I do apologize.'

'Don't mention it, please, Mr Samuels. Only, Gilbert and Sullivan is quite tricky, really.'

The immediate task in hand was to accompany Annette's chorus in a runthrough of the opening chorus:

> If you want to know who we are,
> We are gentlemen of Japan . . .

'Now come along, boys. Let's have some enthusiasm. "If you *want* to know who we are-*hah* – We are *gent*lemen of Japa-*han*." Got it? Once more, then. Miss Purvis?'

She had decided to try out Brian Samora out as Nanki-Poo, the romantic lead. He seemed altogether right. He wasn't bad-looking and his voice – well, maybe it was a point or two ahead of his colleagues on C Wing. At the moment the chorus sounded more like feeding time at the zoo than the D'Oyly Carte Opera Company.

In the stalls front row lounged a few prisoners who had yet to be allotted roles, either in the cast or backstage. One of them, Oswald Snooper, looked around to check the whereabouts of the minders. Officers Jackson, Chiswick and Hully were away at the back of the hall, catching up on the latest news about Keller's resignation. The coast clear, Snooper whispered out of the side of his mouth to Keith Smith, sitting next to him. 'How much you asking, man?'

Remand prisoner Smith had a song sheet raised in front of his face and he spoke as if reading the words. 'It's a high grade. A cockle a crystal. But I can keep the supply coming.'

'You joking, man! Ten quid? I was dealing rocks for five.'

Smith stole a glance at Snooper. The tone of voice told him he had his fish on the line. 'Take it or leave it, friend. But you never had gear this good. There's crack and there's crack . . . And you could earn a few readies for the back pocket before you get out of here.'

Snooper closed his eyes. Mmm. He didn't want trouble and that stuff had had weird effects on him before now. Ten days . . . He walked in ten days. But still . . .

'How many rocks you got, man?'

At this moment, Miss Purvis thumped a series of crashing chords which echoed around the hall. These chords were Nanki-Poo's cue but Samora, with only a few days to go now, was day-dreaming of the moist and connubial acts he would be performing with Sharon within, at most, the first sixty minutes of his release.

'Brian!' said Annette sharply. 'Brian! What's the matter with you? I was even pointing to you. It's where you come in. "Gentlemen, I pray you tell me . . ." Yes? Brian?'

Samora shook his head and looked at the men on either side of him. 'Wha'?'

Standing next to him, Buffy sniggered. 'Waste of time anyway, Miss. He's being released next week. Won't be here for the show.'

Annette dropped her hands to her sides. 'Brian. Is this true? What are you wasting my time for? Everybody's time?'

Samora just shrugged helplessly and offered Annette a lopsided, naughty-boy grin. She clicked her tongue and called to the officers at the back of the hall. 'Will you please take Brian back to the Wing?'

She swung round, eyeing the pool of unemployed volunteers still occupying the front row of seats. They looked depressingly unpromising, but she decided to try the rasta.

'Snoopy, will you come up? I may have something for you to do in a moment. Miss Purvis! Stand by, please.'

As Snooper stood up, holding both arms by his side, palms turned to the back, Keith Smith dropped the small packet wrapped in foil into his curled fingers. He whispered, 'Better not tell her you're going out too, mate.'

By now Miss Bullock was taking the chorus through their song once again.

Three hours later, with the afternoon light waning, Oswald Snooper was bored out of his skull. The gentlemen of Japan had stumbled endlessly in their efforts to understand the two harmonized lines they were expected to sing and Annette Bullock, in her exasperation, had completely forgotten him. So, unnoticed, he'd edged to the side of the stage and then into the gloom of the wings. Out of his skull? So be it.

He pulled a home-made crack pipe from his pocket and unwrapped Smith's merchandise. Half a minute later, hidden from sight by a large stage-flat, he had ignited a butane lighter and taken a hit. Man, Smith wasn't joking. This was zero-zero crack.

Now Officer Jackson had climbed onto the stage and approached Miss Bullock. He coughed nervously, looking back at Hully and Chiswick, who were breaking up, sniggering and nudging each other.

'Er, Miss Bullock. I was wondering. Have you cast any of the staff in the play? 'Cos I'd like to audition, if that's all right.'

Annette looked at Jackson. Huge man, gigantic chest dimension. Might make do as a Pavarotti look-alike. Sound-alike probably not, but, well, he'd make a Mikado.

'OK, Curtis. Have a look at this.'

She handed him a sheet containing the Mikado's song about the punishment fitting the crime. She was smiling. Yes, Jackson might bring the house down with that one: everyone knew he'd been on the training course and he bored for England on penology these days. Next thing to the Chief Inspector of Prisons, he thought he was. Jackson sat down on the edge of the stage to study the song and Annette turned back to the chorus. 'All right, lads, it's coming along. See if you can go through it again without me. I want to talk to Mr Snooper. Snoopy? Is he here?'

She looked round, then caught a glimpse of the dark figure in the shadow of the stage wings. She walked towards him. 'Right, Snoopy. We're running a bit short of time now, and I'm terribly sorry I've kept you hanging about. But I was just wondering – Snoopy? Are you all right?'

She was with him in the shadow now. He was swaying around, grinning, the white of his teeth vivid in the twilight.

'Hey,' he said, in an unnatural, husky voice, 'you been arksing for this, bwan. You been putting out signals. I know. I feel you. I *feel* you.'

Suddenly Annette was alarmed. 'What are you doing here, Mr Snooper? What're you—'

She was cut off as Snooper's large hand went over her mouth. She struggled, trying to force herself into a position where she could get a knee in, or an elbow. But he bore down on her, and then stumbled. He was completely out of it. He almost fell, and Annette, gripped in his two hands, went lurching sideways, hitting her head hard against the metal support for the stage-flat.

'Shut your mouth, bitch,' whispered Snooper. 'You hearing me good?'

He pulled her back and pushed her deeper into the gloom, almost running the three steps it took to reach the wall at the side of the stage. Her face smashed against it, her teeth jamming painfully against Snooper's fingers. The rasta kept her in position with the dead weight of his body as he reached down to wrench up her skirt.

Miss Purvis had tried to lead the chorus through another assault on the gentlemen of Japan. It had been a spirited try. Now the men were arguing among themselves as to whether Eugene Buffy had been singing the right notes. The pianist was mesmerized by the beautifully manicured fingernails of her page-turner. She felt oddly uplifted and she played a little melody as a kind of signing-off tune.

'Mr Samuels, you have been *so* helpful, but I do believe I ought to be on my way. Miss Bullock!'

She continued to play while looking around for the psychologist. Annette had been looking for that man with the dreadlocks. She peered towards the wings, then the tune abruptly ceased as Oswald Snooper erupted from the shadows.

'I want some real music.'

Miss Purvis screamed. Snooper was hopping, dancing almost, in a furious way. His eyes were popping, froth had appeared between his lips. He kicked out, connecting with the upright piano.

'I want real sounds, bwan, not this shit!'

By now Jackson was on his feet and talking into his radio. Chiswick and Hully were moving forward.

'Hello, this is Officer Jackson, the chapel,' shouted Jackson, unsure where Chiswick and Hully were. '*Immediate* back-up to the chapel required. Inmate behaving violently.'

He dived for Snooper and the two men went down, rolling together on the floor. Then doors were banging as six officers in single file cantered into the room. Two had C-and-R gear on. They leaped for the stage, pulling Snoopy off Jackson while the others began herding away the chorus of Japanese gentlemen.

Miss Purvis recovered her nerve sufficiently to walk to the back of the stage and peer into the murk. She stood there, frozen, her mouth half open and a hand plucking at her lip. Jackson straightened his uniform and joined her. 'Where's Miss B— Oh, my God!'

Annette was a pitiful sight. She was trying to stand. Her blouse was ripped open and her skirt hitched up. She pulled at the skirt and the tattered blouse, trying pathetically to cover herself. Her panties were tangled round her thighs. Blood streamed from her nose. She tottered forward and then subsided back to the floor.

Gary Marshall had gone down to the Block to talk to Tarzan, a.k.a. Victor Braithwaite. In only a couple of weeks the spitting psycho had become the talk of Barfield for his incessant bloody-mindedness – and his wolf-howl.

It was the howl that filled Marshall's ears as he stood with Officer Horrocks outside the door of the cell.

'I've begged the bastard to stop, Mr Marshall,' said Horrocks. 'We all have. He won't. He says he wants raw vegetables, raw meat and, well . . .' He looked embarrassed.

'Yes, I'm listening, lad. What did he ask for?'

'Bananas. It was bananas. He was doing his apeman.'

'Oh, Christ!'

Marshall hammered with the back of his fist on the door. 'Come on, stop messing us about. You're getting on everybody's nerves. Victor?'

A muffled roar came from inside. 'Me Tarzan!'

'Well, I'm not your bloody Jane, mate, so shut up. If you don't like the food, send in an official complaint.'

There was more howling. The man was obviously torn

between being an apeman and a werewolf. Marshall tried again. 'Tarzan, you keep this up and you're going in the isolation unit – the Strong Box. You hear?'

'Eh, you, dick-features! Marshall! I want to talk to you. I want a visitor.'

'Oh, yeah, Nellie the Elephant, is it?'

There was a roar of laughter from inside the cell. Marshall looked at Horrocks, cocking an eyebrow.

'No, it's me dad. I want to see me dad. Will you fix that for me, Marshall?'

'Will you put your clothes on for him?'

There was a moment's silence. And, when Tarzan spoke again, the voice was perfectly calm, perfectly normal, perfectly sane. 'All right. Okay. I'll put my clothes on for him. Thanks, mate.'

Marshall shook his head. Weird.

The sudden blessing of silence on the Block lasted no more than a few seconds because another eruption occurred, this time at the entrance to the unit. Hearing the outburst of screaming and scuffling, Marshall and Horrocks ran to assist and found Jackson and a C-and-R team bringing in Oswald Snooper, his wrists secured in ratchet handcuffs, his eyes rolling, his body twitching and jumping and a stream of unintelligible abuse coming from his mouth. Snooper was bundled into a cell and at once the strip-search procedure began.

'What's up, Curtis?' asked Marshall.

Jackson was examining his wrists and hands. There was blood on them. 'Bastard's bitten me all over. Bitten me, he has.'

'I've never seen Snoopy like this,' said Marshall. 'What the hell's he on?'

'It's Miss Bullock, over in chapel. She's in a bad way.

Gov Syons has called in the local DS and it's sealed off as a crime area.'

Marshall stared. 'What'd he do? What'd he do to her?'

'I don't know. I reckon he raped her.'

Marshall couldn't believe it. He roared, '*Raped?* *That*'s not the Snoppy I know. So what's he on, lad?'

Jackson shrugged, and the two men turned to look again into the cell where Snooper now stood, stripped to his pants, his eyes flashing and his breathing heavy, while the officers went through his clothes.

Marshall shook his head. 'He's taken something. But what?'

The voice of Victor Braithwaite called out from the nearby cell. 'Oi! Whatever it is, *I*'d like some of that.'

Helen stood in her coat at the training college reception desk. The duty sergeant was taking a call and, at the same time, holding up his hand to detain her.

'No, as I say, Dr Williams is not here,' he was saying. 'He's gone to HQ. I believe . . . Yes . . . Yes . . . I'll see if she's still here . . . Just a minute.' He put his palm over the mouthpiece. 'It's Barfield, Miss Hewitt. They wanted Dr Williams, now they're asking for you.'

'Me?'

'Yes – it's Mr Marshall, Barfield's Deputy Governor.'

'All right, I'll take it.'

She took the phone. 'Gary?'

'Miss Hewitt, I'm glad you're still there. Is it possible for you to come to Barfield?'

'When – tomorrow?'

'No, today. Now.'

'I'm sorry, Gary, but I can't. Why?'

'You were called over in the hostage situation, that's why I thought—'

'Gary, I don't know what's happened but if you want me you have to contact HQ first – or at least John Bunny.'

'A woman's been raped, Miss Hewitt. We can't get Dr Williams. He's in London.'

Helen hesitated. She shut her eyes. God it was tempting. But then she remembered – she'd resigned, she was serving out her notice period. She couldn't go swanning into Barfield without anybody's say-so.

'Listen, Gary, I'd like to. But do me a favour, not like this. Maybe get on to them, apply some pressure. That's all I can suggest. Sorry.'

Marshall bit his lip as he folded his mobile phone and slipped it back into his pocket. He had to keep a calm head. But how do you find a psychologist for a victim when the victim *is* your psychologist? He hurried outside and along the walkway that skirted C Wing's exercise yard. Heading towards him was an agitated Chaplain Fuller.

'Mr Marshall, I mean Gary . . . Can you come over to the officers' lounge?'

'What, right now? You do know what's happened?'

'Yes, but I'm afraid it's a problem with Mr Morgan. He came back, he said, for a clean shirt. Said he had some appointment or other.'

'Oh, Christ – begging your pardon, Mr Fuller. I'll get along there.'

In the lounge he found two uniformed officers standing in front of the door that gave entrance to the locker and changing rooms. Len Syons was between them, peering in through the toughened glass of the door's window. As Marshall approached he could hear a series of resonant metallic bangs. 'Is anyone in there with him, Len?'

'No. Wait. Come here.' He drew Marshall to one side, out of earshot of the other officers. 'He's very angry. Keeps punching the lockers. I couldn't get through to him and he's doing God knows what to his fist. You can't be rational with him.'

Marshall patted Syons's shoulder and brushed past him. He opened the door to the locker room and strode in.

Morgan was sitting on a bench which ran along beneath the lockers. His own was open and Marshall could see it was empty. All his belongings were spread out on the bench next to him – the uniform, with its wire hanger still in place, cap, shiny black shoes, clean socks, a couple of Wilbur Smiths, squash racquet, tracksuit. A shirt, neatly ironed, was in his hand and he was looking at it strangely, as if at a foreign object.

'What you playing at, you silly bastard? You're supposed to be in hospital. You got them all worried sick out there.'

Morgan was sweating. His assault on the lockers had left the knuckles of his right hand red. 'I needed a clean shirt. Had to have one. I went home but couldn't find one. Had to get a clean shirt. I got to go and see Mr Bunny at Area. Go over the hostage thing. Got to pick myself up and get on with it. Needed a clean shirt.'

'Well?' said Marshall. 'Have you got one now?'

'Yes, got a clean shirt now. I always have one in my locker – in case of need, see?'

Morgan's head dropped. It slumped on his neck like that of a man defeated, the chin resting on his upper chest. 'What's the matter with me, Gary? I don't know what I'm doing any more.' Then he heaved himself up. He seemed normal again. 'I better be going home now.'

Slowly and methodically he began to replace the items in his locker.

CHAPTER 9

'"H IS VOMIT suh-puh-luttered on the thick, hairy rug."' Bloody hell!'

Brian Samora was pursuing his education aloud through the greasy pages of a fat, well-used paperback. Lying in his bunk, eyes shut, Eugene Buffy lay listening to him. Eric Haddock lay on top, stoned, humming strangely distorted selections from *The Mikado*. Hesitantly, Samora continued reading.

'"Sev-ver, severed from its body, the black silky heed – head – of the great horse . . ." Shit, Eugene. It's his horse! They cut the head off of his horse.'

'Oh, shut it, Brian. Everybody knows he found the horse's head in his bed. Didn't you see the film?'

'No, well, I missed it when it came on TV, didn't I?'

There was a short interval while Samora read on, subvocalizing the words by moving his lips. He kept it up for another paragraph before his enthusiasm bubbled up again. 'Reading's fantastic, though, ain't it, Eugene? Whole world opening up to me. Eh! I'll be able to write to you when I'm out.'

'You'll be writing to Snoopy as well, now.'

'Yeah, and we was going to meet up for a curry. Had it all planned out.'

'There'll be no fucking curry with him, mate. They'll never let him out for no curry with you now. Draw at least a six for doing that to Miss Bullock.'

Buffy's voice betrayed his intense bitterness. Snoopy had been going out, that was the point, and to be out was all Buffy wanted, with a desperation that at times bordered on insanity. But Snoopy had blown his chance and that seemed to Buffy much worse than a crime: it was a sacrilege, an enormity even greater than the act of rape itself. And none of the prisoners he'd spoken to doubted Snoopy had raped. It was a notion with which the whole prison was on fire.

'Why'd he do it, Eugene?' asked Samora. 'You was there.'

'Didn't see nothing. They was on the side of the stage, in the darkness.'

'But, shit, I mean, I won't be there, I'll be out—'

'That's right, keep reminding us!'

'Well, I shall. But this'll mean the end of the show, like. They'll cancel it now, won't they?'

'Yeah, they'll cancel it. Be a miracle if they don't.'

Suddenly Buffy punched his pillow, once, twice, hammering his fist into it. Then he turned his back on his friend and faced the wall. The show mattered to him, not because he gave a toss for Gilbert and Sullivan – Motorhead was more his style – but it had been a stimulus, something shining and different amid the grey, indifferent mush of his life. He hated Oswald Snooper for what he had done.

'That bastard better not come back on this Wing. I'll kill him, I will.'

*

Mavis O'Connell sat in Gary Marshall's office, sipping a cup of tea. It was funny, really, but she felt at home here. Who'd ever have thought it from a respectable girl like her? In a prison!

Mavis had been Governor's secretary for years until Keller came in. Trouble was, she couldn't be doing with the man. Well, it had been difficult with Miss Hewitt at the start. But at the end of the day you had to admire the guts of the woman. And she did straighten Barfield out, there was no denying that. Mavis would have been happy to have gone on serving Helen Hewitt, demanding boss though she was, but that smarmy-arse Keller – never. So she'd resigned when he came in, though that didn't stop her calling in now and again to have a cuppa with Gary Marshall and the rest of the old timers.

Marshall, too, was glad of the visit because he knew Mavis was a friend of Nora Morgan and could give him another window on Morgan's mental state. He was looking through it now, and it didn't give him much comfort.

'Well, I'll tell you this, Gary, Nora's been having a terrible time with him. I feel ever so sorry for her. He leaves all the doors open. Goes into a rage if she so much as shuts the front door. Well, I ask you! And she says he's taken all the knives and God knows what to bed with him. Keeps them under his pillow.'

'He's like a stranger to me, Mavis, my oldest mate. Used to go fishing together every other weekend. And when I got to Deputy Governor, it made no difference, not to old Russell. And now this. You know how cheerful he always was. Nothing affected him.'

'Nora says he's been diagnosed as clinically depressed.'

She put the cup down and got up, smoothing her

skirt, ready to leave. Marshall shook himself out of his preoccupations. He hadn't been very welcoming to poor old Mavis, now he thought of it. Just dwelt on his own problems. What job was it she'd said she was doing?

'How you liking the, er, library, is it now?'

'I just can't settle, to tell the truth. And I *was* wondering – with him, Keller, going I might, well, you know . . .'

She looked at Marshall with wide eyes at her own daring. 'He *is* going, isn't he?'

'Yep, but keep it quiet, Mavis.'

'Oh yes, I'll – where is he?'

'Off sick apparently. Called in this morning.'

At this moment a tight-lipped Mrs Gill opened the door, glancing in the direction of Mavis but looking right through her. Mrs Gill was definitely the kind of person who listened at doors, eavesdropped on telephone calls.

'Area Manager's here to see you.' She thrust a sheet of fax paper at Marshall. 'And this is the list of members of the amateur dramatic society needing clearance for *The Mikado*.'

Marshall waved her away, policeman fashion. 'Cancel them. There's no bloody musical any more. Come on, Mavis. I'll show you out. Area's here.'

As she walked past Mrs Gill, Mavis flashed her a smile that would strip paint. 'Nice to have met you, Mrs Gill.'

Royston Andrews had had better days. One of his star young governors – and it *would* be the one with the high media profile – tries to blackmail him into giving her the Governorship of Barfield. Then she resigns when she doesn't get it. And now the Area Manager's on the phone asking for her as a stand-in psychologist at the very same prison. There *had* to be someone else – but, according to Bunny, there wasn't. Was John Bunny up to something?

'John, are you at Barfield now?'

'Yes. Waiting to see Gary Marshall. I'm sure he'll agree with my suggestion of using Miss Hewitt. They work well together.'

'Well, I have to tell you I have a difficulty in agreeing to the release of Miss Hewitt. I've had her in my office this morning. She turned down Williams's job flat. Her ambitions run higher – her old job at Barfield, no less.'

'Yes, I had an inkling of that when you sent her down to report on Keller and the hostage incident.'

'Yes, I'm sure you did. So we can hardly ask her to go in as a locum now. Can't you find someone else to hold the fort for Williams? Otherwise you're placing me in a very awkward position. If there is some ulterior motive, be it personal or professional—'

'There *is* no one else. This is really a very minor operational matter. We're short-staffed in the psychology department and being aware of Miss Hewitt's training and availability, not to mention her knowledge of Barfield, drafting her in makes all kinds of sense.'

Andrews heard another voice in the background now, speaking urgently. It became muffled as Bunny put his hand over the mouth piece. Then Bunny's voice came back on the line. 'Mr Andrews – er – could you hold for just one moment?'

More muffled talk, and then Bunny's voice back on the line. Shaken was not quite the word. He sounded as if a nuclear missile had just cruised past his head.

'Mr Andrews, I'm sorry to tell you this but, er, Gary Marshall has just been with me and apparently –

unknown to me until this moment – there has been another serious incident at the prison. A female member of staff appears to have been raped by an inmate.'

'Did you say *raped*?'

'Afraid so, yes.'

'Who?'

'Well, that's just the thing. You see it's almost unbelievable, given the conversation we've just been having. It's the prison psychologist, Annette Bullock, Cameron Williams's assistant.'

'Jesus Christ!'

'She was producing this play, you see, and some inmate possibly got hold of some drugs and—'

'Drugs *and* rape! No, no, no. Don't go into all the details now. Just stop and think for a minute then send me a secure fax. I want all the circumstances as you know them. I'll get back to you when I've considered. Meanwhile stay put.'

Twenty minutes later, with Bunny's fax in his hand and fighting the desire to hurl his crystal paperweight through the window, Andrews found himself putting a call through to Newgate House. This whole thing was gift-wrapped for the tabloids. Something had to be done, very fast indeed, to stop HMP Barfield becoming a lame-duck prison. The Home Secretary would be in for a roasting in Parliament and who would be blamed? He, Royston Andrews, of course. Yes, much as it riled him, this was the only way out of it.

'Can I speak with Helen Hewitt, please?' he asked, picking up the paperweight and gripping it tight.

Outside Barfield's assistant psychologist's office Dr Harris was wondering what to do. The door was locked,

Annette Bullock was inside and she was refusing all help. Harris knocked as tactfully as possible. 'Annette, nobody is forcing you to do anything. We just want what is best for you.'

Annette's voice was firm, even harsh. 'Then leave me alone, please. All of you, go away.'

The 'all of you' were Gary Marshall and a couple of CID officers, waiting in the background to interview the alleged rape victim. Now Harris left the door and rejoined them.

Marshall led him to one side. 'What she say, Doc?'

'She's Greta Garbo. Wants to be left alone.'

'We can't do that! Not after what's gone down here today.'

'Well, she refused to go to the local hospital to be examined – that's what should have happened. I don't know what else I can do. Bloody ridiculous, isn't it? Did he actually do it?'

Marshall shrugged. 'I don't know, do I? And the bloody Area Manager's about as helpful as a whippet. So, what do we do?'

'Wait until she's ready to talk to you?'

Marshall crossed to DCI Tully and his colleague. 'So far she told the doctor she doesn't want to press charges.'

Tully consulted his notebook. 'Well, I've already taken statements from a Miss Adele Purvis, Officer Jackson and a prisoner, Eric Haddock. I mean, now that you've brought us in you can't hush this up. I have to treat this as a rape case though, admittedly, if she won't press charges there won't be a conviction on that. Shall I have a go at talking to her?'

Marshall was not best pleased at the tone of the copper's voice. 'We're not hushing anything up, right? I haven't even spoken to her yet.'

'Can I suggest somebody does? I've been here for over two hours, you know.'

'Well, I'm sorry to hold you up,' snapped Marshall.

'Hasn't the prison psychologist seen her?' Tully suggested.

Marshall raised his hands in desperation. 'She *is* the prison psychologist.'

The journey from Newgate House to Barfield was normally an hour's run. Hammering down the dual-carriageway, the Range Rover had done the distance in forty-nine minutes and now, drawing into the prison car park, Helen saw that the governor's parking space was free. She swung straight into it, came to a dead stop and was out before the car had stopped rocking. John Bunny had been watching from a window for her arrival. He pursed his lips when he saw where she'd put the car. Who the hell did she think she was?

Waiting in Mrs Gill's area, just outside the Governor's office, the Area Manager greeted Helen non-committally as she walked in, then turned to Mrs Gill. 'Miss Hewitt's come in to see Miss Bullock. We can use the Governor's office.'

He went towards the door but Helen was in front of him, turning the handle only to find the door locked.

Mrs Gill looked flustered. 'Well, I've had no instruction from Governor Keller so I thought, for security reasons, I'd better keep it locked.'

She came forward with a key and, as she unlocked it, Gary Marshall appeared. Helen walked in first, dropping her coat on the large leather armchair. A couple of cardboard boxes had already been filled with Keller's personal items.

116

Gary Marshall noticed them too. He ignored them. 'Miss Bullock's still in her office, door locked. Mr Andrews call you in, did he?'

Helen leaned on the edge of Keller's enormous desk. 'Yes. Can I just look over the reports of the incident? Then you can ask Miss Bullock if she'll see me. Thanks. Give me a few moments, would you, Gary, please?'

'Fine. I'll wait outside.'

Helen looked sharply at John Bunny. 'Mr Andrews is worried about the rape getting into the press. So would I be, coming on the heels of the hostage-taking. Not looking very good for Barfield – or, come to that, for the Area, is it, Mr Bunny?'

Bunny walked to the window and looked out. He could see the Range Rover. He tried to sound lightly mocking. 'I saw where you parked. That an omen or wishful thinking?'

A snide remark by any standards, but it didn't matter. Helen, for once in her life, had the perfect rejoinder. 'Mr Andrews has obviously not spoken to you. Well, I'm very sorry to be the one to tell you but, as from nine a.m. tomorrow, I am the official Governor of HMP Barfield.'

The stunned silence that followed would have done credit to a nunnery. Bunny's mouth dropped open, but even had he known what to say he could not have vocalized it.

Helen allowed the moment to extend to three, four, five seconds and then followed up. 'Just between these walls, may I say it will be up to you to accept the posting – or not. Everyone is replaceable, be they Area Managers or Governors. Correct?'

'I, er, think you may have misinterpreted me, Miss Hewitt, er, Helen. I—'

'No, I don't think so. But whatever personal differences

there may have been between us, I feel this evening isn't the time to hammer them out.'

Bunny pulled himself together. He held out a hand but could not quite control its trembling. 'Con-congratulations. Is this a transitory posting?'

'Certainly not. I will have a three-year guarantee. Now, this report. Do we have details of what drugs were taken from Mr Snooper after the incident was over?'

Helen went down to the Psychology Department with a master key. She found Marshall and the policeman, Tully, standing indecisively in the corridor. A small group of officers had also gathered nearby.

'Please would everybody clear off?' she called, loudly enough for Annette to hear from inside her locked office. 'There's coffee and tea in the Governor's office. Come on, please! This isn't a side-show.'

She tapped on the door. 'Miss Bullock? I'm unlocking your door.' She inserted and turned the key in one fast movement and slid inside.

Annette was sitting behind her desk, sifting through a stack of files. She was behaving nonchalantly, as if this was a normal day.

'Miss Bullock, I'm Helen Hewitt.' She held up the key. 'I hope you don't mind.'

Annette looked up. 'Is that detective still waiting?'

'Yes. Corridor was a bit like a Piccadilly Circus, but I've sent them away. Pitiful, really. But you can also take it that everyone is very concerned about you.'

Helen drew up a chair and sat. 'Can I call you Annette?'

'Please don't talk down to me. I'm the psychologist

here, I do know the routine. All I wanted was to be left alone.'

'I'm sure you do know the routine, but perhaps not from the point of view of the victim. You might not be able to make the right decisions.'

'Because I'm in shock?'

'Yes, of course you are.'

Annette lit a cigarette and Helen looked to see if her hand shook. Steady as a rock. The psychologist inhaled deeply and expelled a thin stream of smoke across the desk.

'This was my fault. I should have been more wary, more watchful, whatever. I allowed myself to be lulled into a false sense of safety. On top of that—' She took another drag and heaved the smoke into herself. 'And anyway, he was drugged up – his eyes, his speech, his aggression – he didn't know what he was doing.'

'But *you* did. Did he penetrate you?'

'Yes. Very briefly. And obviously I want him to be punished. But I don't want to press criminal charges outside the prison itself. I would like this whole thing to be kept as private as possible. I want it finished, over, done with. I want to get back to work, which' – she nodded at the heap of files on her desk – 'is what I've been doing.'

Helen could only admire the woman's poise. God knew where it came from, but it wouldn't be easy to shake. And yet how could she, a woman prison governor, allow a rape to go by?

'I'm sorry, Annette, but you should know that it may not be possible to keep the incident under wraps. OK, there are no eye witnesses and if you don't wish to have the man charged, Mr Snooper cannot be tried for the

119

assault. But, well, you have admitted that it did take place.'

'Of course it did!'

'So, what could happen is that Mr Snooper will get twenty-eight extra days for committing an illegal act within the prison.'

'Twenty-eight days! Is that *all*?'

'Yes, because the illegal act is not rape. The illegal act is having intercourse with a member of staff. And to the member of staff concerned that is also a sacking offence. You could lose your job.'

Annette stood up, staring and shaking her head. 'Oh for God's sake. You can't be serious.'

'It means you're up against it to press charges, Annette.'

Annette flicked her hair from her face and held the back of her neck for a moment. 'Is this what you've come here to tell me? That I might be fired for having intercourse with a prisoner who *raped* me?'

Helen swallowed. Enough of the shock treatment. She realized she was behaving more like the Governor she would become tomorrow than the psychological counsellor who was supposed to be attending to today's incident. But she wanted Snooper dealt with. Memories of how he used to wind her up two years ago were still fresh. He had never been her favourite prisoner.

'We may be able to charge Mr Snooper with dealing drugs, hopefully. It depends on how much of whatever-it-was he had. I just want to give consideration to every angle.'

By now Annette had put on and was buttoning her coat. The half-smoked cigarette was smouldering in the notch of the ashtray. 'I'm not going to press charges. I have no intention of being forced in a court of law to give evidence – or be coerced into making a statement to the police.'

She picked up the cigarette and took a final pull, then crushed it out. On her face, Helen could have sworn, was something like a smirk.

'It was all a mistake. Nothing happened, after all. So you see, Miss Hewitt, I have made my decision. I am not hysterical. I am not, as you suggested, suffering from shock. And now do you mind if I go home? I've got to give a lift to Miss Purvis.'

'Miss Purvis?'

'Pianist.'

Then cutting past the woman who would tomorrow be her boss, Annette let herself out.

Helen stood, arrested by momentary confusion. 'Pianist? What pianist?'

Helen was on her way to the car park with Gary Marshall. The day had been clear and cold but now fog had descended and the perimeter arc-lights shone down on them through the mist.

'Can I ask you something, Gary? I want a straight answer.'

'You never got much else from me, did you?'

Helen smiled. It was true. 'OK. You started the vote of no confidence in Keller, right?'

'Yes.'

'So why didn't you put yourself forward?'

'Not the right rank.'

'But you could have stood, on a temporary basis. Then gone for the promotion.'

Marshall shook his head, not looking at her. 'No. I can't distance myself, not like you can. I don't have the education you have. I'm not a number one, I know that. I didn't before but I do now.'

They walked a few paces in silence, along the walkways that would take them through the main gate and into the car park. The dank night-silence was broken by a single howl.

'That's odd,' said Helen. 'Have they moved the kennels?'

Marshall chuckled. 'Nope. That's Tarzan. And he's high on your to-do list.'

Once through the gate they saw Helen's car. The Range Rover had been sprayed all over with good-luck and welcome-back messages. Helium-filled balloons were tied in bunches to the bumpers and wing mirrors. She looked at Marshall.

'What's this?'

He grinned. 'I tipped off the lads on the gate. Welcome back, Governor.'

CHAPTER 10

Monday, 18 December

ELEN WAS DRIVING to work, thinking about the convicted drug dealer Oswald Snooper, still languishing in the Block. He had asked to see her again, to plead for his release to be reinstated, no doubt. What he'd done to Annette Bullock had defied reason. Not to mention his own best interest, when he was just about to be out. Well, now he wouldn't be out. But, though Snooper had never been an easy customer, he was not a likely rapist. He'd fallen victim instead to the madness of his own merchandise.

Helen hated drugs. Almost all her philosophy had been formed, directly or indirectly, by her father, Jack Hewitt, a farmer who saw the world, its nations, institutions and aspirations, as a farm. And by that he had meant a society of plants and creatures whose common purpose is the decent management of life and death. Factory farming was anathema: her dad could think of nothing more repellent than a factory, with its soulless exchange of time for money, its distant shareholders and interchangeable workers. He was a deeply moral man who believed you waste your inner life by detachment and grow it again by involvement. He never used the word humanity because he thought it was offensive to the beasts he reared and – ultimately – slaughtered. An older and truer word – his favourite word – was kindness.

'Always measure a man's kindness by the muck on his boots,' he once told his daughter.

Her father's other great watchword was progress. If kindness bound humanity and nature together, people alone were capable of progress, and that was fuelled by ideas. If ever you ran out of ideas you got nowhere and nothing, only a living death. On Helen's fifteenth birthday, as he himself lay dying of cancer, she had sat by him in her parents' bare, functional farmhouse bedroom and he had taken her hand. Though the strength he had left to squeeze it with was ebbing fast, he yet managed pressure enough.

'Don't give up on ideas, Hel. Positive ideas are our life-force. Whatever you do in life, fight for ideas as if they were your own children. Positive ideas, I mean. Things that make a difference.'

Helen wanted prisons to be something positive. They must be austere, of course, and when necessary severe. But in the end she believed a penal system must assist, not negate, progress. In America, now holding more than one in every hundred of its adult male population in prison, she had struggled to hold to the positive image of her job. Prison after prison had resembled nothing so much as a machine for crushing the human spirit.

Drugs were the ultimate in negativity. Helen loathed the way the system, for all its protestations, secretly connived at their circulation – especially cannabis and heroin – because they kept the inmates docile. And now, with the Snoopy thing, you had the results of this snivelling policy-by-default. A woman raped, a prisoner banged up for another long time, a family further deprived of its father.

124

Helen had a guaranteed tenure at Barfield, and suddenly she knew what the ruling idea of those three years must be: to rid the place of drugs. And she also knew how she would try to do it – slowly, relentlessly, Wing by Wing. It would be hard. Drug cultures are incredibly tenacious and she knew she'd have a battle just to take the staff with her.

But then again, if Helen liked anything, she liked a challenge.

As she parked the car and walked towards the gate, she was considering which Wing to start with. She handed in her disc and collected her keys in return. The jaunty figure of Brian Samora, carting a fistful of well-stuffed plastic carrier-bags and escorted by a uniformed officer with clipboard, appeared. He was on his way to freedom. She called out to him. 'I wanted to see you before your release.'

Samora stopped. He looked confounded. He swung one of the bags in the direction of the gate. 'But I got all me documents. And me brother's waiting.'

Helen approached him. She felt suddenly light and optimistic. Seeing a man go out could do that. 'I just wanted to wish you good luck, Brian. Nothing heavy. Now, you know the restrictions?'

Samora smiled. He had an attractive smile. 'Oh, yeah. I'm going straight to me probation officer. He's going to help me further me edeecation.'

'Well, keep it up and good luck again.'

He set off once more. She stood and watched him through the gate as he presented his papers and marched out into the big bad world.

A rusty, battered van was waiting for Samora in the public car park, its engine turning over noisily. He ran

125

towards it and hammered on the window. 'Hey, feller. I'm out! I'm free!'

His brother exploded out of the driver's door and punched the air with his fist while wriggling his hips. Yesss! His kid brother was out! Oh, yesss!

'Come on, Bri. Come on, my son! All the lads are waiting in the pub. So gerrin and let's go.'

He and Samora hugged and then the latter was dancing about, intoxicated. His brother flung himself back in the driver's seat and revved the engine furiously.

Samora yelled at him through the windscreen, 'Never mind the lads. I got other plans. Take me to Sharon! Take – me – to – my – baby.' He hammered on the side of the van, shaking himself to the rhythm of some imaginary dance music, gyrating his hips like an Elvis-impersonator. 'Are you in there, babe? Oh bee*ay*by, I do *lurve* you. And I was su-uch a fee*yool*.'

He pulled down the handle of the van door but, by this time, it had begun moving and he had to scramble to get himself inside. The horn sounded in a defiant blast of celebration as the vehicle squealed away, leaving only a cloud of black exhaust smoke to show it had ever been there.

Helen arrived outside her office looking for this morning's Duty Governor, Len Syons, to report on the day's programme. The office door was open and the smell of coffee drifted deliciously on the air. Mrs Gill hadn't made her coffee on a single day last week. Then Helen remembered in a flood of relief. Mrs Gill had gone and it was Mavis's first day back. Shit! Helen had meant to bring her in a pot plant as a welcome-back gift. Oh, well.

Mavis came bustling out, beaming. 'Got your coffee on. Back in the old routine, eh?'

'Hello, Mavis. It's great you're back. Is Len Syons around?'

'I'm here.' Syons had appeared with a clipboard from the corridor. He was all efficiency.

Five minutes later, in the Governor's office, now purged of Keller's worst excesses, he was rounding off his briefing. '. . . and there's three remand admittances for C Wing. Personally, I've never liked this mix-and-match system – remand with sentenced prisoners on the same Wing. Some of the old lags don't like it either.'

'It's called integration, Len. We'll just have to see how it works out.'

Helen wandered across to the plan of the prison, which was pinned on one wall. 'I want to work towards making one wing drug-free. Maybe C Wing . . .'

Syons gave out a curt laugh as he moved across to the door. 'Drug-free? You must be joking.' He opened it. 'Only way you'll ever get a drug-free prison is to stop all visits. That'd do it.'

'Thanks for the input,' said Helen, with a slight sarcastic edge to her voice.

She sat down at her desk as Mavis returned with a pile of documents to distribute around the various trays lined up along the side of the desk. 'You had a call from a Mr Ishmail and another from a Simon Lennox.'

'Did he say what it was about?'

'Wanted an appointment.'

'Simon?'

'No, Mr Ishmail. Don't know what it's about.'

She sounded so cheerful that Helen hesitated to say anything. But she did. 'Mavis, please, I know I've told

127

you this. If someone calls, try to ask what it's about. Or, at least, ask who they are.'

'Sorry! Oh, and there's a lot of complaints about the meals again. And A, C and D Wing Governors would like a staff meeting before the usual weekly one. And that's it, for now.'

Mavis got half-way to the door when she turned round and came back, leaning on the desk. 'I think Mr Ishmail is a lawyer. And I'll check on Mr Simon Lennox.'

Helen sighed. 'Simon Lennox is also a lawyer, as well as my partner, boyfriend, lover, whatever you want to call it.'

'So you won't need his number, then.'

'Yes, I do, Mavis, because he's abroad.'

Mavis favoured her with a wide smile. 'I'll make a note of that.'

Over in C Wing, remand prisoner Keith Smith was using the phone, inside its barred cage. By the gate, Officer Chiswick was rattling his keys impatiently. Smith waved to him and returned his attention to the phone. 'Sandra, that you? I got one thing to say to you, one thing only, so listen good. When I go to court, you get in that box and you'll end up in one. You understand? Don't think just because I'll be inside you'll be safe. You'll never be safe. I got friends. So one word, one! And they'll never touch me for anything 'cause I'll be banged up. That's your choice, my girl.'

'Come on, Keith,' called Chiswick. 'Time's up. Lunch.'

On the second landing, the twos, Jumbo Jackson was standing at the door of the cell earlier vacated by Brian

Samora. Inside Eugene Buffy was lying curled up miserably on his bunk.

'Come on, Eugene. It isn't like you to be late for lunch. Trolley's on the Wing, you know.'

'I'm not hungry. Go away.'

'Not sick, are you?'

'I'm just not hungry.'

Jackson shook his head as he moved away. 'Suit yourself.'

He waited along the landing and was passed by Eric Haddock, who tripped back into the cell with his laden tray, singing: ' "A wand'ring minstrel, I, a thing of shreds and patches, of ballads, songs and snatches . . ." Eh, Eugene. It's hamburgers. And did you hear the musical's not to be scrapped, after all? Isn't that great?'

Buffy raised his head from the pillow and narrowed his eyes. 'Piss off, prick!'

When Jackson reached the office, young Jason Hully was fuming. His ears, as usual, rang with the sound of his own name, constantly sung out whenever he came anywhere near prisoner Keith Smith.

'Jay-son. Jaay-son!'

It either came unexpectedly, whenever Smith could creep past Hully's turned back or, more predictably, when Hully had to walk by Smith's cell door. And that crooning, mewling, mockingbird call was driving Hully to distraction.

'Buffy and Watts not hungry,' said Jackson. 'What's up with you?'

'If that little shit keeps this up . . . He's at it all day.'

'Who's at what?'

'Smith. Keith Smith. Keeps on calling out my name. Calling it out. Calling it out.'

'Oh, well, if that's all you got worrying you, sunshine, we got three new inmates due over.'

'So what do I do?' Hully asked. 'Ignore it, right? Thought you'd say that.'

There was a call from the entrance of the Wing and Jackson swung round. 'Shit, they're here. Get everyone back in their cells.'

Hully got on to the microphone. 'Come along. Move back into your cells. Stop rapping. Back inside.'

The new tenant of Kevin Watts's cell was remand prisoner Barry Jones. This young man had few expectations of life and a perennially innocent expression on his face, which made it all the more amazing that he'd progressed so far within the penal system. The first words that passed his lips, as he looked around Watts's fanatically tidy cell lined with books and poster prints, were in the form of an admiring compliment.

'Hey – nice cell.'

Watts, lying on the bunk, a folded letter on his chest, had served seven months of his sentence. He really hadn't known about the weapons in the boot of the police car he'd hijacked. OK, he'd been escaping arrest and he'd driven a hundred and fifty miles up the M1 to see his girl, Anna, in Leeds. But Jesus, ten years! Ten fucking years! He'd see the end of the millennium inside. And here was this prat coming in and saying, 'Nice cell!', like it was a cosy B & B.

He was about to give vent to his feelings when Officer Jackson came in. 'Everything OK, Barry? I'll be around if you need to ask me anything. And Kevin'll show you the ropes. Did you get some lunch?'

God, it was sickening the way these screws treated the remands. Acted like waiters in a curry house.

'Yes, sir, I did. And very nice it was too.'

Very nice it was too!

'Well, it's lock-up now for an hour, and then we open up again,' said Jackson. 'I'll take you over all the workshop details and you can see what classes you want to sign up for. All right, son?'

Barry nodded his head up and down at least three times. 'Great. Thank you, sir.'

As Jackson locked the door, Jones subsided onto the bed with a half surprised, half-contented smile on his face and zipped open his washbag. 'Not as bad as I thought it was going to be.'

He poked around the bag and withdrew a tube of toothpaste and a brush. 'A bit like the YMCA, isn't it?'

Watts picked up the letter and unfolded it. 'What you in for?' he grunted.

'I'm on remand. Waiting for my solicitor to come and see me.

'Well, lucky you.' Watts had unfolded, and was reading, his letter.

'My solicitor thinks I might get off . . .'

It was probably the twentieth time Watts had read this letter. Anna's handwriting alone had the power to turn him on. But not with this prattle in his ear.

'. . . because, so he says, there was something wrong with the way the police arrested me, don't know what it was, and so—'

Watts raised himself up until he was propped on his elbow. 'Hey, I'm not interested. I do not want to hear about some petty little shit who reckons he's at Butlins. Got it?'

Jones nodded compliantly and started to lay out the contents of his washbag. Watts stared at him, then shook his head and went back to dreaming about Anna.

Two cells away, Terry Mahill was pinning his poster of Pamela Anderson above the bunk which had been Brian Samora's. Buffy was still lying, facing the wall, on his own bunk.

'All right if I put this up? Only I haven't got any sellotape.' He hesitated and looked uncertainly at Buffy. 'I say I haven't got any sellotape. You got any? Or Blu-tack?'

There was a moment's silence while Mahill waited for a response. Buffy whipped round. 'Everything I got is *mine*! Right! You touch one thing of mine and I'll break your sodding *neck*. And you don't speak to me unless I tell you that you can. You got that, ferret-features?'

Mahill sat back on his bunk. The verbal assault had left him almost breathless. 'Sorry, it was just that I—'

'Shut it! Shut it *up*!'

'You settled in, Mr Mahill?' It was Jason Hully at the door.

'Hey,' said Buffy, savagely, 'I asked to be on my own, you bastard. I said I didn't want anyone else bunking up with me.'

'I'm sorry, Eugene, but this is a two-man cell—'

'I said, I want to be on my own.'

'OK, OK, just calm down. I'll talk to the SO about it.'

'You bloody do that. Go on, then. Get out of here.'

Hully's face turned red. 'Don't talk to me like that, Eugene. Just calm down.'

Suddenly, silently, Jumbo Jackson's mountainous form filled the door. 'What's all this?' he rumbled.

'I told him,' said Buffy, his voice rising plaintively. 'And I told you. I don't want to bunk up with anyone. That prick doesn't understand English.'

'Hey! Watch your mouth, Eugene. We've not got a single cell available.'

Buffy went into a paroxysm of fury. He stood up and hurled his pillow at Hully, then he threw himself on his bedclothes, dragged them off the bunk and pitched them into Jackson's face. Books, shampoo, pencil box, Lucozade – all of the items of personal possession so neatly laid out were hurled. Jackson and Hully lunged at him and dragged him out onto the landing.

'I'll smash your teeth through the back of your head. I'll bite your eyes out and I'll stick them in your arseholes, you deaf mutes. You parasites.'

It took less than thirty seconds for Chiswick to come up and help them drag Buffy down the Wing. As they struggled with him past Keith Smith's cell, Jason Hully heard that sing-song voice once again.

'Jay-son, Jaay-son. Jaaay-son!'

CHAPTER 11

'I CAN'T ACCEPT that as an excuse, Mr Snooper. Obviously.'

Helen was sitting in the Punishment Block's small interview room, a space stripped down to the bare functionality of a table, a chair, a strip-light. A dejected, dreadlocked Oswald Snooper stood before her between two officers. He spread his hands in a gesture of baffled remorse. 'It's the truth. I honestly don't remember anything. I mean, I'm due out in four days.'

'Correction. You *were* due out, Mr Snooper.'

'I don't remember what I did. I've been told. And I can't say how sorry I am. But I don't remember nothing about it.'

'Well, it's a very serious charge. You committed rape.'

'But Miss Bullock don't want to press charges.'

'Outside the prison. That doesn't mean we can ignore the assault here.'

Snooper's face was a mask of grief. His request to see the Governor had been a last desperate attempt to reinstate his release. But he was not stupid, he knew he hadn't a prayer.

'I don't *remember*. I swear on my daughter's *life*. I was stoned, Miss Hewitt.'

'Were you under the influence when you left the Wing to attend the rehearsal?'

'No, Miss Hewitt. I was straight.'

'But you are now taking responsibility for having these substances on your person?'

'I guess so.'

'Which is also an offence. Would you tell me how you came to be in possession of these substances?'

'I found them. I just look down and – I was sitting in the chapel – and I look down, they was under my seat. They seemed like sweeties wrapped in jimmy.'

'Nobody gave them to you?'

'I picked 'em up, that's the truth. I wouldn't be stupid enough to bring gear in when I'm going out, right?'

'Wrong, Mr Snooper. The only place you're going is back to a punishment cell. Take him out.'

Snooper's body was seized by a convulsion of panic. He bent, as if punched in the stomach, swivelling his head wildly from side to side.

'You can't keep me here, man. She's not pressing charges. I'm due for release.'

'Take him out, please.'

Snooper's will to resist collapsed and he was led away. Helen turned to Jumbo Jackson, who had crept in halfway through the interview. 'You were late. You have the report?'

'Sorry. It's here.'

Jackson handed Helen an A4 pro-forma incident report, pointing to a detail with his massive forefinger. 'Snoopy had five wraps of crack. He going to be charged with dealing?'

'Hmm. Possibly. What did he mean, wrapped in jimmy?'

'Foil – Jimmy Boyle. Rhyming slang. Reason I was

late, Miss Hewitt, Eugene Buffy threw one of his blinders. You know what he can get like. We had to get him down here on punishment, then I had to go back for the report.'

Helen looked up, interested. She had spent all weekend reading inmates' files, trying to familiarize herself with the worst troublemakers. Buffy's file was extraordinary. He'd drawn a five-year sentence for trying to rob a wine warehouse, then assaulting the police when they caught him in the act. He already had form for passing stolen cheques and burglary and since going down he'd been on report 275 times, a bit of a Barfield record: insubordination, assault, fighting. The Buffy temper was a byword, but recently it had seemed to calm down. Helen said, 'Buffy's been reasonably well-behaved for a long time, I seem to remember, except for that little thing in the exercise yard. What sparked this off?'

'I think he's missing his cell-mate, Brian Samora.'

Helen nodded. 'Oh, yes, released this morning.'

'Buffy's been asking for a single cell. We don't have one on the Wing.'

'So we have one for him down here. Let's hope he's happy.'

Back in her office, a lawyer was waiting for her. He was very English, very smooth, public-school educated and dressed by the best. Helen knew instantly that he was here to make trouble.

She shook his hand briskly. 'Hi, Helen Hewitt, the new Governor here.'

'How d'you do? Anthony Turnbull, acting for George Falla.'

Uh-uh. He *was* here to make trouble. The internal hearing on the hostage-taking was coming up.

'Please sit, Mr Turnbull. What can I do for you?'

Turnbull cleared his throat. 'It seems to me that my client is not yet in any fit state to answer these very serious allegations against him. He is, after all, recuperating from surgery.'

'The operation was more or less exploratory, wasn't it?'

'Nevertheless, and Dr Harris, I think, agrees with me, my client is still feeling a great deal of discomfort further to his operation and, as the allegations against him are of a very serious nature, I think he deserves to be in the best possible health to answer them.'

Helen stood up. 'I think we should continue this in the boardroom, with Dr Harris present. This way, Mr Turnbull, please.'

She let Turnbull stew in the boardroom while they waited for Dr Harris. Meanwhile she phoned John Bunny and told him she might be advising a postponement of the hearing on Falla.

The doctor was about to enter the boardroom with Gary Marshall when she came off the phone. Barfield's Deputy Governor was frowning. 'Don't forget,' he murmured, as Helen opened the boardroom door, 'I've got one of my best officers practically in the nut-house because of this bloke's client.'

'Don't worry, Gary, I won't. Now, Mr Turnbull, it's been almost three weeks – how much more time did you want exactly?'

Turnbull adopted an ingratiating smile. 'This is obviously a without-prejudice meeting. Yes? Well, I hope you will take into consideration the fact that my client was a sick man at the time the situation arose.'

Helen bridled. 'Oh, please! Take a look at your client's criminal record, Mr Turnbull. He had already taken an officer hostage at his previous prison, and on another occasion before that. He has served a number of lengthy sentences for serious crimes. Don't make him out to be some sickly, hard-done-by creature—'

Marshall butted in, unable to contain himself. 'Where do you bastards get off? Right now we have one of the best officers I've ever come across unable to return to work. Your client nearly killed him!'

'I'm very concerned for Mr Morgan,' observed Turnbull serenely, 'but Mr Falla has made repeated requests for his case to be reviewed and the hostage-taking arose out of his frustration. He is exceptionally sorry for subjecting Mr Morgan to—'

'Bloody hours trussed up,' snarled Marshall, 'with a noose round his neck. God! You saying it was *our* fault he assaulted an officer and took him hostage?'

Helen glared at Marshall, who held up his hand in a gesture of apology as Turnbull tapped the table with his finger. 'Governor Keller has resigned, hasn't he? It would appear the Prison Service feels Barfield should take some portion of blame.'

Marshall exploded again. 'Well, if that bastard doesn't pay for what he did—'

'Mr Marshall, please!' said Helen sharply. 'And, without prejudice, Mr Turnbull, I agree to a further two weeks' recuperation time, because I want Mr Falla fit and well to answer the charges against him.'

Turnbull's smile this time was one of triumph and self-satisfaction. He stood up. 'Good. Well, I'm glad we've been able to reach an amicable—'

'Would you please show Mr Turnbull to the gate, Mr Marshall?' said Helen, already standing at the open door.

As they left, Helen detained the doctor. 'Just a moment more, Doctor.'

Harris nodded at the door as it closed behind the two men. 'Nice chap, that, actually.'

Helen raised her eyebrows. 'Really? You astonish me.'

'Yes, yes. I know him. Great rugby forward, too. Cambridge Blue, played for England a few times.'

'Did he, indeed? Well, he's passed the ball to us now and we're sure as hell not going to let him have it back. I want Falla's previous medical reports gone over with a fine-tooth comb. And I want him given such special treatment in Health Care that he'll think he's at a health farm. I want him fitter and healthier in two weeks' time than he's ever been in his nasty, vicious life. And perhaps, Doctor, it would be better if you cut out your rugby-club socializing with our Mr Turnbull until after the legalities of this have been sorted out. Understood?'

The door had slammed after her before Harris could frame a reply. But before she could reach the haven of her office where towers of paperwork awaited her, Mavis executed a skilful interception. 'I've got Mr Ishmail on the phone.'

'Ishmail?'

'A lawyer – something to do with remand Keith Smith.'

'Oh, yes, Ishmail. Well, I've had enough of bloody lawyers for one day. In fact, I've had enough of them for the year. I'll see him after Christmas – make a date early in January. Tell him I'm going skiing or something.' She paused at her office door, remembering Gordon Keller and the golf course.

'On reflection, tell him I'm on compassionate leave.'

*

A prison sentence is rightly known as time, but it is a very specialized time, one that accumulates on top of you. Kevin Watts would lie on his bunk for hours, brooding and dreaming of Anna and the many happy times they had spent together. He longed to be with her when their son was born.

He had got used to his new pad-mate. The only thing that drove you spare about Barry Jones was his enthusiasm for prison life. But then, of course, Jonesy had not even been to court yet and – if you could believe him – he'd be getting off anyway. Meanwhile, Watts was lying here staring at ten years.

'Nosh is quite good, isn't it?' Jones was saying for the umpteenth time, as he carried his supper tray into the pad. 'And I was in the gym today. Great, it is, better than our local leisure centre at home. And I'm going to learn to work a computer, I've put my name down.'

Watts grunted, contemplated without appetite his own food tray while Jones filled his mouth, swallowed and took a long drink of water.

'Got a meeting with my solicitor.' This was said in a slightly mournful or regretful way, as you might announce you were attending a funeral.

Watts turned to him. It would be funny if it wasn't so tragic. 'Why not tell him not to bother getting you out?' He pushed his tray aside, the food barely tasted, and rolled back onto his bunk. 'I got a visit tomorrow too,' he said.

Watts could usually put up a brave face to the world, but now it was all getting too much. He covered his eyes with his hands and began to cry.

Uneasily, Jones glanced at him as he used a lump of bread to wipe up the last of the gravy from his steak and kidney pie. He popped it into his mouth and nodded at the photograph in its frame beside Watts's bunk. 'That her picture, is it? She's lovely.' He chewed for a few more seconds and swallowed. 'I've not got a girl. Haven't got anybody come to think of it. Are you going to finish your dinner?'

Watts sniffed and scrubbed his face with his hands. 'She's pregnant – eight months. Breaks me up, seeing her. Everything's such a mess ... It's a boy. We know it's a boy from the scan and ...' He screwed up his eyes again, the tears welling uncontrollably. 'I only want to see him born!'

Jones leaned over and scanned Watts's tray. 'Can I have your dinner, mate?'

Down on the Block, the resident wolfman was howling again. He seemed to be standing right behind the door-flap because the noise echoed round the area like a fire siren. Eugene Buffy was almost beside himself.

'Oi! Someone! Shut him up, will you? I can't hear myself think in here.'

Officer Horrocks strolled over to Buffy's door. 'You shut up as well, Eugene. You're making as much noise as him.'

'Bollocks. If you can't control him, I'm going to complain. You hear? You hear?'

But Horrocks didn't hear, because he was standing outside the – he had to admit – much noisier cell of Tarzan.

'Come on, Tarzan. Give us all a break. You've been at this for hours and you won't be able to talk on your old man's visit. You'll be hoarse.'

Tarzan's voice, however, was clear and strong. 'Who's complaining? Anyone registering complaints about me?'

'*Yes!*' roared Buffy. 'Me, you big ape! You don't frighten me. You hear? You – don't – frighten – ME!'

Suddenly the howling stopped. It was followed by silence. It was like a blessing. It extended for five seconds, then ten.

'Thank you,' called Buffy, after another twenty seconds of quiet had elapsed.

Instantly there came in response a sound that began as a tiger's growl and ended like a power-saw cutting through a rusty oil drum. It was followed by another long, lone, hungry wolf-call.

On a full stomach, Barry Jones had been doing some thinking. It was true, what Watts had said. Meeting his brief was a nice break in the routine, but the truth was, if he faced it squarely, he didn't want to go out, not at the moment. There was nothing for him. He'd been pretty much homeless, kipping at various mates' places, but he could tell they never wanted him to hang about too long. Then he was on the move again. There'd been more than one night in bus and railway stations, and two in shop doorways. Outside Barfield, he was one step away from Cardboard City and that was the truth.

And then it had come to him. Kev's Anna was about to give birth. Kev was desperate to be there. So who was he, homeless, rootless, friendless Barry Jones, to stand in his way? They could swap places. Kev could escape and he could stay inside for Christmas. Simple.

But when he put it to Watts, the bloke just laughed. 'Swap places? Me for you? Joking.'

'But it could work. I mean, you and me are the same height. And another thing—' He jabbed Watts's arm with his fingers. 'When they brought me in, the photo booth wasn't working.'

In spite of his mockery, Watts was interested. Well, a bloke can dream, can't he?

'Trouble is, the screws know me, some of them do, anyway. I'd never get away with it. No, Jonesy. It's crazy.'

Jones was a little miffed that his great brainwave was receiving such scepticism. He went over and killed the cell light. The only illumination now came from the prison-made candle that flickered on the chair beside Watts's bunk. 'Suit yourself. I offered. I mean, he's certain, the brief, that I'll be out – within a week, that's what he's telling me.'

Within a week! Lucky blinder. Pity he doesn't appreciate it. Watts lit a roll-up from the candle and sat watching Jones as he followed his invariable turning-in routine. Kick off shoes, drop trousers, removing socks at the same time. Pyjama trousers on, shirt off, fold shirt . . .

'Hey, another bloody thing, Jonesy!'

'What?'

'You're covered in tats.'

Jones's arms sported several tattoos of the high-street variety – a mermaid and a shield with the word 'Mum' emblazoned on it were particularly prominent.

'Oh, yeah, I got eight. And two on my thighs. Want to see?'

Watts leaned back against the wall and closed his eyes, placing the thin, brown-stained cigarette between his lips. 'You prat. Don't you get it? They'll have every one of those tats listed.'

Jones stopped folding his shirt. 'Oh! Right. Funny, I never thought of that.'

He fell into his bunk and curled up, an expression of serene complacency on his face. He shut his eyes. 'Hmm! Nice and quiet, isn't it? You can sleep well in here. G'night, Kev.'

Watts knew that Jones would sleep within a minute. He shook his head in amazement. A complete fruitcake, but Watts couldn't help liking him. He rolled another butt and lit it from the dog-end of the other, sitting and smoking quietly. He looked across at Jones, whose breathing came easily, regularly, dreamlessly. In the candlelight, the 'Mum' tattoo was clearly visible on his upper arm. Watts contemplated it with growing interest, trying to trace the lines, to see how the design flowed and twisted.

He reached out to the bunkside table, where there was a mug with pencils and colours. He picked out a blue felt marker pen and slowly began drawing on his own forearm.

CHAPTER 12

Tuesday, 9 January

ANNETTE BULLOCK had begun to come in earlier and earlier, keeping at bay unwelcome thoughts by piling up her work-load. When Helen looked in on her office before breakfast, Annette was already working her way through a toppling tower of assessment reports.

'Morning. Sorry I've not got to any *Mikado* rehearsals yet. How's it going?'

'Fine, but Eugene Buffy is missed. He's a good part of the chorus. Can't sing, but he likes to act as assistant director.'

'He's on punishment. Should be back on the Wing today. By the way, how often have you seen Russell Morgan?'

Annette looked startled. 'Who?'

'The officer held hostage?'

'Oh! Oh, yes. Officer Morgan. I've called on him a – a couple of times, and I've spoken to his wife. I got a bit caught up in my own problems. I can arrange to see him if you—'

'I think you should. How are things with you?'

'Fine, thank you. Fine. Keep myself busy, you know.'

'Mr Snooper, you know, is being held in the Block.'

145

'Yes. I suppose he's unavailable to be in the musical now.'

'I take it that was a joke?'

'Yes. A joke.'

'Are you sleeping all right?'

'Oh, please! This isn't necessary.'

'Well, are you?'

'Yes, Governor. I'm aware that I hold a very responsible position at Barfield. I *don't* like having to reassure you constantly as to my competence. If you have a problem—'

'I don't have a problem. I'm just making sure that you don't have one. You had a horrific experience.'

'And it's behind me.'

'OK.'

'I know you contacted my last – the last prison I worked in. You spoke to Michael Hilliard?' She said the name with a reverence that confirmed Helen's suspicions.

From a reading of Annette Bullock's file, she'd guessed that the move to Barfield was prompted by more than professional reasons. And Hilliard was known throughout the service for being led by his prick.

'Yes, as a matter of fact I did. It's not prying. It's just that I'm responsible for you. And I want you to know that, if you need to talk to me, then I'm here for you. Just as I hope you'll be here for me, should I need you.'

'What did . . . Michael say about me?'

'He was very complimentary.'

But Helen didn't want to go on with this. Not now. She sensed the preliminaries to a gush of confidence. But she was expected on the Block and, anyway, this lawyer chap Ishmail would be here any minute. She retreated to the door. 'Well, I'll try and look in on a

146

rehearsal soon. I hear Officer Jackson's playing a big part in the show.'

Annette smiled. Big was right. 'Yes, but I haven't cast it all yet. Do you sing at all?'

'God forbid. Tone deaf. 'Bye, see you later.'

After a month on Good Order and Discipline Oswald Snooper had changed his line on the incident with Miss Bullock. This was partly prompted by the possibility that he would be made to go on Rule 43, which meant removal to the Wing reserved for vulnerable prisoners, most of them the type of sex offenders for whom other prisoners harboured a particularly vengeful hatred.

Now, when Helen again broached the question of Rule 43, Snooper wailed in near despair. 'With the nonces? Aww, no, Miss Hewitt. No way, Miss Hewitt.'

'Well, there's bound to be bad feeling on the Wing about what you did. You could be in some danger.'

'Well, I never touched her. I never laid a hand on Miss Bullock. It's all lying, all lying . . .'

Helen wasn't going to listen to this. She marched out and proceeded to Tarzan's pad. 'You have a VO for this afternoon, for E. R. Braithwaite. Your father? And you've asked, on compassionate grounds, that the visit is not in the no-contact section. That right?'

Tarzan was muted this morning. His head drooped and his voice was almost a whisper. 'It'll be the last time I see him. He's very sick.'

'Yes, I know that. And if you give me your word you'll behave yourself, I'll agree to it.'

The man who regarded himself proudly as the most violent prisoner in the system lifted his head and smiled sweetly at his Governor. 'Best behaviour Miss Hewitt. Word of honour.'

'Right, then.'

'Thank you for seeing me,' said Mr Ishmail. 'I'm here because of serious allegations against one of your inmates, a Mr Keith Smith.'

Helen watched this neat, brisk little lawyer warily. 'Yes. Mr Smith is with us because he is awaiting trial so I am aware he faces allegations.'

'Yes, for armed robbery. He's a particularly violent and unpleasant man, with two previous convictions for similar offences.'

'And you are his defence counsel?' Helen had not been able to keep a suggestion of mockery out of her voice.

Ishmail noticed and became more officious than ever. 'No. I'm with the prosecution. One of my witnesses, who at one time knew Mr Smith, has received numerous threatening phone calls.'

Helen's eyebrows shot up. 'From here? From Barfield?'

'Yes, the calls have been traced here. And it seems to me quite extraordinary that a man who is refused bail because of his previous record of attempting to scare witnesses at his last trial is given free access to a telephone and is able to use prison-issue telephone cards.'

'I couldn't agree with you more.'

'So, what are you going to do about it? My witness is being terrorized into withdrawing her statement.' Snapping open his attaché case he withdrew a cassette tape and placed it on the table. 'I suggest you listen to this.

148

Mr Smith threatened this witness – I quote – that "if you go into the witness box you will end up in another kind of box".'

Helen picked up the tape. 'Thank you, Mr Ishmail. I'll look into this today.'

'And I shall call you tomorrow.'

Helen desperately wanted to reply, '*Don't* call me, Ishmail,' but managed to fight down the impulse. Instead she buzzed Mavis to show him out.

Barfield's visitor room, like those of all modern prisons, was set out in what is known as the cafeteria style, with tables dotted about and officers distributed in such a way that all visits are observable at all times. To be visited in prison is a right of all inmates and it has been found that an open-plan area allows for more natural social interaction without affecting security. In the old-style booths, watched by officers in their tennis-umpire chairs, conversation would often be carried out in the whisper of a confessional. Now the roar of talk would do credit to your local pub.

Eric Haddock was speaking to his old mum of thespian ambition. 'She hasn't decided what part I'll play. We're going to be cast this afternoon. But I've been singing all the solos. Did you ever see *The Mikado*? I may get Nanki-Poo. That's the romantic lead. The young man who loves the beautiful princess Yum-Yum.'

'Romantic lead, Eric? You? Wait while I fall off me chair. Errol Flynn – bald, was he? Or Stewart Granger?'

'Yul Brynner—'

'Didn't talk cockney and wasn't five foot four with jug-handle ears.'

Not far away a huge, muscled prisoner talked urgently to his brother. 'Can't you get me more of those wank mags, Roy? I'm desperate for something new.'

'Well, it's not that easy, Burt . . .'

'Look, five years without a woman, I'm beginning to forget what it tastes like.'

'I could get you a nice tin of anchovy paste, if you like.'

At the next table, Suzy Mahill was sitting with a pained look on her face, listening to her brother Terry's endless chatter.

'I got this new pad-mate, name of Buffy. Anyway he's a right case. One man mini-riot, he is. Spends more time in the Block than on the Wing. But he likes me, I'm the only feller can make him laugh. I goes, what stands between Norma Major and a night of passion?'

'I give up.'

'John Major's. See? Cracked him up, that did.'

At the next table, Anna was gazing at Kevin Watts through damp eyes. 'He started kicking last night,' she reported. 'I just lay there, couldn't sleep. Cried all night.'

Watts leaned across the table, his face creased in longing. 'I wanna to be with you.'

'I know that, Kev.'

'It's all I think about day in, day out. That he's going to be born and I won't be there . . . But hey, don't cry, Anna, listen to me. I might – I *might* – be able to swing it.'

'What do you mean?'

'I might get out.'

'What? Compassionate leave or something? Oh! Oh, Kev. That'd be wonderful. When?'

'Shush. Not so loud. Can't discuss it now but I'll call you, tell you more then.'

Off the main open visitor room were the glass-enclosed solicitor booths, where officers could observe meetings between lawyers and clients but not listen in. Barry Jones's brief had brought what he regarded as excellent news.

'I am now completely confident, Barry, that, as you were not cautioned and went to the station of your own free will, the charges against you will be dropped. And, in the meantime, I'm very hopeful of getting you bail in the next few days.'

'How long? Couple of days, you said?'

'I'm only sorry it's taking so long. The law is a mill that grinds exceedingly—'

'Oh, it's OK. No hurry. I like it here. I really do.'

The least private conversations, strangely, are the most enclosed. In the closed rooms inmates and visitors are cut off from each other by toughened glass and must speak on the telephone. It was in one of these that Oswald and Meryl Snooper faced each other. Meryl had been expecting her husband home for Christmas but was now facing the indefinite postponement of his release.

'Why?' she asked, her voice high, almost hysterical. 'Why did you do it? I don't understand you, Oswald. You were due out. How can they give you that much time extra on your sentence? Did you get in a fight or what?'

'I don't know,' replied Snooper. 'I don't want to talk about it.'

Normally, unlike Oswald Snooper, Victor Braithwaite would be proud to have to use one of these facilities, as a form of recognition for his special status. But when it came to the visit of his father, he wished otherwise. He had stopped his wolf-howling on the Block once he had

151

persuaded Helen to afford them the comfort of the VIP visiting room.

Tarzan was already inside as two officers brought a wheezing and sickly old Braithwaite to the door in a wheelchair.

'Keep shtum about the wheelie, lads,' said the old man, heaving himself out of the chair and laboriously straightening his clothes. He was carefully dressed in check jacket, polyester trousers and yellow paisley cravat, and his thick, nicotine-stained white hair had had a good dollop of hair cream combed into it. He reached for the door-handle and, with an unsteady swagger, strolled in.

'Here he is,' announced Horrocks. 'Want to sit down, do you, Mr Braithwaite?'

'Here, tea and biscuits,' said Tarzan, jumping up, eager to spoil, helping his father into an easy chair. 'Chocolate-orange ones – you like those. You want sugar in your tea?'

'Yes. Three.'

The old man looked uneasily around at the comfortable surroundings – the cushioned chairs, the smoked glass coffee table with tea and biscuits laid out, the four officers in neat tracksuits.

'Bit different from my day. Very nice. Been on a kickabout, have you? Game of volleyball?'

'Biscuit, Dad?' pressed Tarzan, nettled that so far he had been virtually ignored.

'Ta. You not having one?'

'I don't use sugar,' said Tarzan, stiffly. 'I got 'em for you. Eat the lot, go on.'

Braithwaite looked at the enormous pile of biscuits and turned to Horrocks. 'Want a biscuit, lad?'

The request dissolved into a furious fit of coughing, the crackling phlegm surging up through the old man's airways like hot mud. For a full thirty seconds he rocked in his seat, wordlessly heaving and braying, the son convinced he was about to see his father fall dead or, at least, spew blood.

When the fit had left him, old Braithwaite nonchalantly reached for his baccy tin. 'Want a snout?'

Tarzan shook his head. 'You've got smaller,' he said. 'You've lost weight.'

'I'm seventy-two.'

Horrocks gave him a light for the roll-up he had ready in his tin.

'Ta. Old lag I was in with once, he used to pass out these boiled sweets to the screws. Special flavour they had, according to him. I says, "Hey, what you doing sucking up to them screws?" He says, "No, I ain't, I hate the buggers." I says, "You're a liar. I seen you handing out them boiled sweets." And he says, "Yeah, but every night I stick them up my arse then rewrap them in the morning."'

He put his head back and cackled briefly.

Horrocks looked at the other three officers. 'I'm glad I didn't have a chocolate biscuit, then.'

The old man took another drag. 'Na, that was Parkhurst. Con's gaol is Parkhurt.'

Watching the sickly smoke from his roll-up twisting in the air, he was far away from the others for the moment. 'Nobody ever squealed from there . . . Con's gaol, that's why.'

'You've always been a tough guy, haven't you, Dad?' said Tarzan, sarcastically.

His father's eyes narrowed. 'I know one thing. If I'd done twenty years' stir I wouldn't have got out and been back sixty days later.'

He shook his head, reviving a despair he felt whenever his son came to mind. 'Sitting on the steps of Barclays

Bank with a sawn-off and a balaclava. That's not a tough guy. A prat, maybe. Been banged up so long you didn't know what time the fucking bank opened.'

'I'm writing a book now, Dad. About prison and being moved around every nick in England. They put me in shackles and a body-belt. I have to have six escorts, prison van, patrol cars . . .'

'Proud of it all, ain't you? Your mother always said you got a grin wide enough to fit a banana in sideways. What you calling yourself Tarzan for?'

'Because I'm a gladiator.'

'A what?'

'That TV show, Dad. I reckon I could do that.'

Awkwardly and without ceremony, he pulled a sheaf of papers out of his pocket and shoved them at his father. 'Here, I did these for you. You can keep them, take them home.'

'Home?' said old Braithwaite, bitterly. 'I'm in a welfare place. Going to die there, too.'

For a moment he seemed to drift off. He put the papers down on the table, as if he had not registered their significance. Then he shook his head and turned towards his son. He was shaking, trying to concentrate on what he wanted to say – what he'd come to say.

'Don't die in prison, Vic. You can't beat the system. In the end it beats you. OK, it's a zoo. But your name's Victor, not Tarzan. Victor!'

Then, slowly and methodically, he began wrapping the remaining chocolate biscuits in his son's poems.

Helen was having a mild argument with the cook on her inspection of the trolleys, which were about to carry the men's suppers up to the Wings.

'I eat this food,' he was saying. 'Same food goes into the officers' canteen. We've had so many health inspectors in here they've been tripping over themselves.'

'But you've been changing round the menus, haven't you?'

'Yes. I thought I'd vary it. Surprise them. It gets so boring for me. And my staff.'

'Please stick to the regulated menus that have been devised, will you?'

She flipped open her trilling mobile phone. 'Governor.'

'It's Horrocks, Governor. The Block. Tarzan's asked if he can spend ten minutes in the chapel.'

'How's he conducting himself?'

'Since his visit he's been very quiet. He got a bit upset when his dad wrapped chocolate biscuits in his poems. He knows he won't see the old man again.'

'All right, I agree to the chapel. But the usual escort, Mr Horrocks. No chances.'

'OK, Governor.'

Twenty minutes later, Tarzan stood in front of the altar table, looking up at the large bare cross which hung over it. He scowled, his lower lip jutting, the jaw muscles balled as hard as glass marbles. His three minders stood respectfully near the door.

Feeling it was part of his pastoral duty, but without real enthusiasm, Chaplain Fuller had made a nervous approach behind the inmate's back. 'Er, Mr Tarzan. I'm the prison chaplain. If there's anything you would like to talk to me about, you know that I would be . . .'

The statuesque figure took not a blind bit of notice. His bottom lip began to tremble; his concentration on

155

the cross became even more intense, as if he were trying to set fire to it by just looking at it. Then he swept his arms outwards and up until he held them at ninety degrees to his body, the fingers stretched wide. The chaplain continued to stand hesitantly by his side as Tarzan's fingers clenched and unclenched. He filled his lungs as he tipped his head back, then let fly.

'IS THERE ANYBODY THERE?'

The bellow echoed around the chapel and, startled, the uniformed minders sprang forward. The chaplain, holding his ground, suddenly looked very frail beside Tarzan's enormous frame. They sprinted up the side aisles as they saw Tarzan's arms bend and his hands make massive fists.

'ANSWER ME! IS THERE ANYBODY THERE?'

Two of them caught his arms and held him. He glanced once more at the altar, then let himself be led away.

Candlelight filled the cell, flickering as the two men breathed hard in their excitement. Kevin Watts was sitting in his boxer shorts while Barry Jones added the finishing touches to the tattoo on his right thigh with the blue and green felt tips.

'Come on, Kev, take me through my family again – that is, your family.'

Watts giggled. He was enjoying himself. 'Your mother's name is Barbara, aged forty-three. Sister called Diana, aged six. Address, 44 Elmswood Crescent. Auntie Carol lives with you – Mum's younger sister. Dad left in 1985. Mum works in a laundry. You – I – went to school at, um . . . How do they look?'

'They look great, and the ink's fading just right. Don't forget the dog. What's his name?'

'Archie. But I can't remember where we went to school.'

'Elmswood Comp. Just at the top of our road. Dump it was, too. Then we worked for eighteen months at . . .?'

Watts snapped his fingers.

'Sanders' print works. Got fired and went to the candle factory. Had chicken pox, measles, mumps and . . .'

'Wisdom teeth out.'

Watts stood up and pulled up his trousers. He walked to the cell door, touched it and bustled back. He was wildly excited, shaking with nerves. Sleep was a remote possibility. 'You think they'll ask me that?'

'I'm just telling you what's on my admittance slip.'

'You sure they got no photo when you came into Barfield?'

'Yeah. They said it wasn't working.'

He sat in his bunk and drew up his knees, hugging them. 'So what do we do now?'

'We wait. There's nothing else *to* do.'

Tarzan was taken back to the Block, where he began to scream louder then ever before. His bloodcurdling yells were setting off the other prisoners, and the place was bedlam. None of the officers on duty could bring the situation under control, so the Governor was called in.

Marshall met Helen at the gates. 'He's demanding to be put in the Box. Never heard anything like it before.' The Strong Box was the Block's ultimate stripped cell with not even a bed, merely a mattress on the floor. It had double doors, one opening inwards and the other

157

outwards, making it exceptionally soundproofed. It was used strictly as a last resort.

'I'll talk to him, Gary. Maybe he just needs someone to listen to him.'

Helen approached his closed cell door as he screamed, 'I can't stand the noise. I need quiet. I want to be put in the Strong Box.'

'You are creating the noise, Mr Tarzan. Can you hear me?'

Helen turned to see three of the Specials arrive with their shields. These were men trained to deal with difficult and violent prisoners, and Marshall had called them in. After a moment's hesitation, she decided to use them as her back-up. Tarzan's cell door was unlocked, and slowly, slowly, Helen moved in behind the officers.

With his fists clenched and his muscles straining, Tarzan was moving up and down his cell like a caged animal. On seeing Helen in the doorway, his lip curled and he seemed about to pounce.

Helen pulled her six-foot frame as tall as she could and looked him straight in the eye. 'Will you talk to me, Mr Tarzan?' she said, without a trace of hesitation.

His eyes flicked to the officers then back to her. It was a contest of wills, but Helen did not flinch from his manic glare. Every movement Tarzan made put everyone in the cell more on edge. It seemed as if he would attack them at any moment.

'Calm down, now, come on. This isn't doing any good. But you know that, don't you?'

Tarzan didn't take his eyes off her as he slowly nodded. His body began to sway but still he seemed angry and unbalanced. Helen edged forward and tried again, using all the tactics of persuasion that she taught at Newgate Hall, and which had secured the release of Russell Morgan.

'I understand you must be upset about your father, Tarzan.'

'You don't understand – he never did. Sweetie man!'

Tarzan paced up and down his cell as Helen was told of what had happened in the visiting room.

He began again. 'He wrapped the chocolate biscuits with my poems. He won't even look at them. He's dying, and all he could do was tell me what a hard man he was. Served six months, that's all. I'm so tired of it.' He sat down on his bunk with a huge sigh, his head in his hands.

Helen seized at this display of humanity, and moved just a little closer. 'You're an intelligent man, Tarzan. Why are you demanding we put you in the Strong Box? Now, I have to admit, not many men here would freely ask to be put in there. In fact – ' Helen paused and gave a little laugh – 'I think you're about the only one who ever has. But you know I can't give in to inmates' demands. Next thing we'd have cons asking for extra sugar on their pudding, extra time on association. We can't let that happen, can we? You're a reasonable man, you have to see it from our side.'

Tarzan smiled. She was gradually winning him over; few had tried to talk to him before – it had seemed easier just to get rid of him.

'Nobody knows what to do with me. They're trying to disorientate me, moving me around all the time. I get confused.'

'Tarzan, you've taken officers hostage, you've killed three inmates, you've held three sieges. That's what I would call a record on its own. Plus you've stripped two prison roofs. You could get a job as a demolition man.'

He chuckled, and glanced at her. 'Can I have a cup of tea?'

Helen nodded to one of the officers, who disappeared.

'He didn't even look at my poems . . . We never could talk, and now he's dying.'

'Tell me what you want, Tarzan, and I'll see what I can do. If you want to talk, I'm here and I can come and see you every day, if you want. Just me and you. But you've got to be quiet. You can't keep upsetting everybody else.' She was passed a cup of tea by an officer, which she handed to Tarzan with a smile.

'OK. But I just want to be put back on an ordinary wing, Miss. That's all I want.'

'Well, I'll see what I can arrange.'

'Oh, yes, Miss. I'll be good from know on, Miss. Just you wait and see.'

Marshall couldn't believe his ears. This nutter had been transported to and from more prisons than he'd had hot dinners. He was renowned as the most difficult inmate in Britain. How did she do it? Marshall was once again amazed at this young woman's abilities.

Helen got up to leave the cell, and promised Tarzan that she would look into his case. His enormous bulk filled the cell door as he grinned and nodded goodbye.

CHAPTER 13

Wednesday, 10 January

WITH THREE weeks to go before the rescheduled performance of the show, Annette Bullock had completed casting *The Mikado*, but not to everybody's satisfaction.

'I'm not doing it,' complained Eric Haddock. 'It's not fair. I can't do it.'

But the casting decisions had been posted with a note at the bottom to say the director's decision was final.

Roddy Marsh was trying to look on the bright side. 'But you'll have a wig. And I'm playing one as well.'

'I know that, stupid. That's not the point. I don't want to play that part.'

'No one'll know you in your make-up – lipstick and that. It'll be a laugh.'

Haddock looked at Marsh with distaste. 'You a bloody pervert? You actually want to play one of the three little maids from school, do you?'

Helen was sitting at the back of the chapel, with Gary Marshall. They watched with amusement as the ragged chorus was bullied by Eugene Buffy into their dance steps to the tune of Miss Purvis's piano.

'Gary,' asked Helen, 'have you arranged for Brent to cover on C Wing?'

'Yes, and they need him an' all. Not only because Russell Morgan's away. There's Jumbo Pavarotti Jackson over there, always at rehearsals. Len Syons was worried. He also tells me you asked if we could pull Keith Smith's phonecard.'

'Yes, I did. But, as he rightly pointed out, he'll probably only purloin another. Len says we'd have to withdraw all the cards on C Wing if we want to stop these calls.'

Marshall sighed. 'We can't do that without HQ's say-so. And there'd be a riot.'

Miss Purvis crashed the finishing chords of the chorus that was being rehearsed.

Buffy was haranguing the gentlemen of Japan about their foot movements as Wilfred Samuels, faithfully on duty at Miss Purvis's elbow, took the opportunity to whisper a compliment. 'I do like your cardigan, Miss Purvis.'

The pianist blushed. 'I knitted it myself. I also do crochet and needlepoint.'

'Needlepoint? So do I. I've just got a lovely pattern for a bedspread. Would you like to—'

'Miss Purvis!' called Annette and Buffy together.

'Yes, Miss Bullock?'

'Top of first chorus number again, please!'

At lunchtime, Eugene Buffy was performing his custom-ary act at the meal trolley.

'Is this shepherd's pie, then? It looks like porridge. Is that vegetable soup? That should be oxtail. Where's the carrots? What's this? Parsnips? I hate parsnips, there's supposed to be carrots.' He spotted Officer Brent, just arrived on relief. 'Oi, you. Excuse me! They got the wrong food on here!' He turned to Roddy Marsh, who was behind him in the queue. 'Who's that bloke? He's not been on our Wing before.'

Officer Hully began hustling the queue along. 'Stop nattering there! Move on, Eugene.'

Buffy took his food with deliberate slowness, pedantically asking for the precise ingredients of every selection. The orderly merely shook his head in ignorance.

Further back in the queue, Eric Haddock was pounding a fist on his tray as he discussed Annette Bullock's casting. 'I just don't want to put a frock on, that's all.'

Keith Smith nudged him in the back. 'A frock? You'd look horrible in a frock. Bad enough as it is. But now everyone's going to think you're a poofter.'

Barry Jones, with two trays to fill, was beaming as he surveyed the trolley. 'Is it jam roly-poly today? I like that. Custard, too. Anyone not having their pudding? Because I'll have it.'

Smith turned his ferret face around to find Jones. 'You butlering for Kevin Watts again? What's going on between you two? Not another shirt-lifter like Haddock, are you?'

'No, Kevin's got a migraine, that's all.'

Hully made more hurrying-up noises and Smith's attention switched again. 'Jason! Jaay-son! Jay-yay-son!'

Len Syons appeared and gestured for Jumbo Jackson to join him. He looked at his clipboard. 'Can you tell prisoner 741 Jones, Barry to pack up his gear. He's being released at two o'clock. And I want to see Keith Smith. Get him into my office after lunch.'

Jackson had a request of his own. 'All right if I just take ten? I want to have a word with Miss Bullock about Eric Haddock. He's unhappy and that's an understatement.'

'About the musical, is it? The union wants it scrapped and I agree with them. But go on. Is Philip Brent here?'

Jackson strode off to the Psychology Department, pausing to pass on the good news to Jones.

Syons joined Brent. 'Phil, I'm seeing Keith Smith after lunch. He's in cell 22. He might get into a paddy – we're taking his phonecard off him. Keep an eye, OK?'

'No problem,' said Brent. 'I'll go through the lists, see who's who around here.'

When Jones got back to his pad carrying two lunches, he was in high excitement. 'Kev? I've just been told. I'm out at two.' He put down the trays.

'When?'

'Today. I told you, didn't I? I *told* you!'

A helpless panic washed over Watts. 'Today? But I'm not ready. It's too soon.'

Jones looked at his watch. 'You got an hour and a half.'

The ninety minutes passed at an agonizing rate while Watts ran once again through the intricate world of 44, Elmswood Crescent. When the time came and the door swung open, Watts was still unsure whether he was going to go through with it.

'Barry Jones?' said Officer Brent. 'Prisoner 471. You all packed up?'

In that instant, seeing an utterly strange officer standing there with his clipboard raised, Watts knew that the gods were with him. He had to give it a go.

'Yes,' he confirmed. 'All packed up and ready.'

'Step out, then.'

He did as he was told. The first really dodgy moment would be passing the Wing office, from which any officer

164

who knew Watts might look out. But he could hear a hell of a ruckus going on in there, with Keith Smith's nasal voice almost screaming in fury.

'IT'S A BLOODY LIBERTY! I have not been *sentenced*. I am not a fucking *prisoner*. I am on *remand*. I got *rights*, you bastards . . .'

Under the circumstances, no one took any notice of the man proceeding to freedom behind an armful of personal possessions.

In reception, Brent passed Jones's details across to the duty officer, who barely glanced up. 'All right, Barry, strip your clothes off and take a shower. I'll get your gear.'

As Watts strolled, with all the nonchalance he could muster, to the shower section at the back of reception, the officers chatted among themselves. Safely inside he turned on the water, got undressed and, leaning into the shower cubicle, carefully soaked his head while leaving the rest of his body dry. With wet hair he would look as if he'd had the full shower, which it was imperative not to have. That felt-tip ink might wash off. In seconds he had grabbed a towel and was lightly drying his hair as, without warning, the duty officer popped his head around the corner.

'Blimey – that was quick. Just want to check your tattoos, Mr Jones. We got no pictures when you came in so we're relying on distinguishing marks. Let's see, forearms and thighs. My, my. You got enough anchors, ain't you?'

The officer ticked the form on his clipboard and returned to his desk. Watts wrapped himself in a towel and was about to start back to collect his clothes when his blood froze. Jumbo Jackson's voice was echoing out from the reception area.

'Oi, Phil. Can you hang on here? We've had a call from Walton. We got a return ticket coming in, be here any minute. Eh, you're on C Wing now. Heard about little Eric Haddock? Wanted to play lead in *The Mikado*. Instead she's making him play one of the three little maids.'

Jackson's laugh boomed out. Watts risked a peep through the doorway and glimpsed Jackson's broad back. The duty officer caught sight of Watts and jerked his arm. 'Come on, son! Not got all afternoon.'

Nervously, Watts crept out of the showers. If Jackson should turn round now he was fucked. He approached the desk.

'Over here,' said the officer, leading the way towards a curtained cubicle. 'Trousers, boots, shirt, belt, vest, underpants . . .'

Briefly recoiling at the thought of having Barry Jones's underwear next to his skin, Watts entered the cubicle, pulled the curtain and went through with the pants. The rests of the clothes followed more easily, until he got to the footwear.

'Here's your wallet,' said the duty officer, swishing back the curtain. He was watching Watts struggling to insert his foot into a fancy cowboy boot. 'Too tight, is it?'

'Feet must've swollen,' Watts whispered, conscious of the sweat starting to form on his brow. He was praying Jackson wouldn't suddenly think of something he must tell the duty officer and walk over.

'Happens to the best of us. What did you have in this?' The officer waggled the wallet between his fingers as, with a mighty thrust, Watts got the boot onto his

166

foot. The toes were crushed uncomfortably but he would be able to walk.

'I had, er, a five-pound note, a bus pass and a diary. Also had seventy-five pence in change. I took a tenner out when I was—'

'OK, OK. Go on, take it. They're waiting at the gate so hurry up.'

He returned to the desk as Jackson strolled over to join him there. Watts forced on the other boot and picked up his prison clothes.

Jackson was still talking show business. 'They had this idea of changing the names of the characters to suit the prison staff. So the Lord High Executioner is Mr Marshall and Pooh-Bah, Lord High Everything Else, is Miss Hewitt . . .'

Watts had started across the space between the cubicle and the double doors which led out to the open air. He was flushing hot and cold, his stomach churning. He might spew at any moment. He was only a few yards away, and Jackson's back was still turned to him—

'Oi! You!'

The duty officer's bark made him freeze in his tracks. 'You forgot to sign out, son!'

'Well, I better get back on the Wing,' Jackson was saying with a sigh, wandering away from the desk again. 'Nice talking to you.'

'See you, Curtis. Right, son. Sign there and over the page, on the back.'

Jackson having moved away, Watts, in relief, had taken his place at the counter. But as the officer reached the door leading to the Wings, he met someone. The new voice freaked him out.

'Gassing again, Jumbo?' asked Len Syons, in a loud, authoritative voice. It sounded as if the C Wing Governor was in no mood to piss about. And he knew Kevin Watts perfectly well – and Barry Jones as well. 'Go on, hop it. You know who's coming in from Walton, by the way?' He showed Jackson his clipboard.

'What, already?' said Jackson. 'I don't believe it!'

The duty officer walked over to take a look at the name for himself. 'Oh, Christ, not him.'

'Yes, him,' said Syons grimly. 'Oi – you! You still here?'

He suddenly noticed Watts, still lingering over the form at the desk. The duty officer returned and squinted over Watt's shoulder. 'Come on, sign it, son. Right there.'

Watts began with the K of his first name, then remembered and hastily converted it into a B. He finished the rest of his assumed name exactly as practised back in the cell.

'That's it,' said the duty officer. 'He's just got to go out the gate now, Gov.'

Syons took a step towards them. 'I'll walk him through.'

Watts's head dropped almost to the counter. Shit, shit, shit! He was trembling, and sweat was dribbling down inside his shirt. It was Philip Brent who came to the rescue.

'No, it's OK. I'll do it, Gov. Who is it, anyway? Who's coming in from Walton?'

'Oh, you won't know him but he's famous on C Wing.'

Brent marched ahead of the hunched Watts, who stumbled along in his too-tight boots. Seconds later they were in the open air, away from reception, away from Governor Syons and almost away from Barfield.

Ahead of them a prison van had swung into the

reception yard and was unloading its cargo. Watts looked to see who the arrival was. The glasses looked familiar, so did that faintly uncoordinated gait. Oh, Jesus! Oh, no! It was Brian Samora.

Watts stood at the gate window, presenting his papers. Samora, with two escorting officers, approached him. The gate guard looked over the papers with exaggerated care, then handed them back to him. He hardly dared to turn round. He knew, could sense, that Samora was right behind him. He waited for that high-pitched voice going – surely it would: 'Hey, Wattsy! Is that you? What you doing getting out?'

But at that moment a Range Rover drew up, the engine throbbing in neutral and Watts heard the Governor's voice. 'Brian! What on earth happened?'

Watts thanked the gate guard in a whisper, then swivelled in such a way that his back would be towards the car. He could hear Brian's voice, sing-song-sorry. 'I'm sorry, Miss Hewitt. But it was Sharon's fault. She ditched me and I got drunk. Don't remember anything. So – you and me, we're both back now, eh?'

It was the last Watts heard of Samora's downfall. He didn't care. It wouldn't happen to him – or not until he'd seen his son born. He stood at the side door with Brent, thanking him. Then he was through into free air. He walked a pace, then three more, then another ten. His feet pinched but didn't hurt. He was walking on air. No, he wasn't. He was walking on water – because this was a sodding God-Almighty miracle. He was out.

CHAPTER 14

Thursday, 11 January

HELEN'S ACTION plan for Barfield had taken shape slowly on Simon's state-of-the-art Power Macintosh. Its owner was still away sorting out legal tangles in Hong Kong so there had been little to distract her during the long evenings in his mansion flat with only black coffee, the black cat and Wordperfect Version 3.5 to keep her company. Now she had compiled a detailed fifty-page report outlining all her ideas on drugs in prison and their control.

'A relatively permissive attitude to drugs has informally come about in the prison service,' she wrote in the introduction, 'because, in some eyes, they are thought to be inevitable, unstoppable and even perversely useful, as they keep the prisoner population in a compliant state. We should not be blinded by these false arguments.'

There was no doubt that drugs in prison were a hot potato for politicians and a huge headache for any government extracting a big chunk of its vote from law and order. Recent estimates put the problem at crisis levels, with seizures of drugs in prison doubling, and then doubling again in four years. Two out of three prisoners were on something illegal, and one in five on heroin. In his report on HMP Styal, Judge Tumim found virtually all inmates using cannabis and 80 per cent also on heroin. Meanwhile cocaine and crack, with their much greater potential for disturbing the peace, were gaining ground everywhere. Where would it end?

A lot of anti-drug literature takes its tone from 1950s rhetoric – of the 'Evil Weed Saps Moral Fibre of Youth' variety. But Helen wasn't interested in attacking drugs *per se*. For her, they simply represented an obstacle in her path, a check to her ideas for Barfield. In the report she explained why.

'The spread of drugs is far more dangerous in a captive population than in society at large and therefore to eliminate them is a major prerequisite for any successful penal system. This is true for the following reasons. Narcotics use in free society, like alcohol use, is usually self-limiting or self-regulating. In prison it is not. Starting as a subculture, it soon bids to be the dominant culture – a cancer capable of subverting all normal institutional life. It can grow so fast that, if left alone, it becomes a terminal disease.

'In spite of the obvious negative influence of drugs on the health of the men, it is the economic and social effects of drugs that do the worst damage in prison. The prisoner economy is distorted to an unbearable degree. Extraordinary power is held in the hands of a few of the most ruthless inmates, resulting in huge increases in violence. And a large class of civilian accomplices, acting as couriers or 'mules', is created. All three effects bring the authority of the prison and its officers into disrepute. I therefore want to see drugs eliminated from use in Barfield, and I outline below my programme for doing so.'

At the heart of this programme was the establishment of a new deal with the inmates. Of course, there were repressive measures she could take – systematic testing, electronic sniffer devices, but these would not reach the roots of the problem: boredom, addiction, bullying. There would have to be a massive detoxification programme as well as comprehensive psychological support. But Helen's new deal was to go further than this. She was planning to curtail the inmates' most prized privileges, then reintroduce them in reward for compliance with the drug-free programme. One was the phonecards. These rectangles of plastic were the prisoners' money: they didn't just buy phone-calls. In prison you could buy almost anything under the sun if you had enough phonecards.

She knew she would have a hard time pushing this through the staff – notably the Prison Officers' Association. Yet she believed – with a kind of perverse idealism which her father, for one, would have liked – that the prisoners themselves would like to be rid of drugs. They knew that a drug addict is slave not only to the substance but to the person who supplies it. In prison, the effect is multiplied. To be a prisoner of Her Majesty is bad enough. To be the prisoner also of Sammy the Smackman is like doubling up your sentence.

Yes, thought Helen, as she made her way up to her office at eight thirty to have her second cup of coffee of the day, it was a good report. Its logic was compelling, its vision bold. At this moment her officers were chewing it over at specially convened Wing meetings. There was only one snag. If *only* Mavis had printed up enough copies in advance . . .

Arriving on her floor of the Administration Block, she found Mavis with her head inside the photocopier, trying to retrieve a sheet of paper that had stuck.

'Mavis, any more copies of the report on the way? They've run out in the boardroom, apparently.'

Mavis's voice was muffled. 'The Xerox machine's acting up. I called the engineers and it'll be two hours at least.' She emerged from the bowels of the machine, her face red from the effort.

'Simon Lennox called. And Detective Inspector Tully's on his way.'

'Tully? What's he want?'

'Couldn't say.'

From the stairwell Annette Bullock appeared. 'Can I see you for a moment?'

Helen was half inside her office: the aroma of coffee was calling her. 'Have a word with Mavis, Annette, fix a time. Bit busy at the moment.' She went in and shut the door. She would just have time to phone Simon and welcome him home.

In the officers' lounge, C Wing's meeting, chaired by Len Syons, was proving an undisciplined affair.

'Hey! Hey! Let's try and concentrate. Curtis, what was your point?'

'All I'm saying is,' said Jackson, 'if you start removing prisoners' privileges on this "snakes and ladders" basis, it's going to make our lives very difficult.'

'All right, thanks. Now look, what about the proposal to withdraw phonecards? By the way, anyone listened to the recordings lately? That bastard Keith Smith's been making threats to a prosecution witness. Anyone heard that?'

Officers shook their heads.

'That's why he's not allowed near the Wing phone.'

Jackson was buried in Helen's report, looking with the zeal and patience of a bloodhound for anything with which he could disagree.

'And what about this suggestion?' he suddenly bellowed. '"Extra enforced exercise periods." You start making some of the old lags do even a couple of press-ups and they'll bloody riot.'

'I think it's directed at the younger inmates, that,' said Syons. 'But look at the third paragraph on the same page. "More confrontational therapy programmes." Everyone know what that is?'

Jackson shook his head and muttered into his beard. 'Load of crap, I do know that . . .'

'It all costs,' Syons was saying. 'And we've got cutbacks as it is.'

'She doesn't mention extra funding, that's for sure.'

Chiswick's deep voice echoed the sentiments of most of them. 'It seems to boil down to a lot of extra work for us. But I couldn't quote from it, because I haven't got a copy, have I?'

'Well, I have,' said Jackson. He flicked the report with his fingers. 'We're already doing long hours at the same wage. Everything here is aggravation for us. Where is more security, more protection for staff? It's down to our goodwill and our stress-levels.'

Brent laughed. 'It's ridiculous, isn't it? Right now, we got three full-time psychologists working for the inmates and bugger all for us.'

'We got Mother Hewitt!' suggested a voice at the back of the room, triggering a flurry of laughter.

Syons held up his hand. 'So consensus is, Miss Hewitt wants to get tough but we'll be the ones taking the brunt of it – right?'

'Right,' said Chiswick, and half a dozen other officers.

'Well, I'll tell you one thing,' sang out Jackson. He stood up and raised his fists to his chest. 'Get tough? I'm all bloody for it, mate.'

Helen was on the phone as Mavis bustled in. 'Police are here. It's about the escapee. And I've still not got it working.'

Helen said into her phone, 'Hang on a minute, Simon. Have they found him, Mavis?'

'How should I know? Anyway, Miss Bullock said she needs to talk to you about Miss Purvis. And I'm off to try the Art Department.'

'Miss who did you say?'

'Purvis – piano player.'

'Oh – Simon, look, I'll be there early and I'll pick up the shopping on the way ... Yes, of course I'll cook, you must be jet-lagged. See you later.' She giggled briefly and hung up just as Mavis showed in two CID men. DCI Tully and DS Marsh. Immediately Helen became businesslike. 'Ah, hello. What news of Kevin Watts?'

'His girlfriend's gone into labour. From what you told us, the fact she was pregnant had a lot to do with why he did a runner.'

'It was what his cell-mate told us.'

'Well, the family – of course, you know they're reasonably local? – is saying Kevin hasn't made any contact. We're waiting for him if he shows.'

Annette could be heard raising her voice outside the door. Helen said, 'Excuse me. I think that's something I should deal with. Won't be a moment.'

Annette was flustered. She also looked pale and hollow-eyed. 'Look, I'm sorry to interrupt your meeting, but it's with regard to Miss Purvis and prisoner Wilfred Samuels. I think you should—'

Helen touched Annette's arm to interrupt her. 'Just a moment. Miss Purvis is?'

Annette sighed as Mavis approached, coughing loudly.

'Governor?' said Mavis.

Annette said, 'The pianist for *The Mikado*. I have reason to—'

'Governor!' repeated Mavis urgently. 'It's the Area Manager. He's – he's here!'

Annette clicked her tongue. 'You see I *believe* Miss Purvis is visiting a prisoner.'

'Samuels?' asked Helen.

'Yes, and I just think it should be checked out – or *he* should be.'

John Bunny breezed in after running up the stairs.

'Morning!' He looked unacceptably pleased with himself.

'Mavis,' said Helen sharply. 'Please give Mr Bunny a copy of the report, will you?'

Mavis grimaced. 'I can't. I'm trying to get some more printed up. But the Art Department are still using their copier –'

'Please, Miss Hewitt!' Annette was becoming agitated. 'This woman is my responsibility. She's very naïve and—'

'All right, all right, all *right*! I'll have a word with Mr Samuels on my rounds. OK, Annette? Excuse me, Mr Bunny, I have the police in here. Be with you in a moment.'

176

'Well, for Christ's sake!' muttered Annette.

'Annette,' said Mavis, 'can I use your Xerox machine?'

But Annette Bullock had already left the room.

Not many miles away a red Ford Mondeo drew up outside a terraced house. A young man got out of the driver's seat, locked the door, and walked up the path towards the front door. He rang the bell and waited, rubbing his hands and stamping his feet in the cold. He ignored the presence of the police squad car, parked on the other side of the street.

'Colin Watts,' said one of the two policemen inside. 'Kevin's brother. The grandma's housebound, uses a Zimmer frame. This is her now.'

The door opened slowly and they glimpsed beyond Colin the glint of aluminium and the pale colour of a well-washed cotton print apron. As Colin went in, one of the policemen got on the phone.

'Car oscar-zero-ten. We're in position outside 14 Arpington Avenue. Over.'

At Barfield, Helen was walking with John Bunny past the Punishment Block's exercise area. They could see a tracksuited Tarzan working out alone, doing press-ups. They paused and watched through the wire mesh.

'A strange character,' Helen said. 'One moment he's a human chainsaw, the next he's Mother Teresa. I don't get him at all. He wants to be moved back on a normal Wing.'

'I don't think you should risk it,' said Bunny, shaking his head.

Helen flashed him a defiant glance. 'But we should at least try it, don't you think? The cost of moving him from one prison to another is astronomical. Twenty-eight prisons in eighteen months – with police escorts . . .'

Leaping up from the ground, Tarzan spotted them and jogged over. His breath flowed like smoke from his mouth in the cold air. By the time he reached them they had started on their way again.

'Miss Hewitt . . . Any word yet about me going back on the Wing? *Miss Hewitt!*'

Helen walked another couple of paces. In front of Bunny, she didn't want to be seen to pander to any prisoner. Then she swung round and called to him, 'It's under review.'

'How long will I have to wait?'

'Just keep up your good behaviour and I'll let you know.'

Tarzan growled quietly to himself, bounced off the mesh fence and began jogging again, high-stepping around the perimeter. Two officers stood on duty inside the fenced area. Outside it another guard and a dog watched his every move.

Helen entered Wilfred Samuels's pad on E Wing and glanced around at the clutter. He had two talking budgies named Whiskey and Soda. He had a needlepoint bedspread, which he'd made himself. He had an easel and all the paraphernalia of oil-painting. The current production was a portrait of a child with a teddy bear, copied from a photograph that was attached to the corner of the easel frame with a drawing-pin. On the wall were other paintings, some featuring scenes from the Bible, and numerous snapshots carefully arranged on pinboards – girlfriends, wives, mums and dads, kiddies, household pets, living-room groups, all waiting to be painted.

Oil-painting, needlepoint and teaching budgies to talk are time-consuming activities, but Samuels had a lot of time. He was just fourteen years into an eighteen-year stretch for armed robbery and murder. Appearances can be deceptive.

Helen was looking at the display of photos. 'These your commissions, Mr Samuels?'

The lifer smiled to cover his uneasiness. He had guessed why Helen Hewitt had come to see him. 'Yes. Inmates give me these and I paint the portraits – Christmas, birthdays, you know. I keep these photos as souvenirs.'

Helen bent to examine the work in progress and casually asked, 'And you're working with Miss Bullock on the musical, aren't you?'

'Yes, Miss. I don't sing, so I'm helping out – doing props, scenery-painting and stuff like that.'

'Helping Miss Purvis?'

Samuels stuttered. He knew she was not there just to admire his work. 'Yes, yes, I do. I turn the music for her, sometimes she has to play fast. Can't turn the pages herself, you see.'

'And I understand Miss Purvis has visited you outside rehearsals. Twice.'

'Er, yes.'

'And you write to her?'

'Yes, Miss Hewitt.'

'Does she know why you're in Barfield?'

'No, Miss Hewitt. She just knows I've been in for a long time.'

'But not exactly how long. Is she aware that you're not likely to be up for parole for some considerable time?'

'We haven't discussed it.'

Helen considered. 'And prior to this you haven't had any visit for four years?'

'That is correct. And I appreciate her kindness. She is a very nice, respectable, trusting lady.'

Helen went back to the cell door. 'So make sure you don't abuse her trust. Or the trust we have in you by allowing you to take part in the show.'

'I won't. I appreciate the kindness very much.'

'Good. Thank you, Mr Samuels.'

It was Helen's last call on E Wing, but she had another to make on C Wing before the morning's rounds were over.

Kevin Watts's hideout was dark, damp and smelt of Three-in-One oil. Colin had made it as comfortable as he could: cleared a space for the camp bed, found a sleeping bag, which probably hadn't been used since Kevin had last gone on a school journey, laid in four crates of lager.

Barfield's most recent escapee was fairly relaxed at first, lying on the camp bed, listening to his grandma hobbling around upstairs, all oblivious to her grandson's presence. They didn't confide in their grandma. She was pretty far gone; she'd probably invite the plod in for a cup of tea and say have you met my little boy Kevin, he's down in the cellar mending a fuse. She never even knew about the escape.

Kevin's optimism began to wane as soon as Colin told

him that Anna had gone into labour. He went on and on at his brother to bring a cellphone, but Colin wouldn't. 'Mobile's not safe. But don't worry, she's in good hands. Mum's there as well. You should see her. They put her in a white overall thing and a surgeon's mask.'

'I want to be there. I want to talk to Anna.'

'You can't, Kev. Police are outside the hospital. They're outside here. They're waiting for you to make a move. They're *sure* you're gonna move on the labour ward, so what you got to do is stay away.'

Kevin groaned.

'Tell you what I'm gonna do,' said Colin. 'I'll video his birth, right? The doctors said I could. Lots of people do, apparently. So I got the camera ready and I'm waiting for when they tell me it's time to go down there. Meanwhile here's a packet of biscuits and the *Sun*. There's sod-all in it, but you got page three to keep yourself amused. Want some Kleenex?'

'Fuck off, you!'

'Colin!' It was a querulous voice from upstairs. 'What you doing down there in the cellar?'

'Just coming, Gran.'

He picked up an adjustable spanner to justify his absence and moved towards the stairs. 'I'll bring you the video as soon as he's born. You'll see it all. So just stay put, Kev. No one knows you're here except me. You're safe.'

Kevin inclined his head towards a steel box on the wall. 'Until they come round to read the gas meter,' he said.

C Wing's probation office was a plain room with few embellishments. Annette Bullock would have liked something more dignified – easy chairs, the odd pot plant and Impressionist print. Some hope.

She was sitting with Burt Threlfall, watching him chew his fingernails while he complained. 'I mean, what am I supposed to do? I go into exercise and he's starting on at me. I go into the showers and he's goading me, like, trying to make me lose my rag. I'm telling you, unless he's moved I'll have to take him. I can't keep on turning away, understand? I'm losing face. And it's nothing to do with *me*! I can't sleep for thinking about it.'

Annette's voice was soothing. 'But, Burt, you know it *is* to do with you. You become aggressive very easily over the smallest thing. Now this recent altercation. You're saying it started because—'

'He stole my chair. Brian Samora took my chair in the TV lounge. He knew it was my chair. I always sit in that chair.'

'But you don't, Burt. You've only just moved onto the Wing. Maybe you took Mr Samora's chair.'

'You're not listening to what I'm saying. I'm being *got* at.'

'Burt, will you try and do something for me? Tonight, when you're watching TV—'

Threlfall raised a massive, tobacco-mottled forefinger. 'I'm telling you. I'll wrap the chair over his head. I'll put my foot through the TV. I just won't be able to stop myself. People are always getting at me.'

The door was partially glazed and, walking past, Helen paused to glance in, smiling at Annette and beckoning. The psychologist stood up. 'Excuse me just a moment, Burt.'

She crossed to the door and let herself out.

'I've seen Mr Samuels,' said Helen, in a low voice. 'To be honest, there's little I can do. If Miss Purvis wishes to visit I can't really refuse.'

Annette shrugged. 'If you wanted to you could.'

'No. I've no grounds.' Helen jerked her head at the probation office. 'How's he coming along?'

'He isn't. He's suffering from deep paranoia. I don't think he's stable enough to be on an ordinary Wing.'

Helen considered. From her own contacts with Threlfall she knew him to be deeply unbalanced. Yet he'd got hold of the idea that he was something special: according to him, he was got at because people envied his magnetism and debonair looks. She said, 'Make sure the Wing Governor knows and we'll see where we can move him.'

Helen left Annette and moved down the Wing towards the cells. From a ground-floor pad she heard a voice, in sing-song, calling: 'Jaay-son! Jay-yay-yason!'

It provoked an angry response.

'Shut up! SHUT UP!'

Helen looked. Officer Hully was hurrying away from the cells with clenched teeth.

'Officer Hully! Over here.'

Hully joined her, still looking deeply agitated.

'You settling in all right? Only I noticed just now . . .'

Hully was breathing hard, trying to control his emotion. 'It's Keith Smith, Miss Hewitt. Ever since I got here he's done it. Drives me nuts. I know I'm supposed to ignore it, but I can't. Listen!'

And sure enough there was the voice of Smith again, calling out through the flap of his cell door. 'Jason! Jason! Your pants dry now, Jason?'

'Try not to let it get to you, Mr Hully.' She patted his shoulder and moved off to the gate, leaving Hully staring after her. Was that all she could say? It was all any of them ever said. Right, he wasn't going to let it get to him. He was going to *do* something about it.

By special arrangement, Mahill had been moved and Samora and Buffy were reunited in the same pad on the threes. At this moment Buffy was holding up a small hand-mirror, checking his appearance, while Samora lay on his bunk, thinking aloud.

'Soon as Sharon did what she did I was on my way back, I reckon. Maybe, Eugene, it was psycheelogical. Sort of sublime. Me getting banged up again. You know what I mean?'

'Yes. I know what you mean. You mean you're a pillock.'

A screw's key rattled in the lock and the door opened. Buffy didn't turn round. In his mirror he saw Officer Hully look left and right along the landing and then come in.

'Look, I – um – want you to do something for me. I'll – I'll pay you in smokes.'

'OK,' said Samora, simply.

Buffy butted in fast. 'Hey, wait a minute, Brian, wait a minute. What do you want us to do, Mr Hully?'

Hully cleared his throat. This was embarrassing, even humiliating, but hardly worse than the treatment he was already enduring.

'It's that prick Keith Smith. He's been having a real go at me ever since I came here and . . .'

He looked at Buffy, who was still using the mirror to eye Hully suspiciously. 'And what?' he said.

'I'd like him given a bit of a thrashing.'

Abruptly Buffy turned round. 'You'd like us to beat him up?'

'Yeah. I mean, not too much. Don't want him hospitalized, just . . . I don't have to spell it out, do I?'

Buffy rubbed his chin theatrically. 'Keith Smith? Well, I don't know. He's down on the ones, we're up here, how we going to get him?'

'I'll leave his cell unlocked. Maybe just after association.'

'And another thing. He's a cockney. Got a lot of mates up here. We go in and give him a couple of whacks, they're going to know about it, aren't they?'

Samora raised himself up on one elbow. 'He wouldn't know who done him if we had masks on. Can you get us balaclavas?'

Buffy glowered at his friend. 'Don't be dumb, Brian.'

But Hully was already nodding. 'Yes, I can get you some. I'll do that.'

Hully backed out. 'OK. Thanks,' he said, and left, locking up after him.

'Is he on the level?' whispered Samora. 'If he is, we'll get more than a few smokes out of this, I can tell you.'

Buffy went over and spat in the toilet. 'We're not going to do it. You crazy? You realize what he just asked us to do?'

'Yeah. And you've been threatening to knock Smith about anyway.'

'That's different. That's between cons. Not a screw paying us. It's a bloody liberty, Christ! If you can't trust a screw who can you trust?'

'I hate screws too, you know.'

'I know. That's just normal, but this one's different. This bastard's bent.'

185

He frowned. A thought hit him. He said, 'We got a bent screw, Brian.'

They exchanged looks. They smiled. A bent screw, and only they knew about it. It was knowledge worth having. It was knowledge that might, just *might* get them transferred out of here and into a more cushy nick.

The squad car's vigil at Arpington Avenue had been a long one, almost an entire shift. The two coppers watched Colin Watts bring out the rubbish, go down the road to the cornershop, come back with a copy of the *Sun* and a packet of ginger biscuits.

Now, after they'd been there several hours, Colin appeared again.

'What's he been doing all afternoon?' asked the sergeant.

'Not making a casserole for his gran's dinner, anyway,' said the constable.

'Or dusting the ornaments. Watching Channel 4 racing, more like.'

'Look up his file, did you? He got form?'

'They all got form, the Wattses. Even old Gran.'

'What, GBH with a Zimmer frame? Eh! Here the boy comes now.'

Colin let himself out of the house. He had changed into clean jeans and a fresh bomber jacket and was carrying a nylon zipper-bag slung from his shoulder. A black plastic object was grasped in his hand.

'What's he got there? Looks like a—'

'Video camera.'

'What's it mean, then?'

Colin got into the car, revved the engine and drove

away. The sergeant got on the radio to report. When he'd finished he said, 'I don't know, but I can guess.'

'Go on, then.'

'Her waters broke. She's ten centimetres dilated. Another little bent Watts is about to come into the world.'

The constable was excited. 'I get it, I get it! The camera's to tape the birth, for posterity.'

'Not posterity, Cliff. For absent friends. For Kevin.'

CHAPTER 15

Friday, 12 January

HELEN HAD NEVER found it easy to deal with Oswald Snooper. The huge rastafarian had an attitude born from years of crack-dealing on the rough Peckham estates and was as arrogant as they come. He was used to women being whores or wives, not Governors, and he found it hard to give Helen any respect. She, though, was determined to crack him and let him languish on the Block for a month. She then put him on Rule 43 in the Vulnerable Prisoners' Wing. She knew he would regard this as even worse than the Block but she wanted to teach the man who had smoked crack and raped a member of her staff a lesson. And, in any case, there was good reason to suppose he might be attacked on a regular Wing, as she told him when she went down early in the morning to see him, shortly after he had been placed on Rule 43.

'But I hate it down here,' he raged. 'I want to go back on C Wing.'

'You're here for your own protection. That's what Rule 43 is for. Prisoners who are in danger of being attacked by other inmates.'

'Miss Hewitt, I tell you who is in danger of attack – from me! Every morning I have to face that sick, queer, pervert killer East in the next pad from me. He gloats. He's got guys working for him. He gets all this *fan* mail! It's sickening. I don't want to be anywhere near him.' He took a drag on his snout. 'And all these queens in here won't leave me alone.'

Helen sighed. 'I'm sorry, Mr Snooper, but this is the way it has to be.' She started to move towards the door.

'Wait,' said Snooper. His voice was playing a tune of true desperation now. 'What if I make a deal with you? Just so as I can get moved away from here.'

'I'm not here to make deals with you.' Helen's back was turned – she was half-way out of the door.

'Yeah? Just listen. I know every major drug dealer in this nick.'

Helen stopped in mid-stride. She reached up for the door frame and, using its support, turned in one smooth, graceful movement.

'Go on.'

'I know who brings it in and who passes it out on the Wing. All of it.'

His eyes met hers and they completely understood each other. For Snoopy to trade bodies with straight white society was going so far out into no man's land that the trail back to his own place was going to be a daunting one. But Snoopy had a daughter. To be forced to live next door to a man who'd raped children of the same age was a living torment to him. He would do anything.

And, as it happened, he held in his head the one class of information that Helen desperately wanted. She smiled ironically. So it turned out she *was* here to do a deal, after all.

'I'll see about a transfer, Mr Snooper. To another prison.'

Then she left.

*

Annette had asked the show's pianist to come and see her a few minutes before the morning's rehearsal. Let down by Helen's refusal to do anything to protect Miss Purvis, she had decided to intervene herself.

'Is there anything between you and Mr Samuels?' she asked, trying to control the shrillness in her voice.

'What do you mean?'

'Have you been writing to each other? Have you been visiting him?'

'Oh, that! I didn't think—'

'No! You certainly didn't think.'

'I meant, I didn't think there was anything wrong with it.'

Annette preferred not to meet Miss Purvis's eyes which, she knew, would be looking at her in innocent distress.

'I just can't believe you'd go behind my back. I'm responsible for you. For your being at Barfield.'

'I just didn't think it was necessarily anything to do with you.'

'How can you say that? You know what happened to me. You saw it.'

'Well, Mr Samuels is a trusty. And we do have officers around us at all times.'

'Miss Purvis, you have no knowledge of prisons. You've never been inside one before this. You are not, to my mind, able to make judgements about whether a man is trustworthy.'

She risked a rapid glance across the desk. Miss Purvis's head had gone down and she was groping for a Kleenex. Her voice was trembling on the edge of tears. 'But he's got no family. And he's had no visits for years. And—'

Annette was not going to spare her. She said sternly, 'I don't expect he mentioned why he's here?'

Miss Purvis blinked. Tears were welling in her eyes. Annette knew she shouldn't tell her the details of Samuels's crime and sentence. In fact, she could lose her job for it. She didn't care. 'Mr Lover-boy Samuels is here to serve eighteen years for a particularly vicious armed robbery. *And* a concurrent sentence of life for the murder of a police officer. You are here to play the piano, nothing more. Remember that.'

The meeting of Barfield's six Wing Governors had been in session for forty minutes, and Helen had not had much in the way of an endorsement of her plans.

'If we get ministerial approval for the withdrawal of phonecards, how do you all feel about it?' she asked.

'Don't like it. None of us does.'

'It's their money, their unit of currency, you're talking about. There'll be riots.'

The six men seemed unanimous in their disapproval of Helen's idea. She shut her eyes and took a deep breath before continuing. 'If there are to be no changes, then you're all saying that Barfield is running without any problems whatsoever. In fact, however, it's blatantly obvious we are just filling up the cracks.'

She looked around. Len Syons lit a cigarette, sucked in and spoke with the exhale. 'Maybe if you'd implemented more staff, more officers to start your programme, then there would be some leeway.'

'It's not just a question of more staff. You're simply using that as an ex—'

She looked up at the returning Gary Marshall, who had been out taking a phone call. He murmured to Helen, 'Mavis asked me to tell you Turnbull, George Falla's legal beaver, is in your office.'

191

'Oh dear. Right. Yes, Charlie?'

E Wing Governor Bradshaw had been longing to have a say. 'Facts are facts, Governor. We've got a full house. And we've *not* got a full quota of officers.'

'I'm not advocating we begin this overnight, Charlie. Only gradually. Look, I've got an appointment so I'm afraid I must . . .' She rose and picked up her file. 'But what if we just try it in practice on one Wing only?'

They looked at each other.

'Why not?' said Syons. Then he wished he'd kept quiet.

'Good,' said Helen, cheerfully. 'C Wing it is, Len. Thanks for volunteering.'

And before anyone could react she'd walked out. After a moment's surprised silence at the way they'd been outmanoeuvred, Bradshaw burst out laughing. 'You walked into that one, Len. Still, you'll need a bit of help with Tarzan moving in.'

Syons was gobsmacked. '*What?* On my Wing?'

Bradshaw had fished a clip of banknotes from his pocket. He stripped a blue one from the wad and wafted it between two fingers. 'Yup. The Governor's trying to rehabilitate him, treat him like a human being or something. And this fiver says he won't last a day.'

Syons threw his head back in scorn. 'Fifty, I can handle Tarzan.'

'I've seen my client Mr Falla, Miss Hewitt.'

Turnbull wore a confident smirk on his face. What on earth flowed through his head apart from an endless hymn of self-praise? Helen wondered. 'Is he in good health?' she asked. 'I most certainly hope so, as he's been coddled for the past three weeks and more.'

'Well, I'd like to set a date for the police to interview him, obviously with you and SO Russell Morgan present. Monday – morning or afternoon – would suit.'

Helen leaned across and snapped down a key on her intercom. 'Mavis, do you have my diary for Monday? Mr Turnbull would like to set up the inquiry into the hostage situation. I'll need at least two hours.'

Mavis's piped voice came back with rare efficiency. 'It'll have to be in the afternoon. You're booked up all morning.'

Turnbull had his attaché case open on his knee, and a leather-bound desk diary open inside it. He scribbled a note, shut the book and brought down the lid of the case. 'Monday afternoon it is, then.' He snapped the brass catches of the case. 'How is Mr Morgan?'

'Neither as fit nor as able as your client. He is still on sick leave. Is there anything else?'

'I don't think so – unless . . .'

'Yes?'

'Unless you're free for dinner one evening?'

Helen was astonished and it showed. 'What?'

'I'm asking you out for dinner.' That smirk still played around his sleek mouth.

'I'm sorry. I'm not available.'

'I didn't say when.'

'It's immaterial. I am not available.'

She was aware of speaking curtly. There was a moment's silence. Had she been unforgivably rude? No, to hell with it, she wouldn't say anything to soften it. And then the phone rang. 'Excuse me,' she said. 'The phone.'

It was Mavis, in a whisper. 'Do you want rescuing? There's Officer Jackson with inmate Brian Samora wanting to see you.'

'Oh, all right, if it's important.'

Turnbull rose and gave a stiff, ironic little bow. 'Thank you for your time.'

At the door, Jackson stood aside to let Turnbull pass, then walked in with Brian Samora in tow. With exaggerated care, the officer closed the door and nudged Samora towards the Governor's desk. 'Go on,' he urged. 'Tell Miss Hewitt. Tell her what you just told me, Brian.'

Samora stood in front of the desk like a small boy called to the head mistress's office. He cleared his throat.

'Well, Brian?' she asked. 'What's this all about?'

'You got a bent officer, Miss Hewitt. And he's bringing in balaclavas.'

The costumes had arrived and rehearsals were developing into something like a toddlers' one o'clock club, with inmates diving into the two big wicker baskets to try on hats, wigs, false beards, kimonos and wooden sandals, then cat-walking around the stage and screaming with laughter.

Miss Purvis and Wilfred Samuels busied themselves sorting out music. 'I think I'd better not see you again,' she murmured. The words came with difficulty, tears not far away.

'It's all right, Miss Purvis, I understand, no hard feelings. But can I give you this? They're just some poems I wrote.'

From his shirt pocket he extracted a few sheets of paper, folded in four, and proffered them. Miss Purvis averted her face. 'Better not take them, Mr Samuels.'

He tucked them into the pile of *Mikado* music. 'I'll leave them here for you.'

'Come on, now! Please don't mess with the costumes,'

shouted Annette. She hurried round, trying to assemble the three little maids from school, including Eric Haddock. He hadn't had so much fun since Cub Scouts.

The costume skips were close to the Wings and stood partly in shadow. One inmate had pulled out a kimono and was starting to undress to try it on. As Annette approached the skip, he shrank further into the shadow and in the corner of her eye, as she touched the skip, she saw him stripping off his shirt.

Suddenly she froze. Her heartbeat thudded and stopped, then thudded again. She saw Snooper there, pulling her into the darkness, pulling at her clothes. She screamed and screamed again.

'Hey, Miss Bullock,' said Jumbo Jackson, coming up behind. 'What's the matter?'

She flailed out at him, thrashing with her arms when he touched her, then going down, half screaming and half sobbing. The prisoner stood a few feet beyond her with his mouth open.

'I never touched her! I never touched her!'

'Hully?' said Syons, incredulously. 'But he's a good steady lad.'

Helen had cornered the C Wing Governor near the coffee machine in the officers' lounge.

'Not quite so good,' she said. 'He has apparently asked Eugene Buffy and Brian Samora to beat up another prisoner.'

'Who?'

'Does it matter who? It's Keith Smith, actually.'

'Did they tell you themselves? I wouldn't trust those two little bastards.'

'We'll have to listen at least to what they've got to say.'

'I'd prefer just to front it out with young Hully.'

'He'll deny it, won't he? Now, Buffy's at the rehearsal. I want to wait till he's back on the Wing and then see them both. In the meantime – do not inform Officer Hully, understood?'

Gary Marshall came in to refresh his cup.

'Ah, Gary, I have an update on the Watts escape.' Helen drew him to one side as Syons, miffed at being left out of things, muttered about getting back on the Wing.

'Have they picked up our tattooed wonder, then?' asked Marshall.

'No. But the police think he'll try to see his girlfriend. She's given birth this morning. So maybe we'll be welcoming him back any time.'

'Bad news about Miss Bullock, Miss Hewitt. She freaked out during rehearsals.'

'Oh, my God, what happened?'

'Jackson saw it. Says nobody touched her, she just flipped, started screaming.'

'Where is she now?'

'Her office. Doc Harris is with her.'

She was sitting with a cup of machine-made tea, her feet drawn up under her, in one of the easy chairs. Davyd Harris sat opposite her, his elbows on his knees.

'You just bottled it up, Annette. And then by refusing to—'

'Face it? Please!'

'Annette, listen to me. There's a colleague of mine, not in the Prison Service, who might be able to—'

'A psychologist? What the hell do you think *I* might

196

be? I don't need therapy and, if I do, I'm more than capable of dishing it out to myself.'

She jumped up and walked to the window. It was late afternoon. A weak, wintry sun had broken through the clouds and made the damp asphalt of the exercise yards gleam. Two prisoners were running about, tagging each other and laughing. It was weird to see them enjoying themselves. She had been afraid that, as a result of all this, she would end up hating all inmates. That, at least, had not happened.

'Annette,' said Harris in a severe voice, 'I would suggest you take leave – at least two weeks.'

'No, I refuse to. I don't need that. I need to work.'

'Well, I'm sorry, but as chief medical officer I will have no alternative but to have you ordered off duty.'

Annette drained her cup and dropped it into the waste bin. 'You know, I counselled rape victims for two years. I thought I knew exactly what they were feeling. I advised, cajoled, encouraged them to talk, talk, talk about it. So, like a good counsellor, every night I've gone over it. And every morning I wake up thinking about it.' She clenched her hands. 'I know it isn't the physical humiliation, the brutishness, even the loss of control, that eats into you. Do you want to know what it is?'

Harris looked steadily at her. 'Go on.'

'It's the fear. I'm frightened, and I can't make it go away.'

There was a rap on the door. As Helen came in with Gary Marshall, Annette was standing by the window, sobbing. Dr Harris was sitting down, his hands resting, palm up, on his knees.

Helen said, quietly, 'Could you leave us alone?'

After they'd left, she stood behind Annette, patting

her shoulder. 'Shush, it's all right. It's all right. You'll be OK.'

The two women continued to stand silently, for a while, looking out over the exercise yard.

CHAPTER 16

'I MISSED YOU, I missed you.'

Simon had crashed into the flat, calling her name. He'd dropped his suitcase, hurled his briefcase at the sofa and run through to the bedroom, where Helen sat in a dressing gown, making up her face.

'Oh,' she said, in delighted disappointment, 'I was going to be all ready and dressed for you.'

'You're overdressed for what I have in mind.'

They hugged and staggered in an undignified way towards the bed. He was undoing her dressing gown.

'Come on, you,' she said, 'let's get your kit off too. Fair's fair.'

Three-quarters of an hour later, they were half-way through a bottle of champagne and Simon had brought her up to speed on his trip. 'Anyway, it was hellishly frustrating with the case dragging on far longer than anyone expected. But it could make me a junior partner.'

She kissed him lovingly. 'You brilliant man.'

She rolled from the bed and wrapped herself back in the dressing gown. 'Right, you can finish your drink, have a shower. Give me twenty minutes to prepare you a delicious meal.'

She walked across to the dressing table and picked up

a prison file. 'And wrap that intellect of yours around this. I need to talk about it.'

'Sure. What's in it?'

'Details about a prisoner and a hostage.'

'Where?'

'Barfield.'

Colin's video camera was jammed to Kevin's eye as he watched the playback. His baby. He was beautiful, but he had a look on his face that reminded Kevin of his mum when she lost her temper. Anna was sitting up in the labour-ward bed, covered in sweat, cradling him. Her eyes were shining. She looked up at the camera – at Kevin!

'He's eight pounds and five ounces. Can you see, Kev? Got all his fingers and all his toes. He's beautiful. He's perfect, just . . . perfect.'

The camera wobbled and then zoomed onto the face of the baby. His son filled the little viewfinder – but the image became fuzzy as Kevin's eyes filled with tears, and then it went black. That was it. The third time he'd seen it.

Colin was whispering urgently, but Kevin hardly heard him. 'I can't replay again, Kev. I've got to go. They're right outside, man.'

'Give me that phone. I've got to talk to her. I've *got* to.'

Colin hesitated, then handed over his portable. Kevin keyed in the number he'd biroed onto the back of his hand.

'For God's sake, be careful. The cops are watching her.'

He got a connection immediately. 'Hello? Anna? Can

you talk? . . . Yes, yes. I've just seen it three times. He's beautiful . . . I love you, Anna. I love you both. Hello? Hello? Fuck! Cut off.'

He shook the phone, tears glistening on his cheeks and started to dial again. Colin grabbed at the phone but missed. 'Oh, come on, man. I've got to go.'

Kevin got a second connection. He spoke urgently, fast. 'Listen to me, Anna, I'll come and see you, I don't care how I do it, I'll see you, I'll see him, I will. I love you.'

And he shut the phone down, folded it and handed it back to Colin.

The squad car had returned to Arpington Avenue duty late in the shift and it was dark. Now, as he ate a sandwich and sipped from a flask of tea, the sergeant was passing on to his colleague the result of some research he'd carried out earlier in the day.

'Apparently, when they arrested him originally they got him in the back of a patrol car and the officer stepped out to say something. Next moment Watts had slid over the back of the seat into the front and drove off.'

'You kidding? The bugger nicked a patrol car?'

'Yep, but there's more. It was one of the specials. A flaming arsenal in the boot. He drove it around for hours, clocking up Christ knows what mileage, then dumped it – back at a police station.'

'Wondered why the Gov's gone out of his way on it.'

'Too damn right, mate – it was his patrol car.'

'Is that what he's banged up for?'

'No way. He pulled a few blags. He's a nasty little bastard. Look out, he's coming. Colin Watts.'

He got on the radio. 'Suspect's brother just left. We tail or stay put? Over.'

The sergeant started his engine as Colin Watts's Mondeo accelerated away. Then control came back to them. 'Stay where you are. Watch the house. We got another car on the tail. Over.'

Meanwhile the constable was looking at the house. 'Hang about, Sarge – light on top bedroom, see that? From the hall, light on, now it's off again. Wait, wait – another light, see?'

'For someone on a Zimmer, the old bat's moving around fast.'

The bedroom light snapped off again and the sergeant opened his door. 'Going to take a look. Stay in the car, get on the radio.'

He strode up the front path.

Kevin's gran was in bed. He'd made himself scrambled eggs and tea, then popped up to Colin's bedroom to collect a book. Now, as he moved back through the hall towards the cellar again, the door chimes stopped him. He knew it was the filth even before he heard the voice calling through the letterbox.

'Can you open the door, love? It's only the police.'

Kevin opened both his hands, unable to control them, and the eggs and tea crashed to the floor. He ran into the kitchen and shut the door as the chimes sounded again. He crossed the kitchen, catching his foot on the ironing board, which clattered over, and then he was out of the back door, across the small paved yard and inching open a wooden gate.

He stuck his head out, looking first one way, then the other. Nobody. He bolted out and sprinted along the alley. If the cops had any sense they'd have the end of the alley covered double quick. He had to get there first.

In the dark, he didn't see the heap of black plastic bin bags and tripped, taking a rolling fall. As he went over, he fell on a half-open rubbish bag and sliced his knee on the sharp-edged lid of a baked-bean tin. Within seconds he could feel his leg wet. But he thought he'd landed in a puddle and ran on. Before he had reached the end of the alley he had cannoned into a metal rubbish bin, which crashed loudly to the ground.

The alley bent to the right and ended a dozen houses up Arpington Avenue from his gran's. There were parked cars in the street. He turned and could hear a commotion from around number 14 – the police calling out, neighbours coming to their windows. He tried a car door. Locked. He walked on, his leg throbbing. A second car, a third. Kevin was an experienced car thief. He knew that he'd be lucky to find one open in twenty-five he tried – one in fifty in some areas of town. But, after all, it might be his lucky day. He persisted, looking back. Tried another door, the fifth. He glanced back again. The squad car's engine was running, the lights were on. He came to a sixth car. It was open.

He crawled in and shut the door as quietly as he could. He lay in the dark, among the pedals, breathing heavily, trying to listen to what was going on. The voices were too faint to make out, but he didn't care. It must be his lucky day, the day his son was born.

CHAPTER 17

Saturday, 13 January

HELEN'S WARM balsamic corn-fed chicken and prawn salad was usually a triumph, and this one, with garlic bread and washed down with a fantastic bottle of white wine, had certainly tasted great. But there must have been something wrong with the prawns because Helen was sick before she went to bed and again in the morning. For a while Simon had pretended to be cross – sex-deprived. There had been nothing wrong with the prawns he'd eaten. But now he sounded his usual cheerful self. 'Just the one prawn can do it, you know. Break a camel's stomach.'

She lay with a damp facecloth on her forehead.

'You want me to call the doctor?'

'No, I'm better. In fact, I think I'll have a whiskey to settle the stomach. Got any of that bourbon I like, Wild Turkey? Get one for me, get one for yourself and join me in bed.'

'You want a whiskey at eight o'clock in the morning?'

'Why not? It's Saturday.'

'Well, all right, why not indeed?'

The penalty for the next hour of self-indulgence was the washing up. When Simon saw the state of the kitchen he blanched.

'Jesus, it looks like a bomb's hit it. I don't get it – you didn't really cook anything.'

'I did. Crème brûlée!'

'But my God, Helen, is there a pan you missed?'

'Oh, shut up, you!'

Helen stood and watched him scrubbing away, still sipping her drink. She said, 'I bet Anthony bloody Turnbull doesn't wash up as well as you.'

'Yes, well, I'll be interested in what he might try to pull over the Barfield business. And if he succeeds.'

'Succeeds – you mean in proving it was Senior Officer Morgan's own fault he was taken hostage? You're joking.'

'He just might, Helen. Don't underestimate him. I wasn't joking when I said Turnbull's one of the élite. He's one of the very best there is . . . quite apart from being a brilliant rugger player.'

Helen swallowed a sip of whiskey and then felt a twinge in her stomach.

'Oh God.'

She bolted for the bathroom.

Hospital casualty was quiet on the Saturday morning. Kevin Watts was sitting in a cubicle, with his damaged leg resting on a sterilized plastic sheet. A nurse was sitting on a stool wrapping the bandage gently with her practised fingers.

'We used clamp stitches as the cut was quite deep. And Doctor's writing out a prescription for some antibiotics.'

'Thanks,' said Watts, blankly. It had been an unpleasant night, with not much sleep. He had found a woollen scarf in the car and managed to staunch the flow of blood with it. Getting the scarf out of the wound had not been pleasant.

'Nurse,' he said, 'is the maternity unit close to here?'

She tipped her head towards the ceiling. 'Two floors up. Not pregnant as well, are you?'

She finished the bandage and stood up. 'I'll just be a second, dear. See if I can get that prescription. You get dressed again.'

She swept crisply out and Watts eased himself off the bed groping for his trousers. They were torn and caked with blood, but he had no others so he put them on gingerly. He looked around. A curtain divided his cubicle from the next one. The curtain was slightly open, and he could see a white coat draped over the bed. A stethoscope hung out of the pocket.

Cautiously, Watts poked his head into the cubicle. Empty. He reached for the white coat, drew it into his own cubicle and put it on. A badge on the lapel said 'Dr V. Patel'. He wrenched it off and jammed it in the pocket, then hung the stethoscope round his neck. He was ready. Dr Watts limped out into the corridor and went looking for a public telephone.

Detective Chief Inspector Tully was in a fury as he left home, following the phone call from control to say Watts's hideaway had been located. His empty stomach didn't help, though, God knows, to be called out before breakfast was situation-normal as far as he was concerned. What bugged him was that it was the grandmother's place – the one Watts family house they never got a search warrant for. *And* the little bastard had got away.

He snatched up his radio. 'Any news on the car taken from Arpington Avenue yet?'

'Yes, Gov. We think we've got it. Abandoned outside St Mary's Hospital.'

It took five minutes through the light Saturday-morning traffic.

'We found it in a side-street, just over there,' panted a uniformed officer, running over when he saw his boss drive up.

'And? *And?*'

'Seat's covered in blood. I got someone checking out Casualty now.'

They were joined by the crew from another patrol car. Tully leaned in and jabbed a finger at the driver. 'Right, you, get on the radio. I want all the hospital exits covered. He's here! He's either injured or – worst case – he's got a wounded hostage. So I want the armed-response team. I'm going to talk to Casualty.'

Tully took off almost at a run. The driver of the patrol car picked up his handset as his mate said, 'Bit strong, isn't it?'

'You kidding? He nicked the Gov's patrol car. This is personal. It's called "get-the-egg-off-my-face". Car alpha-zero-foxtrot to base . . . request AR team to stand by, St Mary's Hospital . . .'

Watts had been aware of the increasing police presence for the last hour and a half. It was inevitable. They'd have found the car and, of course, the blood would bring them into the building even if they didn't already know about Anna and the baby being here.

He still had the labour-ward phone number written on his hand, so he'd called up and told Anna he was in the coffee shop off the main reception. She promised she would come down and bring the baby, as soon as she could. That had been two hours ago. He'd had three cups of tea, read the *Star* right through three times and played hide-and-seek with the police. Meanwhile he watched the lift, his heart rising to his throat whenever it opened. And now, at last, she was walking unsteadily towards him. She wore a dressing gown and was carrying in the crook of her arm a blue-blanketed bundle.

She didn't see him at first. Various patients and hospital staff bustled about and she stood in the middle of the cafeteria, looking uncertainly around. He hurried towards her.

'Anna. Oh, Anna.'

He wanted to touch her but they couldn't embrace because of the bundle in her arms. He stroked her cheek and looked into her face. The eyes were frightened.

'You all right?'

'It hurts to walk, a bit. But we're here, anyway.'

They found an empty corner and sat side by side on two scuffed easy chairs.

'What took you so long?'

'There's a policewoman posted on my ward. I had to wait ages till she went to the toilet. Oh, Kevin!'

'Shush, shush. It doesn't matter. Did anyone see you leave the ward?'

'I don't know. But you're mad to come here. There's police everywhere.'

'I know, I know. I'm going to give myself up. But I just wanted to hold him. Can I hold him?'

She swung round gently so that he could open the blanket and see his son's face. Then she held the baby out to him, whispering, 'I'm going to call him after you. He looks just like you. Even his hands are the same. Look.'

Watts parted the blanket a little more and found a

miniature pink fist. 'Hello, Kevin! I'm your daddy, yes, I am.' He lifted the baby from her. He was so light and small. He settled him into the sling of his arms and rocked him from side to side.

'I love you, Anna. And I love my baby boy. He's all mine. He looks like me, doesn't he?'

Much of the police operation was being carried out in hushed tones. Tully had interviewed one of the café counter staff and showed her Watts's mugshot.

'Looks like him.'

'But is it him?'

'Yeah.'

'Sure?'

'Yeah. But he was wearing a white coat. I thought he was a medical student.'

Tully rejoined his colleagues in the sister's office. 'I've got a confirmed sighting. He's dressed as a doc.'

'Gov, the WPC on the postnatal ward lost Anna. She's gone AWOL. Taken baby with her.'

'Oh, great. All we need. I suppose the WPC went for a wee, did she?'

'Well, at least it means something's happening.'

Ten minutes later Tully took a tour of the coffee shop. It seemed a normal crowd in there. Then he spotted Anna, coming from some recess at the back and making her way through the people. She walked quickly, a bundle in her arms. Tully backed off, tracking her with his eyes. Another officer had also seen her.

'Gov, she's going to the lifts. She got the baby?'

'I don't know. She's carrying something . . .'

Tully took the radio handset. 'Hold positions, let her go. Nobody make a move until she's in the lift.'

He listened to his earpiece. 'She's back on postnatal? With the baby? What? Well, has she or hasn't she got the baby?'

He raised his eyes to the ceiling. 'Believe this! They don't know if she's got the baby. Right, seal off the café. Let's collar this bastard.'

The ring of officers around the reception block moved in tighter. The customers and staff in the cafeteria were evacuated. The armed-response team waited just outside in an ambulance bay.

Suddenly Watts appeared from the recess at the back of the café. He carried a bundle wrapped in a blue blanket. He glanced round, saw he was the last one left in the place, then spotted Tully standing in the middle of the reception hall. He called, 'Oi, copper. Stay away from me. I mean it. You make one move towards me and I'll drop – I'll drop him.'

Tully's insides were churning with anger, tension, desire to smash this bastard's head against a wall. But he'd been here many times before. He knew how to play it – calm, kind, reasonable. 'Nobody's going to do anything, Kevin. We just don't want any harm to come to the baby.'

He snapped his fingers and a woman officer came forward, holding out her arms. 'Let me take the baby now, Kevin, please.'

Watts thought it difficult to imagine a less motherly looking figure than a female police officer. Something to do with the chequerboard scarf they wore and that daft hat.

'No, I won't! Get this. I want to walk out of here. I want to get into a patrol car outside. I will not be dragged out.'

Tully motioned the officer back. Get into a patrol car? And what happened last time this little sod did that?

'All right, all right. Let him walk. Go on, Kevin son. You keep walking. There's a car just outside.'

Watts moved towards the exit. As he reached the bank of lifts a chime sounded and one of the doors slid open. Oblivious to the drama she was stepping into, a nurse walked out. She was carrying a tray laden with samples. Watts's reaction was as swift as it was unexpected. He did a U-turn and shoulder-charged the nurse whose tray crashed to the ground. The test-tube contents flowed across the lino as Watts leaped into the lift. The doors slid shut.

Tully sprinted forward and hammered the lift-call button. 'Cut him off! Get up the stairs, one body on every floor.'

He looked at the lights above Watts's lift as they went through three, four and five. The highest number was six.

He turned to the nurse who was standing, shocked, beside the debris from her tray. 'What's on the sixth floor? Is it a ward or what?'

'No, it's a – a – utility floor. Fire escape!'

The sixth-floor indicator lit up and stayed on.

'He's on the bloody roof!' shouted Tully.

It was a long way down. Watts could see a police cordon defined by yellow tape, with idle spectators and evacuees from the hospital marshalled behind it. Patrol cars were parked at various angles, their identity codes in large black figures on the roofs. There was also the armed-response van, and a trio of dog handlers with their Alsatians. Everyone, including the dogs, was craning up to watch him mounting the fire escape. As he reached the roof, still holding his blue bundle close to his chest, he heard two men climb onto the fire escape a few stages below. It was Tully with a uniformed man.

'Kevin,' called Tully, 'we're all a long way from you. Nobody's going to harm you.'

Watts stepped off the fire escape, crossed a narrow leaded portion of roof and came to a slated section. He began to clamber down towards the guttering. Tully turned his head and hissed at the uniform just behind him, who mouthed into his radio. Down below, the police marksmen started to climb out of their van, their weapons ready.

'Kevin. Just come away from the edge of the roof. Kevin. Bring us the baby, son. You don't want to harm the baby.'

Watts now had one foot resting on the slates and the other on the guttering. He felt it give a fraction – perhaps the fixings were rusty or loose. At this moment he didn't care much. He looked back at the coppers, who had panted up the cast-iron stairs and were watching him from the flat part of the roof. Then he leaned forward, peering down at the stick people and toy cars below. He wobbled, then started to laugh. He lifted the blue woollen bundle high above his head and looked up, watching an airliner's shining vapour trail as it crawled across a section of cold clear sky. He started laughing loudly, turned once more towards Tully to make sure he was watching, then swivelled back to the people on the ground.

'Catch! Catch!' he yelled, and tossed the bundle out and down.

Everyone watching gasped, but then the bundle started to unravel. The blanket peeled off and, caught by the wind, flapped and floated sideways. Inside it was nothing but a tabloid newspaper – the pages pulled apart and then crushed together haphazardly to increase their bulk – and a scatter-cushion from the hospital. The wind soon separated the paper and blew it away in every direction. The cushion spun in the air until it thumped onto the roof of a car.

'You big pillock, Tully! Conned you again, you git. It wasn't my baby! Think I'd do this with my own baby? You're all stupid bastards. I wouldn't hurt him. Come on you bastards, I'll take you all on!'

Tully, incandescent with fury, clenched and unclenched his fists. Nobody, but *nobody*, messed with Vincent Tully like this and got away with it.

Three hours later, Helen was at the Barfield gate-lodge, handing in her disc and receiving her key-ring from the pegboard. Jumbo Jackson caught sight of her as he was running out to collect a spare packet of fruit gums from his car.

'Miss Hewitt,' he called, 'there's been a lot of bad feeling with the show being cancelled again. You know, we all – officers and inmates – put a lot into it, we really did.'

Helen sighed. 'Mr Jackson, I've just been called in on my weekend off. I'm not feeling my best and there is an emergency. This bloody musical is the last thing on my mind. Who cancelled it anyway?'

'I don't know,' said Jackson, momentarily dumb-founded. 'Not you?' he added under his breath as Helen marched away towards inmate reception.

She said, 'Watts.'

The desk officer said in a subdued voice, 'Hospital, Miss Hewitt.'

She could feel her stomach playing up as she walked up the stairs to the Health Care Centre. Gary Marshall – talking on his radio – and Dr Harris were waiting. 'What's the problem?'

Marshall wore an even more lugubrious expression than usual as he shut down his handset. 'We need a camera because this didn't happen our end. He arrived in this condition.'

'What condition?'

Harris went ahead of her towards a curtained cubicle. He drew back the curtain and ushered Helen inside. Marshall followed. 'We were only told he resisted arrest and had to be restrained. He didn't seem too bad, just a bit fuzzy, and then we undressed him.'

Kevin Watts's face was unmarked, although a black bloodclot showed through his hair above the ear. He lay there not moving, except for his eyes which were open and responsive. His lips quivered but no sound came from them. The doctor drew back the sheet and began to unbutton Watts's pyjama top. He opened it to show the chest covered in bruises, many turning black, and a number of deep scratches, which had been cleaned and treated with ointments.

'This is only what you see,' said Davyd Harris. 'There are also traumatic injuries to his testicles, shins, thighs, back and buttocks. Bruising, contusions and swelling, fractured ribs. This, in my opinion, is all consistent with a very severe beating indeed. He's also had a blow to the head, which may prove to be more serious than all the rest.'

Helen compressed her lips. She had forgotten her own

214

sore stomach. 'Right, get him photographed. And I want a list of all the Barfield officers who were in reception when he came in.'

'None of our officers did this,' said Marshall. 'I am absolutely—'

'I'm not making any accusations, Gary. But somebody did it. He should never have been accepted back into Barfield in this condition. But he was, so now he's our responsibility. Is he conscious?'

Harris leaned over Watts's face. 'Yes, just. He's trying to say something.'

Helen sat down on the chair beside the bed and put her ear near Watts's mouth. The sounds were barely audible.

'Ke – Ke – Kevvy – nnn – buh – buh – bayy . . .'

On their way back to the Admin Block, Marshall told her he'd seen this sort of thing before in the case of recaptured escapees. 'I doubt if we'll ever find out who did it.'

'You want to bet?' shot out Helen. 'I want to see everyone involved – reception officer, Duty Governor, Wing Governor, principal officer, the lot. Oh, and, Gary! Who cancelled *The Mikado*?'

'I suppose I did.'

'Look, I had a tough enough fight with the union to keep it on. So you can relay to all those concerned – and especially Mr Jackson who I know will otherwise make my life a hell – that Gilbert and Sullivan will go on at Barfield as arranged.'

'But Miss Bullock is – I mean, who'll oversee it?'

'We'll come to that later. I will, if necessary. It's about

time I made my presence felt around here. It's about time everybody realized that *I* am Governor of Barfield.'

'Show goes on, then?'

'Yes, most definitely. The show goes *on*.'

CHAPTER 18

Monday, 15 January

TARZAN CAME through C Wing gates like a warlord. He walked between two officers, carrying his pile of possessions with ceremonial gravity and staring straight ahead, as if it would demean him to look either to the right or the left. The sight of him stopped Officer Jackson in his tracks as he officiated at breakfast-tray collection. He bolted for the Wing office where Len Syons was printing out a memo.

'How come we had to have him?' said Jackson. 'With all the excitement over Miss Bullock I never did find out.'

'Don't say a word,' said Syons, laying his finger alongside his nose. 'That bugger Charlie Bradshaw's stitched us up – laid fifty quid Tarzan won't last more than twenty-four hours on my Wing.'

He laughed as he picked the memo out of the laser printer and selected a pen from his pocket. 'So let's see if we can cope with him for forty-eight. We'll clean up.'

'We're still lumbered,' said Jackson anxiously. 'Where you putting him?'

'Number four. It's ready.' He signed the memo and walked out into the association area to pin up the notice. Cell number four happened to be beside the board.

'Morning, Mr Tarzan,' Syons said briskly. 'I'm Mr Syons, your Wing Governor. This is Officer Jackson.'

Abruptly Tarzan's face changed. He broke out into a broad, beaming smile as Syons took his papers from the minders and nodded at the empty cell. 'Get your kit sorted. It's lock-up now, until ten thirty.'

Tarzan cleared his throat and spoke. Incredibly, his voice was tight, as if afflicted with nerves. 'Will I be allowed on the Wing for association, sir?'

'You're no different from anyone else on this Wing, Mr Tarzan. Same rights, same obligations.'

'Want to bet?' muttered Jackson, as he perused the noticeboard to read Syons's latest memo. It concerned an insignificant aspect of tray collection. As Tarzan moved into his cell, Jackson's eye moved on to another memo, which appeared over Gary Marshall's signature. 'Eh, when did this go up? Musical's back on, is it?'

Len Syons locked Tarzan's cell door, lifted the flap and looked in. 'OK, Tarzan?'

He dropped the flap and strolled past Jackson. 'Governor's orders, the show goes on.'

They heard a booming, cheerful voice from cell number four. 'Musical? What musical? I can sing, you know.'

A resonant bass voice issued from the cell. 'Holy, holy, holy, Lord God Almighty!' Cutting through it, Syons heard the crisp tone of Helen Hewitt's 'Governor!' as she stood at the gate, awaiting unlock.

Ten minutes later, after Jackson had brought Buffy and Samora into the probation office for a meeting with Miss Hewitt, the allegations against Officer Jason Hully, who was currently not on shift, were reviewed. Helen made copious notes.

'. . . and Officer Hully then said he would bring in the balaclavas?'

Eugene Buffy lounged in front of her, feeling that an over-respectful attitude would compromise his status as the Deep Throat of C Wing.

'Officer Jason Hully then said he'd bring them in and he would leave Keith Smith's cell door open so we could get in there to beat him up.'

'And this was on . . .?'

'Last Friday morning.'

'Three days ago. And has he reapproached you, or discussed this further with you in any way?'

'No, because we have not encouraged him. Not until we spoke to the authorities. Because we know our word against the screws doesn't count.'

'But as things stand, that is exactly what it would be, Mr Buffy. Your word against Officer Hully's.'

'Right,' broke in Samora excitedly. 'We know that – which is why we're prepared to prove it.'

'Yeah,' said Buffy coolly. He remembered that Deep Throat doesn't get excited. 'What we propose to do is tape his next visit. Then you got proof – and we got proof. Understand?'

Helen checked her watch. It was a chock-a-block morning.

'Thank you, both. Either I or the Deputy Governor or Governor Syons will talk to you again.'

When the prisoners had been escorted out, she said to Syons, 'No one has spoken to the officer in question about this?'

'Not as far as I know.'

'Well, then, let's tape him. If there's no truth in this, he'll be exonerated. Agreed?'

Samuels had been working on his most ambitious work yet, the portrait of Miss Purvis as a famous concert pianist, seated at the keyboard and in full evening dress. Samuels remembered, as a kid in the war, hearing Dame Myra Hess playing on the radio. He had formed a vivid mental picture of the pianist herself, based on nothing but his imagination. She wore a chiffon gown which showed to advantage her beautiful swan-like neck, as did the string of large pearls and the gleaming permanent wave. His portrait of Miss Purvis owed much to this image – the same dress, the same jewellery, the same long, elegant hands. In point of fact, Miss Purvis's rather stumpy fingers had always been a source of chagrin to her, but what was reality compared to the nobility of Wilfred Samuels's dream?

He was in a jaunty mood today. A grave depression had descended over the weekend when he heard *The Mikado* would be cancelled. Now the show was on again and his heart soared back into the realms of springtime and a young man's fancy. He was just working on a delicate carmine-tinted fingernail when the cell flap clacked and he heard a key in the lock. Quickly he threw the old shirt he used as a paint-rag over the work-in-progress and turned to face his visitor.

'Oh,' he said in surprise, as the Governor swept in. 'Miss Hewitt – I, er, was sorry to hear about Miss Bullock.'

'Yes, we all are. Now, you have requested a visitor's order to be sent to Miss Purvis, yes?'

Samuels was shaking. He sat down on his bunk. He didn't fancy the businesslike tone the Governor had adopted. She sounded in a tearing hurry, which meant if she was going to knock back his hopes, he'd not have much time to argue back. He scrabbled in his pocket, talking fast. 'Yes, Miss Hewitt, and I have this to show you, this letter from Miss Purvis that came today, and she says she wants to see me.'

He proffered a sheet of decorative notepaper. Helen took it and read, but Samuels was afraid of allowing a silence to develop. 'She knows why I'm in Barfield and she just says it doesn't make any difference to our friendship.'

Helen handed him the letter and returned to the door, turning round before she let herself out. 'Have a nice visit, Mr Samuels.'

And she was gone.

'Thank you. Thank you very much, Miss Hewitt,' said the lifer to the door.

One inmate Helen had to see on the VP Wing this morning was Oswald Snooper, and on her way over she radioed to have him put in the probation office to await her. She found him twirling a roll-up, then running his tongue along the adhesive edge of the skin.

'All right if I smoke? There's no ashtray.'

Helen turned on her heel and fetched an ashtray from the Wing Office, placing it on the table. She fixed Snooper with a long look. 'I think I've arranged a transfer, but it has not as yet been confirmed.'

'Will it – if I keep me end of the deal?'

Whatever she might think privately, Helen could not

allow this kind of open talk. 'I'm not making any deals with you, Mr Snooper. But if you have any information which will assist me, it will be gratefully accepted.'

Snooper hunched over his snout, dragging hard. 'I just want out of this asylum, man. There's guys on this Wing that should be . . . I mean, you put a mad dog to sleep, right? I never come out of me cell on association. Too risky.' He leaned forward towards her confidentially. 'There's stuff going down on this Wing that's disgustin'.' He grimaced. 'Dis-*gus*-tin'.'

'Well, I don't have much time, Mr Snooper. Could we get to the main business of this meeting, please?'

Snooper had a tremor in his hand. He was acting very edgy, glancing up at the door, pulling his dreadlocks, twitching at noises from outside, tapping his foot.

'Right. OK. Look, you know how it goes down? Each Wing has a main dealer. Wing baron. He shells out on his runners, maybe two, three, four, and they act like street dealers. So, if you just pick up a runner, that doesn't do that much because it's only a matter of time before the gear is being passed by another runner. Right? You with me?'

'Yes, I am with you.'

'An' the main men never, ever put themselves at risk. No way. They got lists of inmates, guys they can use that need money for trainers, rations, coffee, chocolate, whatever. Weight-trainers all want steroids now. It's big, big, big business, Governor. Big money. It's got to be, for all the couriers from outside need a bit of organizing. The barons pressurize the inmates to get their families to bring in the drugs.'

He opened his eyes wide and shook his head, amazing even himself at the extent of it. 'Big, big business.'

'Mr Snooper, this is all very well. Very interesting too.

But you're giving me information I already have, at least in outline. I need names.'

Snooper considered. He was muttering to himself, shaking his head. He looked at her, his eyes still wide. 'I do that, Miss Hewitt, then I will *have* to be moved. There's a lot of users down here – guys needing protection because they're in debt with the barons over the other side.'

He was whispering now – whispering and shaking like a sick man.

''F I give you information like this, them users gonna pay their debts by selling me ass. I would be dead meat.'

Helen said, 'You'll be all right. Have you got writing materials in your cell – paper, pencil? Good. Then I'll expect to hear from you again. Meanwhile I shall continue to hold that prison transfer in abeyance. Clear?'

Miserably, Snooper nodded then pushed his head down towards his knees. He dropped the butt and crushed it out under his trainers then stood up wearily. An officer was waiting to take him back but Miss Hewitt had already gone.

In the officer's lounge, Russell Morgan had been greeted by all with slaps on the back and a bear-hug from Jumbo Jackson. He was in a just-pressed clean uniform to face the inquisition of DCI Tully about the events around his hostage incident. Helen came in to have a quick word in advance.

'Russell, you'll be all right if you stay calm. Don't let him get to you. If at any time you want a break, you just say. If you don't understand any question, don't be afraid to ask for it to be repeated. You are not on trial, not in *any* way. This is just a preliminary inquiry into the hostage situation. There will be two police officers asking the relevant questions, but it'll be mostly Tully. All right?'

She couldn't be sure that he had been listening. Morgan often had that look these days: absence, pre-occupation. He was sitting there sweating, looking nervously at Gary Marshall who was sitting in on the briefing. Marshall gave him a reassuring wink.

Davyd Harris walked in, wearing his Sunday-best suit. He produced a bottle of medicine from his pocket and put it on the low table in front of Helen. 'This is for you. Mavis said you had a tummy upset.'

'Oh! Thanks. Yes, I do need something.'

She squinted at the label then got up and drew Harris aside, shaking the medicine. 'What about Kevin Watts? He saw the neurologist?'

'Yes, and there's no brain damage. But they're worried about his symptoms. His speech is very slurred.'

Helen unscrewed the cap of the medicine and smelt it. It was white and thick. She put the bottle to her lips and swigged. 'Ugh! All right, I'll come up to Health Care to see about him later.'

While Helen and the doctor consulted, Morgan stood with Gary Marshall by the door, waiting. 'Are they talking about me?' said Morgan suspiciously. 'Because I'm sick to death of people talking behind my back about me.'

It was lunchtime on the block and the cons were agog to see Tarzan. During association earlier he'd been offered drugs by Keith Smith.

'I don't approve of drugs,' he'd said loudly, ramming a ping-pong ball in Smith's mouth then slapping him on the back. The ball had flown and Smith had scuttled away.

But if most of them wanted to get an eyeful of the big man, Eugene Buffy was an exception.

'He's over there behind us,' said Samora excitedly. 'See him? Can you see him? He's coming into the line-up now.'

Buffy kept his face averted. 'Don't keep pushing me round like that, you prat. I don't want him to see me. I gave him some verbals in the Block.'

But Samora was not to be denied a chance to bask in the rays of Tarzan's fame. He had turned round to face the back of the queue and was jumping up and down.

'Hi there, Tarzan. Over here. Welcome on to C Wing, Tarzan. Remember me?'

Buffy pummelled him. 'For Christ's sake, Brian! Don't bring him over here. Just shut *up*!'

Tarzan did not deign to join the back of the line but, bypassing the queue entirely, walked serenely to the front. Nobody argued. He turned and eyed the rest of the inmates. They fell silent, subdued by his gaze.

'I don't approve of drugs. I want no drugs on this Wing.' Having spoken, he turned to the meal trolley and began to help himself. Eric Haddock, at the front of the queue which Tarzan had barged, tapped the huge man's elbow.

'I'm Eric,' he said.

Tarzan looked down at him, as at a lower form of life. 'Hello, Eric. Now get out of my face.'

Behind Eric was Roddy Marsh who had already started piling up his plate. Tarzan watched him through hooded eyelids. 'Oi, you! Shouldn't have the potatoes, or the pudding. Just soup, meat, veg. You're overweight and unfit. Get fit. Eat just protein, no carbs for you!'

He moved across to the tea urn and filled his mug. Then he turned to make another general address. 'Anyone want to work out with me in the gym? One-on-one training?'

'Yeah! Me,' said Samora. 'I'll work out with you.'

Buffy looked at his feet and muttered, 'I'm on medication, me.'

Now Tarzan had his meal and he proceeded with his tray back towards his cell, where Jumbo Jackson was standing in amazement by the noticeboard, arms folded.

'I've never known them so well-behaved at dinnertime. Everything all right, Tarzan?'

'So far, so good, Mr Jackson.' He nodded at the notice about the resumption of work on *The Mikado*. 'I want to be in this musical.'

Jackson shook his head. 'Too late, I'm afraid. It's all been cast. I'm the Lord High Executioner. But you can come to the show, all right.'

Tarzan nodded judiciously. 'Good. Want to be a part of everything. Take part in everything.'

He moved into the doorway of cell four. 'When do I see this show, then?'

'Not for a while. Ten days. We're still rehearsing.'

'How many performances?'

'Just the one.'

Tarzan raised his eyebrows. 'Just one? Better be good, then, hadn't it?' And he disappeared inside.

CHAPTER 19

'YOU'LL NEED TO speak to Dr Harris and all the officers who were on duty including SO Morgan – correct?'

DCI Tully sat with Helen in the boardroom, going through the interviews the policeman would be conducting. If criminal charges were to be brought against George Falla for his treatment of Russell Morgan it was time to start the investigation. Gary Marshall, going out to check that everyone on the list was lined up, met John Bunny coming in, late and flustered.

'Sorry, have I kept everyone waiting?' He took his seat and started to unpack papers from his briefcase. He looked up at Helen. 'Oh, yes! Would you call Mr Andrews at HQ, Miss Hewitt? Perhaps when this meeting is adjourned?'

The door opened energetically and Anthony Turnbull sprang into the room, eager for battle. 'Ah! We're all gathered? Good. Where shall I park myself?'

Helen showed him the empty chair opposite to herself. Another vacant chair stood next to it. 'As you see, there is a chair ready for Mr Falla when he is called.'

'I would like him present throughout.'

'I don't think Mr Morgan should be subjected to facing him across the table.'

Suddenly, Turnbull whipped a large white cotton handkerchief from his pocket and held it out to Helen, smiling. 'You have something white on your upper lip.'

It must be a smear of Dr Harris's stomach medicine. Helen was damned if she was going to accept Turnbull's handkerchief so she quickly wiped her lip with her finger.

'I'll kick off with Barfield's security and transfer arrangements on 22 November, which is the day my client is accused of taking Senior Officer Russell Morgan hostage.'

God! thought Helen. His client was accused of doing that because that is what he *did*! Turnbull was playing this like a barrister in court number one at the Old Bailey.

'Could you outline them for me, Miss Hewitt, or – as you were not actually in charge of the prison at the time – perhaps you would care to delegate?'

Gary Marshall said, 'As Deputy Governor I was Acting Governor on that day.'

'Hmm. That would be because the then Governor of Barfield was unavailable as he was playing a round of golf?'

John Bunny interjected, 'Mr Turnbull, Mr Keller is no longer with the Prison Service.'

'Well, now he's retired he'll have plenty of time to perfect his swing. Mr Marshall, could you take me through the transfers of prisoners from their release – in Mr Falla's case from Parkhurst – to their reception here at Barfield?'

'HQ issue the movement order, which would have been faxed through to here to Governor Keller. The timing of the relocation would be decided between the two prisons. Officers accompany the transportee. In this case, Mr Falla was in a wheelchair but he travelled in a Cat A reinforced van.'

'And when he arrived here, did the Hospital Wing, or did it not, get the relevant information regarding my client's previous prison and security records?'

'No, they didn't. I think something—'

'They remained at reception and were then sent to the Governor who was, as we know, absent. With the result that officers in the Hospital Wing—'

'We call it the Health Care Centre, Mr Turnbull.'

Turnbull clicked his tongue impatiently. 'Health Care Centre, then. Officers there did not possess vital information about my client's prison records?'

'That turned out to be the case, yes.'

'Good. Thank you. Perhaps we should bring in Senior Officer Morgan now?'

Russell Morgan had been sitting in the officers' lounge, wearing his uniform. He felt hot. Years ago, prisons were always cold but now everywhere you went they seemed to be over-heated. He never thought it would come to this, but he felt grossly uncomfortable in the uniform, confined in it, as if it was too tight or too stiff. He'd been wearing jeans and sweatshirts every day for weeks, that was the trouble. Getting soft.

He was waiting almost alone. Brent had passed by for a brief chat but there were few staffers with nothing to do at this time of day. It was different at shift changeover when the place was a mill of guys charging around, arguing the toss, changing their clothes, arsing around.

He appreciated the quiet, really. Not like the Wings. He remembered, when he first joined up, thinking he'd never get used to the noise, the constant shouting, howling and cursing of caged men, most of them violent and desperate. But in the end you didn't even notice it. And, then, it was the quiet you noticed, like now. Funny, that.

'Mr Morgan, would you come through into the boardroom now?'

It was one of the woman officers who had come to fetch him. What was her name? He couldn't for the life of him remember, though he knew her face all right. That was another innovation, female uniformed in the men's nicks. Funny idea, to his way of thinking. Men were only going to get disturbed by it, worked up. Most of them spent 90 per cent of their time thinking about what they couldn't have anyway. It was one of the things that made prison the punishment it was – no sex. Well, not with women.

He followed the officer along the corridor towards the boardroom. Suddenly he was seized by fear. What if Falla was in there? He hadn't seen him since that day. Would he have to face him now? He saw Gary Marshall lurking just outside the inquiry room, waiting to intercept. Morgan managed a smile. 'He in there? That bastard in there?'

'Who, Falla or his lawyer? Because they're both bastards. No, Falla's not in there, matter of fact. You OK?'

'I'm fine.'

'Come on, then. Let's get on with it.'

'Do I have to answer the lawyer's questions?'

'No. Me and Miss Hewitt are coming out and the lawyer's agreed he'll come out too. The copper, Tully's the one who'll talk to you, with the Area Manager in there with him.'

Morgan glowered at Turnbull as he and the Governor

withdrew from the boardroom, then he went in and took his seat opposite the policeman.

Tully started gently by taking him through the events of the morning prior to Falla's arrival, that he'd been on shift on C Wing all night, the process of cleaning and preparing the cells. Then he asked Morgan what happened when he put Falla into his cell, prior to Dr Harris's medical examination. 'Did you notice anything wrong about the cell at all?'

'Er, yes. I saw this broom or mop left against the wall. I crossed to collect it.'

'Because it should not have been in the cell?'

'Yes. As I got to it, Falla slammed the cell door and struck me from behind, pushing me forward on the bed.'

He was sweating freely now. Surely it was too hot in here? Like an oven. He tried to remember what to say next. He'd rehearsed this often enough.

'He then broke the mop handle in two pieces, he smashed the bottoms off two medical bottles and stuck them by their necks on the end of the two bits of wood. He used them as weapons, like one of those, you know . . . bullfighters, jabbing at me.'

'Breaking the handle and doing all that would take some time. What were you doing?'

'I was dazed from being hit and – and – I was telling him not to be foolish.'

Bunny looked up from the notes he was writing. 'Were you not, Mr Morgan, very scared?'

'Yes.'

'Had you ever been taken hostage before?'

'Yes.'

Tully turned back a few pages in his notes. 'That was when you were held in a closed cell and forced to get down on your knees and beg?'

'Yes, but this time I had a broken bottle rammed in my neck.' He began frantically pulling at his collar, loosening his tie and fumbling with the shirt button. 'You want to see the scars. You want to see what he did to me?' He pulled down the collar and they could all see the thin jagged white line of the injury.

'Mr Morgan,' said Tully, 'I am not in any way making light of your injuries and the terror you must have felt. You had also, as you've said, been on duty for eighteen hours.'

'Right. Hot in here, isn't it?'

John Bunny frowned. There was a hysterical edge to Morgan's voice, and he sensed danger. 'Mr Morgan, would you like to take a break now?' he suggested, in a voice which did not expect the answer 'no'.

Outside the boardroom there was a small waiting area. The female officer came through to tell them Bunny had suggested a break.

'Senior Officer Morgan should have taken more than a break on the morning of the twenty-second of November last. If he'd had one—'

Gary Marshall was not going to sit here and listen to this. 'Eh! Senior Officer Morgan is *not* on trial here, Mr Turnbull. His work has been exemplary for more than ten years in this job and I for one—'

Marshall turned, realizing that Russell Morgan himself had come out of the inquiry room and was standing behind him. 'That's right,' Morgan said, in a husky, tense voice. 'Ten years plus. And a fat lot it stands for. You bastards can bring me here for this so-called inquiry but it's not for *my* benefit, is it? It's for the prisoner who did it to me. And me, I can't work, I can't sleep, I can't

232

eat. All I can think of is what happened in that cell. Should I have done something different? Could I have changed the course of it? You tell me. Who's taking care of me?'

He jabbed the air with his finger. 'Who's looking after my *wife*?'

Helen stepped towards him with her arm stretched forward, palm up. 'Come and sit down.'

Morgan flinched away, as if afraid she would touch him. 'No I'm sick of the lot of you. You think I don't know, don't you? Well, I do know. You're going to let that evil bastard off the hook. Well, screw you! The lot of you! The *lot* of you!' He turned and rushed away.

Twenty minutes later, Officer Chiswick was crossing to the Admin Block with some workshop reports when he was surprised to see Russell Morgan in full uniform, standing in the centre of the exercise yard in the pale mid-afternoon sunlight. Morgan was very much his usual self, at least in appearance, an upright military figure, swivelling on his heel to keep all the men monitored, barking a warning when it looked like a fight might be starting, bending his head to acknowledge a word from an inmate walking past, and finally checking his watch and calling the end of exercise: 'Come along, back to your cells. Lock-up! Let's be having you – lock-up. LOCK-UP!'

The voice was the same, too – well, perhaps a little more wispy than before, but that was understandable after all he'd been through. There was only one thing. The inmates from B Wing, who had been out there half an hour ago, were already locked up. Who this bunch were, Chiswick couldn't even guess, because only Russell

Morgan could see them. Senior Officer Morgan was standing alone in the exercise yard shouting at ghosts.

When the meeting in the boardroom reconvened it did so without Russell Morgan, who had been driven home. Now it was George Falla's turn to take the limelight. He strolled in and took a seat beside Turnbull. Unlike Morgan, he looked fit and feisty.

Turnbull said, 'May I take my client through his background? Mr Falla, would you tell everyone a little of your history – your medical history?'

Fall coughed drily and then launched into his tale of woe. 'When I was twelve years old my father became very ill, diagnosed as having cancer of the bowels. It took him nearly two years to pass on. I saw him become a skeleton – unable to feed himself, dress or do anything for himself. It left me with a deep emotional scar.'

He stopped talking. He had seen Helen's face. It had gone chalk white as, despite herself, despite her loathing of this man, she found herself there with him, reliving her own fifteen-year-old horror. Like him, she had watched her father slowly transform from a solid, real person into a corpse.

She got up and looked around, aware that every eye was on her. 'Look, would you all excuse me, I have to be on C Wing.' She smiled. 'Prison life goes on, regardless, I'm afraid.'

She hurried out. She felt sick again. Falla made her sick and so did his story.

'Mr Falla,' said Turnbull. 'Please continue. How did that emotional scar manifest itself?'

'I had a deep terror of illness in myself, especially anything to do with my bowels. It went on and on.'

'And did you have any serious, er, bowel illnesses?'

'Mr Turnbull—' began John Bunny, with a pained look on his face.

'Not at first,' said Falla, ploughing on. 'And then six years ago when I was in Brixton I had to have an enema – for constipation, it was. You see I couldn't go to the toilet for—'

Bunny tutted. 'Look, really. We do have Mr Falla's medical reports in front of us, Mr Turnbull.'

Turnbull turned to him with that half-mocking smile of his. 'I am aware of that, but you do not have in detail the emotional reasons or the deep-seated fear – which is why my client has acted in—'

'Your client, Mr Turnbull, has also been sentenced for three terms for his part in armed robberies.'

Falla showed his first sign of temper, his face flushing red. 'I have always maintained my innocence. Always . . . Well, on the last one I have.'

Turnbull tapped Falla's arm sharply and he lapsed into silence. 'I think at this stage we should continue to give Mr Falla the opportunity to explain his state of mind.'

Helen had given a small tape-recorder to Governor Syons to bring into Buffy and Samora's pad. Thrusting from her mind the unwelcome images conjured up by George Falla, she walked swiftly down to call C Wing and check whether Len Syons had got the recorder in place.

He told her he had.

The two inmates had tested the recorder and were ready when Jason Hully unlocked and walked in.

'Hi,' he said, standing just inside the door. 'Look,

I . . .' He clenched and unclenched his fists nervously and turned his head to the side. Indecision was written all over him. 'Look, I don't know about the balaclavas. I mean, I'm not sure about this at all. Maybe wait a few days.'

Buffy was sitting on his bunk, hugging his knees. 'But you said you wanted us to knock Keith Smith about. And we're prepared to do it. But you got to play your part.'

'I know, I know. I don't know when, though.'

Buffy persisted. He had Hully wriggling on his line and was enjoying himself. 'Look, Mr Hully. We're all set. Will you leave his door open? If you do, and get the masks, we can do him for you. It's no problem but it's up to you.'

Hully compressed his lips. He still wouldn't look at either man. Samora was sitting with his mouth open in suspense. Buffy caught his eye and opened his own mouth, circling a finger around in it. Samora snapped his lips shut.

Finally, Hully spoke. He'd made up his mind. 'OK. I'll get the masks. But don't do anything until I tell you.' He pulled a rolled newspaper from his hip pocket and handed it to Samora with a packet of Bensons. 'Here's some extra smokes and today's paper for you.'

Then he turned round and left. They waited until they heard the lock-up and Hully's footsteps going down the landing. Buffy's eyes were shining with anticipation. 'We *got* him!' he said.

He unfolded himself and took the Governor's tape recorder from its hiding place, rewound the tape a short way and pressed Play.

'*OK. I'll get the masks. But don't do anything till I tell you. Here's some extra sm—*'

He snapped it off again. 'We bloody got them all now.'

Samora leaned across to his own mini ghetto-blaster in which a tape had also been running. He rewound and listened to the high-speed gibberish before pressing Play.

'. . . *But you got to play your part.*'

'*I know, I know. I don't know when, though.*'

'Thing is, Eugene,' said Samora, removing the second tape from the machine and slipping it into his shirt pocket, 'when they know we got this, they'll do a strip-search and find it. It'll never get us a deal for an open nick.'

'I thought of that. We give it to Tarzan, ask him to protect it for us.'

'That's brilliant! So who's going to give it to him?'

'You. He's your mate, isn't he?'

The lock rattled and the cell door swung outwards. It was Syons. 'Well?' he said.

Buffy held out the cassette tape. 'You wanted proof?'

Syons took the tape and held out his hand for Helen's recorder. Samora had been sitting with his mouth open once more. Now he roused himself as he saw Buffy passing across the small, expensive-looking machine.

'Can't we keep it, Mr Syons?' he said.

'No. Hand it over.'

Syons left with merely a grunt. His face had told them everything they wanted to know about how he felt about the subterfuge used against one of his officers, Governor's orders or not.

'Brilliant,' said Buffy. 'We're on our way to an open nick.'

*

In the boardroom, Tully was questioning inmate Falla.

'Is it right that you threatened and assaulted Senior Officer Morgan?'

'No comment,' said Falla. He then leaned across and murmured to Turnbull, 'Still all right to say nothing?' Turnbull nodded without looking up.

'But you did slash his throat with the weapon you made from the bottle and the wood?'

'I deny *slashing* his throat.'

'Do you accept you could have caused an injury in the throat area?'

'No comment.'

'Do you accept you made various threats to kill Officer Morgan?'

'No comment.'

'Do you accept that you tied Officer Morgan to the chair?'

'No comment.'

John Bunny had started taking notes but by now he was completely fed up. He tossed his pen down onto his legal pad.

Tully sighed. 'Mr Falla, by persistently making no comment to these questions, are you saying that you do not wish to answer? Or are you denying the allegations?'

'It's my right not to answer questions.'

Bunny looked at his watch. Turnbull smiled. 'Did you wish to say something, Mr Bunny?' he asked, turning to the Area Manager.

Bunny grimaced and clipped his pen into his jacket pocket. 'No comment,' he said grimly.

Tarzan, true to his word about wanting to join in with all the activities, had signed up for information-technology classes. It was taught by Zania Tullbrooke, who was black and generally reckoned to be the most beautiful instructor in the education block. The entire group sat in the IT room, their eyes fixed with intense concentration on Zania's jeans-encased bottom as she reached the dummy QWERTY-keyboard down from a high shelf.

'The keyboard on a word-processor,' she was saying, 'is the same as an ordinary typewriter except there are quite a few extra keys.'

She looked around and advanced on Samora, whose eyes lit up.

'Can you type, Brian?'

'No.'

Samora was sitting next to Tarzan. He had the tape in his pocket but he hadn't had the courage to ask Tarzan to take it.

Tarzan raised his enormous mitt. 'I can. I can type.'

'Really? Mr Tarzan, isn't it? Do you have a speed?'

'What?'

By now Zania was standing over the two of them with the dummy board. She turned around and raised her voice. The noise in the room had risen to a considerable hubbub. 'All of you, please! Don't talk among yourselves.'

While her back was turned Samora leaned across, plucking the cassette from his shirt and pushed it towards Tarzan under cover of the desk. Out of the corner of his mouth, he said, 'Can you take care of this for me, Tarzan? I'll explain later.'

Tarzan frowned, but he took the tape as Zania turned back to them and leaned over the desk. 'How much typing have you done before, Mr Tarzan?' She put down the dummy keyboard in front of him. 'You want to show me? Do you touch-type?'

239

It was too much for Samora. Her tits were inches from his face. 'I'd like to touch you up,' he murmured.

Tarzan didn't even look at Samora, he merely backhanded him. Samora fell off his chair, landing in a heap on the lino. 'You behave yourself, son. Or I'll put you through that wall.' He half rose and subdued the class with a ferocious glare. 'Shut up, the lot of you. Anyone talking gets a thrashing.'

Helen asked to see DCI Tully once he had finished in the boardroom.

'How did the interview go?' she asked, as she poured him a cup of tea.

Tully laughed bitterly. 'There was no interview. Just no comment.'

'Well, it's not that I want to talk to you about. It's the escapee prisoner, Kevin Watts.'

'What about him?'

'When he was returned to us he had severe bruises covering almost half his body. Did he in any way require to be restrained by your officers? Sugar?'

'I'm sorry?'

'Sugar in your tea?'

'Oh, yes, please. What are you implying about my officers?'

'Did Watts require to be restrained?' She handed him the tea.

Tully sipped and shook his head. 'I have no knowledge of any extra force being used to restrain the man. Has he filed a complaint?'

'No.'

'Nothing more to be said, then.' He immediately

drained his cup. 'Must be going, Miss Hewitt. Thanks for the tea.'

Helen was annoyed to find Turnbull still hanging around. But at least it gave her a chance to give him a piece of her mind – a chance she didn't pass up. She cornered him in Mavis's office where he was helping himself to the services of the now mended copying machine.

'Mind if I say something?' asked Helen. 'Without prejudice, of course.'

Turnbull nodded and continued with his copying.

'Well, you're going to try and prove Falla is mentally unstable, aren't you?'

'He's obviously greatly distressed and very desperate to get the correct medical assessment of his illness.'

'Bullshit! He's a nasty, vicious bastard with a string of convictions and a history of violence towards prison officers – as well as inmates. What are you trying to *prove*?'

Turnbull smiled. He said, 'That everyone held in Her Majesty's Prisons has the legal right to have the best medical treatment – and not be forced into taking drastic steps to ensure he gets it.' He collected his copies from the delivery tray, tidied the stack and slipped them into his briefcase. 'Miss Hewitt, I must thank you for your co-operation. And the copies.'

'They should be ten pence per copy.'

He was half-way to the stairs when he turned and waved. 'Put it on my account. 'Bye.'

Turnbull was amazing. He seemed to have no notion of how unpopular he was around Barfield.

241

'Mr Turnbull! You'll need to be accompanied to the gate. Mr Marshall will take you.'

'Helen, I'm sorry, but you won't persuade or cajole me into doing anything I don't want to do.'

Simon was sitting at his desk in the flat, sorting papers for a case he was dealing with tomorrow. It was late and he wanted to be in bed. Helen was standing behind him in her dressing gown, sipping a glass of warm water.

'You're a lawyer, aren't you?' she said simply. 'I mean, are you so inundated with work you won't even consider it?'

'I've only just been made junior partner, for God's sake!'

'You'd have been senior partner if you showed more initiative.'

He closed his eyes and sighed. 'Helen, just because you run Barfield doesn't mean you run either my career or my life. This chap – what's his name? – Morgan. He's got nothing to do with me.'

'He has a lot to do with me. All right, forget it. Just forget it.'

She walked to the window and about-turned and walked back.

'Will you give me your professional opinion, then? You see, I think the Prison Service was Russell Morgan's life. I doubt if he'll ever be fit enough, mentally I mean, to work for it again. He's such a nice man, Simon, such a good officer . . . Is bloody Turnbull the reason you won't even consider this?'

'No. You may know a hell of a lot about running a prison but you know bugger all about the law.'

'Turnbull is making Russell Morgan feel it's his fault he was taken hostage.'

Simon looked at her, speaking with exaggerated patience. 'No, Helen. He is attempting to prove that his client was in a serious state of ill health—'

'He wasn't, he had—'

'And that without the correct medical attention his client was forced to take the action he did.'

Helen started angrily towards the door, then turned once more. 'Whose side are you on, Lennox?'

'Yours. Look . . .' Simon stood up and put his arms around her waist. 'Morgan could sue the Prison Service but he'll get little or no compensation because it isn't to blame for the cutbacks which led to the events at Barfield. Now. There *is* another possibility, but it could have bad repercussions for you.'

She looked at him. 'You don't mean sue the Home Secretary?'

Simon nodded. 'Exactly. Go right to the top. But listen. If Morgan takes on the Home Office and I represent him, they'll know the encouragement is coming from you, don't you see? They won't like it, Helen, not one little bit. It could be the kiss of death to your brilliant career. Do you still want me to take the case?'

Helen laid her forehead on Simon's shoulder, then lifted it again. She had that grin on her face, the grin that said, You'd bloody better.

CHAPTER 20

Friday, 19 January

HELEN HAD BEEN rooting through the pile in her in-tray looking for HQ's last memo about George Falla. She found it underneath an unaddressed manilla envelope which she couldn't recall having seen before. She looked inside it and pulled out Eugene Buffy's cassette tape. She shut the office door and played it through. She played it again. Then she called Gary Marshall and Len Syons to come in and see her at once. 'When was this cassette recorded?'

'Monday, I believe,' said Marshall, glancing at Syons.

'You might have got it to me sooner.'

'I did. I sent it in a plain brown envelope.'

Marshall pointed. 'That envelope.'

'Oh, all right. What do you think?'

Marshall grimaced. 'Well, they said they'd get the proof. Question is, can we keep this internal?'

Syons shook his head doubtfully. 'That might be difficult.'

'Oh?' asked Helen. 'Why?'

'Buffy's been sounding his mouth off on the Wing all week. Says they made a second copy of the conversation with Hully, using their ghetto-blaster.'

Marshall considered. 'They both got visits today –

Samora and Buffy?' he asked. 'If they have, Len, you give their cells a spin. It's got to be in there.'

'Right.'

Helen picked up a fax that had just come in. 'Oh, Gary, while you're here, this memo from HQ. Falla's to be transferred until his trial. HQ feel it would be more beneficial if he was sent to a more relaxed prison.'

Marshall opened his palms and shrugged his shoulders. 'Nobody'll be sorry to see him leave here, except the Gov at his new prison – right?'

Eugene Buffy didn't often get visits but today Aunty Betty had come down to tell him his granddad was dead. Great. Visits should be positive events, not an endless litany of family deaths, illnesses and disasters. He needed stuff to cheer him up, not bring him down.

He returned to the Wing in a morose state. The sight that met his eyes put him in a much, much worse one. The cell had been trashed. The bedding was everywhere, the books were on the floor.

Those bastard screws!

Suddenly he flipped over into a blind rage. He knew what this was all about. The second tape. They knew about it, someone had grassed him up. He picked up a handful of books and hurled them at the door. He viciously kicked the ghetto-blaster. He overturned the table, crashing everything on it into the heap of blankets and pillows on the floor.

'BASTARDS! Had a search while I was on my visit? You slimy SODS!'

Officer Jackson heard the disturbance. He came to the door. 'Hey, calm down, Eugene. Calm down.'

'Looking for that second tape, were you? Well, let me

tell you, fatso. Yes, we got another tape. But you won't find the bleeder. You – won't – fucking – find it!'

Jackson didn't appreciate references to his bulk. He drew himself up to his full height and jerked his thumb backwards towards the landing. 'Right, Eugene, step out. Out, Eugene.'

'Tell you what – you never found the Semtex, did you? Never found the bloody Semtex, eh? Eh? You prats.'

The row brought two more officers to Jackson's assistance. They went in, dodging Buffy's kicks and bites, and pulled him out.

'It's not just one,' he yelled. 'All screws are bent. Every one of you.'

By the time Samora came up after half an hour with his brother, he couldn't believe what he found. 'Who wrecked our drum? Where's Eugene?'

Jackson had returned from his escort duty, Brent with him. He spoke in a low, warning tone. 'He's down the Block, Brian. He wrecked the cell himself. You going to clear it up?'

Samora swivelled round and launched his boot at Officer Brent's nuts. It connected and Brent sagged at the knees, his face contorted with pain.

'You bastards,' yelled Samora. 'You done our pad over. You *trashed* it.' He punched Jackson as hard as he could in the stomach. He was shouting almost in falsetto now. 'I know what you're bleeding looking for. But we got it hidden. *Well* fucking hidden.'

He launched himself on Jackson again, flailing at him. Jackson was pushed backwards out into the landing.

'Son, come on, don't do something you might regret.'

'*You*'ll regret! You'll regret doing this.'

Brent, somewhat recovered, moved in to grab Samora, who started ducking and diving until he was facing them, his back to the winding stairway that led down to the twos. Brent ran at him vengefully, but before he got within grabbing distance Samora lost his footing and toppled down, rolling over, his head striking the edge of a step. For quite some time he didn't get up again.

For the second time in a day, Syons and Marshall were in her office. Helen drummed the desk with her fingers. She was tired after another nausea-filled night. 'I don't think this looks good, Buffy being held in the Block. In fact, it stinks.'

Marshall was adamant that the right thing had been done. 'Officers have a right to strip-search a cell. The little bugger said he had Semtex!'

'Oh, come on, Gary. We all know this was about the second tape. Semtex, indeed.'

'Yes, he mentioned it, we have to take it seriously. It's not unknown. They found some at Whitemoor in a box of poster paints.'

Syons had been very quiet but now he said, 'I agree. We have to take the reference to a high explosive seriously, Gov. We have to strip it out again and have another look.'

There was a knock on the door. As Helen strode over to open it, she said, 'If Eugene Buffy has got Semtex he should not be in the Block at all. He should be in a Special Secure Unit with the terrorists. Still *got* an SSU at Barfield, have we?'

Marshall and Syons exchanged a here-she-goes-again look as Mavis was let in. 'Officer Hully is in the boardroom waiting for you,' she said.

When they put the whole thing to Hully, and played him the tape, the lad simply folded. He slumped in a chair, utterly downcast. 'I wasn't serious. I was joking, I swear.'

Helen look hard at him. 'But you do admit that the prisoner, Keith Smith, was—'

'Constantly having a go at me? You all know he was. Look, I know the recording makes me look – sound bad. But it was just a silly joke, it was! And, anyway, I've not been sleeping, I'm depressed, I—'

Helen shook her head. Two unrelated excuses: now she knew he was lying. 'Officer Hully. You are relatively new here, but this is a serious – a *very* serious allegation against you. And, with this kind of evidence, I have no choice . . .'

Hully was not really listening. He was looking down at the floor, muttering, his face plum-red, 'I don't believe this. I just don't believe this.'

'. . . but to tell you that, until it is determined what the next step will be, you are suspended from duty.'

Hully stared at his boots and shook his head. 'Shit! This is so unfair. *So* unfair!'

And there were tears in his voice.

Since Tarzan had embarked on the new, saintly phase of his life in C Wing, an almost balmy quietness had temporarily settled over the Block. Then Eugene Buffy was brought down.

'I WILL WRITE TO EVERY NEWSPAPER, YOU

CHEATING LYING BASTARDS! I WILL CONTACT THE PRISON WATCHDOGS, THE PRIME MINISTER, THE POPE. YOU'RE NOT GOING TO GET AWAY WITH THIS.'

He kept up a continual stream of threats and abuse for most of the day, punctuated by hammerings and kicks on the cell door. In the early evening, Gary Marshall and Helen Hewitt came down to see him.

'Mr Buffy!' said Marshall, outside his door. 'I have the Governor with me.'

'I DON'T CARE IF YOU GOT ELVIS PRESLEY WITH YOU. I'LL HAVE YOU FOR THIS! I WILL! YOU DESTROYED MY CELL. YOU DRAGGED ME DOWN THE BLOCK.'

'We want to talk, Eugene,' said Helen. 'That's all. We can't talk like this, can we?'

Buffy fell silent at last. Marshall nodded to Horrocks to open the cell door. Buffy was bathed in sweat, panting, his voice hoarse. 'I should not have been brought down here.'

Helen nodded. 'I agree. I don't think you should be here either.'

Buffy swallowed. Had she really said that? 'Pardon?'

'But you stated that you were in possession of Semtex and—'

Buffy took a step back. The cords on his neck stood out as he started yelling again. 'Is THAT it? Well, I tell you what. I'll BLOW the lot of you to smithereens. Just piss off! Go on. PISS OFF OUT OF HERE!'

Helen moved out of the doorway and said to Horrocks, 'Shut the cell door. I'm not going to waste my time here.'

As they walked away, they could hear the tirade continuing.

'YOU'LL NEVER FIND IT! YOU CAN SEARCH TILL YOU'RE BLUE IN THE FACE. WHAT I GOT IS EXPLOSIVE. EXPLOSIVE. AND YOU BLOODY WELL KNOW IT!'

'We got to take this seriously,' said Marshall, in a low voice.

Helen nodded, thinking. She stopped and rubbed her aching head. 'Strip down his cell on C Wing. Do it tonight.'

In Health Care it was cocoa time. Cells were unlocked and a trolley with an urn and plates of biscuits was wheeled in by a couple of red-band orderlies – inmates with the red arm-band denoting their status as trusties. They set off down the landing with a list of prisoners who were either not allowed or unable to collect their own mugs. 'Cocoa time! Trolley on the Wing! Hot cocoa!'

Dr Harris was making sure the medication was correct before distribution at lights-out. Each dose was in a small clear-plastic beaker and he was checking them off against a list on his clipboard. Helen stood with him. Health Care was, oddly enough, one of her favourite Wings in the prison, perhaps because it was the one place with an unambiguous need to temper punishment with compassion. Some of the men in here were never going to come out. They had utterly fouled up their lives, lost every loved one they ever had, been abandoned by every friend. And now they were dying. If ever there was a case for replacing the relentless negativity of prison life with something positive, it was here.

Apart from the odd deviant episode – the hostage-taking incident was the worst it had known – this Wing had a relative quiet about it, almost a peace. Dr Harris had done a good job.

'How's your stomach?'

'Fine. Look, Davyd, is Brian Samora well enough for me to have a quick chat?'

The doctor crossed to a glass-fronted medicine cabinet and took down a large jar of pills. 'Not much wrong with him, but we're monitoring him through the night. We ought to be careful as he fell on his head.'

At this moment a yawning, scruffy Samora, with feet bare, hair disordered and in an enormous pair of pyjamas, came tottering out towards the cocoa urn, scratching behind his ear. He told the orderly, 'Eh, I want extra milk. Doc's orders. And I'm starving hungry – give me a couple more of those biccies.'

Helen walked quickly up to him. 'How are you, Brian?'

Samora hadn't seen the Governor. He did a double-take, and then assumed a pained look and seemed to shrink even further inside his pyjamas. 'Shocking poorly, Miss Hewitt. Fell right on me head. No, *pushed*, actually. I were pushed.'

He took his cocoa and a fistful of Abbey Crunch then allowed Helen to draw him aside. 'You were very upset about your cell being strip-searched, is that right?'

Samora leered. 'Yeah, and we all know what *that* was about.'

'Do you know anything about explosives?'

He took a pace away from her. 'Ho! ho! It's explosive, all right. I'm not saying nothing. Eugene told me not to. But you won't find it and whoever does'll get throttled, I'm telling you.'

'This is not a helpful attitude, Mr Samora.'

'It's not meant to be, Miss Hewitt.'

'I would like to see you in the morning, please. Good night, Mr Samora.'

'G'night, Miss Hewitt.' He stood sipping his cocoa, watching her march off and out of the Wing. Funny woman. She was quite fanciable, too. What made her want to do a crappy job like this, dealing with all these shitbags day in, day out? It beat him.

'Hey, take this down to Sixteen for us, will you?'

An orderly was holding a mug of cocoa towards Samora.

He shook his head. 'No way. I'm not going near that Aids lot.'

'No, this is for Kevin Watts.'

'Oh, right!' He put down his own mug, picked up Watts's and trailed with it down the landing. He put his head through the curtain. 'Eh, Kev mate! Got your cocoa. And I can bring you your biccies, but if you don't want them, I'll have them. Kev?' He edged towards the bed.

'Bloody hell, Kev! What happened to you? Been run over? You're a right bloody mess, worse than me.' He sipped the cocoa he was holding as he contemplated the battered form of Watts, whose pyjama jacket was open. The multicoloured effect of the bruises was dramatic. 'I fell on me head, not serious. Acting up, like. Cushy down here, isn't it?' Absent-mindedly he sipped the mug of cocoa again. Wattsy recognized him, all right. But he seemed to have trouble speaking.

'Ma-ma-guhmm . . .'

'What, Kev? What you say?'

'Gi-gi-give . . . me . . . mafuckin' . . . cocoa!'

The cocoa trolley stood at the end of the landing, unattended, ready to leave Health Care. The officers on shift were down at the other end, checking and relocking cells. The red-bands were chatting with an orderly nurse at the nurses' station.

Brian Samora went back to finish his cocoa, which still stood on the trolley. He drank it, then glanced quickly around and bent down and grabbed another handful of chocolate digestives from the trolley's lower deck. He crammed them into his pyjama-jacket pocket, then started back towards his own cell, a few yards away. He was almost at the door when a prisoner moved out of the opposite cell and came up behind him fast and quick. In one movement Burt Threlfall, supposedly drugged and in Health Care as he was too unstable to be on a normal wing, put one hand over Samora's mouth and hooked the other under his crotch. Then, lifting him bodily, he silently carried his captive into the cell. Samora could do no more than squeak under the huge hand. He tried to wriggle free but was helpless in Threlfall's powerful grip.

Inside the cell, Threlfall eased the door shut with his foot and whipped his hand away from Samora's mouth. He opened it to yell, but before he could issue a single sound, he was thrown arse-up onto the bed, his face was mashed into the bunk pillow and held there, the heel of Threlfall's left hand jammed against the back of his skull. Threlfall's knee was in the small of his back as the big man yanked Samora's pyjama bottoms down to his ankles and then hastily loosened the button on his own pyjamas.

Helen locked her office door and caught up with Gary Marshall on his way out. 'Specials find anything, Gary?'

'Not a jellybean. We also checked every tape in their cell. Nothing but music, and lousy music.'

'So they were lying?'

Marshall paused while Helen put out the lights in the

outer office. 'It means we could keep this balaclava business internal.'

'No, Gary. I've been thinking about it. Every officer in Barfield must be trusted. What Hully did was a criminal offence.'

Marshall threw up his hands. 'I stand corrected.'

They set off side by side along the deserted corridor.

'Cell searches are within our rights. Even more so when inmates are threatening to blow up Barfield with Semtex.'

Davyd Harris, coming down a darkened flight of stairs, heard her. He, too, fell into step beside his Governor, commenting drily, 'It would, on the other hand, get rid of a lot of aggravation. So anyone fancy a drink before home?'

Helen laughed. Why not? 'Best offer I've had today!'

She linked arms with the two men and they went jauntily on their way as she hummed,

'Three little maids from school are we
Pert as a schoolgirl well can be,
Filled to the brim with girlish glee –
Three little maids from school!'

On Health Care, Threlfall was standing at the trolley when Officer Brent came bustling up. 'Come on, now, we're running late here. Get in.'

'Never got my cocoa.'

'Just get back to your pad, Burt. You know the rules.'

Threlfall surveyed the trolley. One mug of cocoa was still there. He picked it up, sipped it, and casually took it back to his cell. Brent, one step behind, banged him up.

'Crazy sod!'

Brent crossed the landing again to Samora's cell. The

door was slightly ajar. He looked round it. The bedding was humped over the inmate. Samora – asleep already? Must have exhausted himself with all those antics.

'Night, Brian.'

And he banged him up.

Samora was not asleep. He was lying facing the wall, his face the only part of him not covered by blanket. His lips quivered and he wept, silently.

CHAPTER 21

Monday, 22 January

GARY MARSHALL had advocated that the threats from Buffy about Semtex must be taken seriously but he had not thought that Helen would trump him. When she'd talked about reclassifying Eugene Buffy as a Category A – exceptional risk – prisoner and sending him over to the Special Secure Unit, he thought she was joking. But she was deadly serious.

'I won't let that inmate make monkeys out of us, Gary. This reclassification may turn out to be temporary but until we're sure about the Semtex, SSU is the only place for friend Buffy.'

By mid-morning the fax had been working overtime, the paperwork was complete and now Buffy, with Gary Marshall behind him and two Punishment Block officers hemming him in on either side, stood at the electronically operated gates of the SSU. He had a pile of his possessions in his arms and he had not stopped creating noise since they'd marched him out of the Block.

'I'm gonna write to Lord Longford, the Lord Chief Justice, the Inspector of Prisons, the Attorney General, Richard Branson, Judge Dredd and the Kray brothers. I'm gonna write to fuckin' everybody.'

Marshall called to the electronic surveillance camera and microphone over the gate. 'Eugene Buffy, reclassified prisoner from C Wing, for admittance.'

The gate opened and Buffy was taken in. His papers were handed across and signed for. His property list was checked. And still he kept it up.

'In with the big boys now, am I? Found the Semtex, then, Mr Marshall? What about the ammo, though? The machine gun? Sorry, that should be *two* machine guns, yeah? Because Brian Samora's got an Uzi up his jumper. He going to be reclassified too, eh? Is he?'

The Punishment Block escort retreated with Marshall and the gates clashed shut behind them. The Deputy Governor looked back. Temporary? Maybe. But, in the meantime, Eugene Buffy had disappeared into the nearest thing to a Black Hole that the Prison Service had yet devised.

Buffy doesn't belong here, he thought. He's not heavy mob. Oh, well.

Helen had brought all those involved in the show to the chapel for a full morning's rehearsal, with Officer Jackson acting as temporary director and Miss Purvis as music director. These two were enjoying their new authority, although they knew they were about to be supplanted by the volunteers from the Midlands Mummers amateur troupe, who were due any time now. Helen had thought it advisable that she see them first in her office.

Mrs Ellison was a large woman with vast breasts and a deep, richly enunciated voice. In her younger days, prior to her marriage to a local accountant, she had played in provincial rep under her maiden name of Hermione

Follett, but she was never good enough for the West End. Rupert Hallam, on the other hand, had appeared in London in *There's A Girl In My Soup*. He had also spent the 1970s as a minor *Archers* character and the chief voice-over for Zipzit, the anti-acne cream. Eventually he, too, had subsided into alternative employment but, for a tourist guide, business is quiet in the English Midlands in winter, leaving Hallam time enough to spare for the Mummers.

'Yes, *Mikado* is a jolly good show,' the Ellison woman was saying, after she and Helen had shaken hands. 'We did it with the Mummers – a few years ago admittedly – but we are familiar with it, all right. No problems there, am I right, Rupe?'

'And you are right, and we are right, and all is right as right can be, Hermione. *Mikado*? That show's a bloody miracle, Miss Hewitt.'

Hallam's voice was loud, warm, country Yorkshire overlaid with dollops of Shaftesbury Avenue camp. He wore a huge floor-length coat, a fedora hat and a long white-fringed scarf.

'Would you excuse me? I'll just see if your two colleagues are here yet. Please do help yourselves to more coffee.'

Helen let herself out fast, holding her face tightly together. She went up to Mavis. They looked at each other and burst out in inadequately suppressed laughter.

'Oh, Christ! I thought I was going to crack up in there. This could be a major fiasco!'

'Excuse me! We're here to see Governor Hewitt.'

Helen swung round. Two women had come in, both around thirty. The one who spoke had a head of wavy blonde hair that would have done credit to a shampoo commercial. She was wearing black leggings, a brown

258

mini-skirt and a silk blouse under a fur jacket. Her friend had gleaming chestnut hair and wore tight black leathers. 'I'm Carol Baker and this is Meryl Sharp. We're with the Midlands Mummers.'

Helen stared. Jesus Christ, what was going to happen when Barfield copped a look at these two? She snapped out of it and pushed out her hand. 'Helen Hewitt.'

Carol hesitated. 'You're the Governor's wife?'

'No, just the Governor,' said Helen simply. It was the girls' turn to be gobsmacked. 'Come through to my office, won't you? Mr Hallam and Mrs Ellison are already here. I should brief you four about security arrangements and a few other matters before we go down to meet the cast of the show . . .'

When Helen brought in the four Midlands Mummers the looks on the faces of everyone from Officer Jackson to Eric Haddock had been all she had hoped. The rucking in the chorus to get close to them would, as Gary pointed out, put Hull Kingston Rovers to shame.

'I'm getting front-row seats for this show,' said Len Syons loudly in the officers' lounge, when she returned there from the chapel. 'We need a good laugh around here and this is going to be hysterical.'

Helen had collected a fax on her way through Mavis's area. She waved it. 'Prison Service! They wish to reserve seats for *The Mikado*. That's the good news.'

'Is it? Is it?' said Horrocks, at the far end of the room.

'Bad news is,' said Helen in a much lower voice, for Syons's and Marshall's ears only, 'they want a detailed report on the tape-recording made by Eugene Buffy and Brian Samora. Officer Jason Hully could see himself in court!'

Marshall grunted and Syons said nothing. Helen knew what they were thinking. Hully was wet behind the ears. Lad had made a mistake like everyone does, especially at the beginning. But did he really deserve this?

Before anything could be said, Horrocks had joined them. 'Have you seen what's going on in the exercise yard?' he said. 'Tarzan's got all the younger lads on C Wing working out. It's a heart-warming sight, I can tell you.'

Helen turned to Syons. 'How's he coming along? You won your bet, anyway.'

'Yeah. Tarzan's surprised us all. He's signed up for every single educational programme – guitar lessons, fitness, computer with Zania over there . . .'

Zania Tullbrooke had come in and was unrolling a poster. She called out to Syons. 'Complaining about me again, are you?'

'No, we were discussing Tarzan.'

She joined them, still holding the roll of paper. 'He's very intelligent, you know. He's got the hang of word-processing and he's written some very good short stories. Exceptional, in fact. He was even entered for the Koestler Prize for Prisoners' Writing when he was at his last prison.'

'Who, Tarzan?' said Marshall incredulously. 'Pull the other one.'

'Yes, I mean it.'

Marshall shook his head.

Helen, on the other hand, didn't seem surprised as she put down her cup. 'Well, good luck to him. It's about time we had a success at Barfield. OK. I'm back to the grind. Is that one of the *Mikado* posters?'

Zania unrolled it. 'Yes. Brian Samora helped make it, using the graphics program. What do you think?'

She showed Helen. 'Hm. Samora was it? Good. But there's only one "k" in "Mikado".'

Back in her office she started signing her name on a series of letters, one to the relatives of a prisoner who had died yesterday, one to an MP who had requested a tour of the prison, one to Turnbull about Falla's transfer. A memo to John Bunny summarizing food consumption at Barfield over the past year. A reply to the editor of a women's magazine requesting an interview. A memo for the file of a prisoner in the VP Wing. An enquiry to HQ about Oswald Snooper's transfer. A requisition slip for new basketballs. A memo detailing the job specification for a new gardener. Release papers, visiting orders, psychological-assessment reports.

Mavis knocked. 'Miss Purvis is waiting. Pianist.'

'Thank you, Mavis, I know who Miss Adele Purvis is now. Two minutes. Oh, and will you please make it a salad for lunch today? I've put on pounds with your sandwiches.'

Mavis approached the desk and put Helen's bottle of alkaline stomach medicine down. 'Have you been to your doctor – about the upset tummy?'

'No, I'm fine at the moment. It just seems to have been coming and going. Maybe I'm getting hooked on this.' She picked up the Bisodol and shook it.

'Comes and goes, you said? Any time of day, or just one particular time?'

Helen unscrewed the cap and picked up a teaspoon from the tray of dirty cups on the windowsill. She wiped it clean with her thumb as Mavis ploughed on, rather self-consciously. 'Only you said you'd put on weight so I was thinking, well, you couldn't be, you know . . .'

'Couldn't be what? Ugh! Still tastes like liquefied chalk.'

'Pregnant.'

Helen looked at her secretary, horrified. 'Mavis! For God's sake, woman. You think I wouldn't know? And besides, I've had my period every month.'

Mavis was half-way out of the door. 'Well, you should see a doctor – your own doctor, not Dr Harris, nice man though he is. This has been going on far too long. Suppose you have an ulcer.'

As Mavis let herself out, Helen considered. It was a thought. It wasn't as if she didn't have a thousand things to worry herself sick about.

Adele Purvis came in with a nervous smile on her face. 'Thank you for seeing me, Miss Hewitt, because I know how busy you are.'

'No, you don't,' said Helen, with a smile. 'I bet you I'm a lot busier. Is it about the rehearsals? Everything's all right with the Midlands Mummers, isn't it?'

'Oh, yes! They're lovely. Well . . . a little *surprising*, that's true. But they really do know their business and Mr Hallam has a wonderful singing voice.'

'So how can I help?'

'Er, well . . . It's about a prisoner, an inmate, Wilfred Samuels. I'm not sure of his number.'

'I know Mr Samuels, Miss Purvis. What about him?'

'We want to get married.'

'Just like that. She says, "We want to get married."'

Simon was lying on the bed next to her. She was in it, with a glass of white wine in her hand. He said, 'And do you?'

'Do I what?'

'Want to get married?'

'Oh, my God. You want the Range Rover back, yes?'

'Can you stop joking? I'm serious.'

'I was talking about Miss Purvis. Now you're talking about us. You and me?'

'We're not exactly at Charing Cross, Helen. There's only you and me here.'

'I thought I might be asked – if you're asking – in a more romantic location.'

'We're in my bedroom – our bedroom. We're living together. You use my car more than I do.'

'So you *do* want it back?'

'And you don't want to marry me?'

Helen sipped her wine. Her heart was beating hard, as it always did when this subject came up. 'I love you. Why don't we just keep things as they are?'

'Why not go one step further?'

'Because, right now, I can't.'

Simon fiddled with his tie, rolling it up and down, a thing he only did when he was nervous and upset.

'OK, OK, let's change the subject. Russell Morgan. I talked to him again on the phone. And, also, my partners think we may have a good case against the Home Office.'

'Brilliant, Simon. *Brilliant*. How is Morgan, by the way?'

'Not so good. Still very depressed and, to make matters worse, his marriage is falling apart, I think. There's one thing I need which you can get for me.'

'Yes?'

'Everything you've got on record about that first time Morgan was taken hostage.'

Suddenly Helen was filled with tenderness. She rolled

onto her side and put her arms round him. 'Simon? Just give me time . . . I do love you, you know. But I need time at the moment.'

'I know,' he said. 'And you've got it.'

CHAPTER 22

Tuesday, 23 January

'IT'S JUST NOT Buffy's scene.'

Gary Marshall's prediction was proving all too true. And the reasoning was simple. The inmates of Her Majesty's Special Secure Units regarded themselves as an élite, and élites don't easily admit new members they have never heard of. Some of the men in the Barfield SSU had made international headlines for terrorism or for the exteme violence with which they expressed hatred or greed. They were often big celebrities in their own right. Others were just big.

Billy Howel, for example. He was in his mid-thirties, a man who had run riot with a sawn-off shotgun after ram-raiding building societies in the Newcastle area. His body count was two. Limping Terry Fowls, whose scowling, razor-scarred face was a chilling reminder of the methods he used to settle scores, had run a large drugs gang in North London. In the small hours of one morning he'd firebombed a house in which a rival gang was having a party. Body count: three adults and a child. Salim Patel, an opulent Yorkshire drugs baron, was responsible for commissioning murders and selling large quantities of contaminated smack. Body count: anybody's guess. Tony Paulso, in his mid-forties, was a

London-Italian heavy with a body so muscled up it made him look like a human pitbull terrier. He behaved like one, too – he was a contract killer for the Mafia. Official body-count: three. Micky Beck, stocky and disarmingly scruffy in appearance, was a ruthless bank robber who had been caught after kidnapping and killing a branch manager and his wife. Body count: two.

These were the men who were caged in this prison-within-the-prison, a tiny zoo whose horizon was never more than thirty metres away. No facilities were shared with the rest of Barfield. The unit had its own visiting rooms, laundry, kitchen, workshop, hobby-room and gym. It was surrounded by its own double-thickness weld-mesh fence and a five-metre wall crowned by an inwardly curving plastic 'beak' to make it difficult for climbers.

The SSU inmates were not looking at getting out for twenty years or more and their lives were dedicated to making things as cushy as they could. That meant dominating their warders and making sure the inmates, not the prison staff, called the tune. It should have been impossible but it was easy. Confident the unit was escape-proof, officers reckoned they could afford to be lax about security. They spent long hours in close proximity to their prisoners and the unit ran itself, anyway. The officers were more often than not bored out of their skulls.

The result was that security-drift had crept in, a by-product of what the Prison Service called 'conditioning' among officers who are not given sufficiently varied duties. Conditioning was fine, as far as the assorted killers and gangsters were concerned. Just fine.

It meant that no one really noticed the slow accretion of luxury creeping into these men's lives. The cells were stuffed full of designer sports clothes and accessories, electronic consumer goods and luxury foodstuffs – cooking was regarded as a positive hobby activity, and there was nothing that said they had to stick to the Asda One Hundred Basic Buys. Officers would even agree to go on specialist shopping expeditions for the inmates to buy dried field mushrooms, quail's eggs, fresh pasta, fillet steak. There were even times when Chinese take-aways had been ordered from the town. The Special Secure Unit was special, all right. Buffy could hardly believe it.

There were other surprises, too. Frightening ones. One of them occurred in the laundry where, after stuffing clothes into the washing machine, Buffy shut the door and pulled open the powder drawer. Looking around for detergent, he saw a row of packets on a shelf above and took one down, shaking it to loosen the lumps. The carton felt oddly heavy and seemed to have a particularly large lump in it. He opened the flap and peered inside, shaking the contents aside. There was something else in it. He stuck a hand in and his fingers met a polythene bag wrapped around cold metal. Were they putting free gifts inside the soap powders now, like they did in cornflakes? He half withdrew the object and then suddenly understood.

There was a noise behind him and Buffy turned. Billy Howel was standing there, chewing gum. 'The boy with the cell stuffed full of Semtex, eh?' He came close, reached out and pinched Buffy's face, his fingers and thumbs gouging uncomfortably into the cheeks and pushing the lips out in a grotesque pout. 'Well, you keep *this* tight shut. *Comprendo?*'

He took back the powder, replaced it on the shelf and selected another. He held it out to Buffy. 'You want soap powder, don't you? Take it.'

Dumbly, frozen with fear, Buffy did so. Howel came even closer, so that Buffy was pinned against the washing machine, the smell of Howel's gum in his nose.

'You're really in it now, sunshine. And I'll be watching you . . . every move you make, every breath you take. Got it?'

Tony Paulso wandered up to the door holding a pool cue, which Howel took before he walked out and said in a whisper, 'Move that thing out of the soap powder, you stupid git. Four-eyes here found it.'

Howel went back to his game of pool while Paulso advanced on Buffy. 'Oi, motor-mouth.'

Officer Becker was passing the internal window. He glanced in. It looked as if the new lad was getting informed of the house-rules.

'You been sent in here to blab off and I'll tell you what. If you do, I'll cut your fucking tongue out your filthy khaki-coloured head.' He glanced round to see if Becker had passed. He had. Paulso spoke close to Buffy's ear. 'Got our Semtex, have you? Find the stash?'

Buffy shook his head desperately. 'Semtex? I don't know what you're talking about. I mean, that Semtex thing was just a joke.'

'I don't like stupid jokes. I like jokes to be funny, wanker. Now listen. If you want to go to sleep at night and wake up in the morning, remember this: you see and hear *nothing* that goes down around this unit! Do you copy?'

Brian Samora had been sent back to the Wing first thing on Saturday with an apparently clean bill of health. But he had not turned up for Zania Tullbrooke's class that afternoon or on Monday and, hearing from Eric Had-

dock that he was holed up in his cell, she had asked Dr
Harris if he might still be suffering from the after-effects
of his fall. So, following his morning round on Health
Care, Harris had a look through Samora's medical file
and then dropped down to C Wing to visit the lad.

'Any headaches, Brian?'

'No.'

They were sitting in the probation office and, not for
the first time, Harris wished it was a more cheerful room.
After all, this was a modern prison, supposed to be.

'You look depressed.'

'Do I?'

'Are you sleeping?'

'Suppose so.'

'That doesn't sound very positive. Is anything worrying you?'

'No.'

'You sure, Brian? Anything you want to tell me stays
between us, you know that, don't you?'

'Nothing's worrying me.'

'Do you miss your pal Eugene Buffy since he's been
reclassified?'

Samora raised his eyes to the doctor's face. They were
suddenly blazing. 'No, I bloody don't. Just what are you
trying to tell me? I'm not queer. I'm not a bloody nonce,
OK? Now, I want to go back to my cell.'

'Brian, what are you getting so het up about?'

Samora jumped up, his body rigid with tension. 'I'm
not a nonce. I'm not a nonce. I got three more years and
I don't want nobody calling me a *nonce*!'

Back in Admin, Harris met Zania on her way to her
class. 'I've no idea what's wrong with him. Nothing
medically, as far as I can see, anyway. And he says not.'

Zania's brown eyes were big with concern. 'It's just

he's not been in class for so long, and they're telling me he won't even come out on association. I wondered if that fall might have done something to him that wasn't picked up.'

'Don't think so, but I'll see him again. On the other hand, if there's anything bothering him, he's not wanting to talk about it. Maybe one of the psychologists should have a word?'

'Well, if I hear any more – Oh! Miss Hewitt!'

Helen was passing by. She stopped.

'Hello, Zania, Davyd.'

Harris noted her pallor. 'How are you?' he asked.

'Fine. But Mavis is insisting I go and see my GP for a check-up.'

'Can't do any harm. Well, I must be off, see you later.'

Helen, too, began to move off but Zania followed her. 'I've got some good news, Miss Hewitt.'

'Let's hear it.'

'I had a phone call from my friend on the Koestler Prize panel. They're so impressed with Tarzan's work they're adding him to the short-list.'

'What? Tarzan? You serious? He really can write?'

'In my opinion. He's my best pupil.'

Helen smiled with delight. 'Wonder of wonders. And Mr Bunny's visiting today. It's always nice if I have something good instead of the usual tale of woe and mayhem to tell him. Thank you, Zania.'

They were opposite Mavis's domain and, hearing Helen's voice, she shot out with a message. 'Your doctor called. Said he can see you at six, Thursday evening.'

'At six?' Helen sighed. 'Mavis, it's the musical. He can't see me then.'

Flustered, Mavis put her hands to her cheeks. 'The musical? Oh, sorry, sorry. I forgot!'

270

'See if he can make it earlier, will you, please? What about four?'

'You've got a Wing Governors' meeting at four.'

'Mr Marshall can take that. Go for four o'clock and say it's an emergency.'

During association on C Wing an unaccountable tension was in the air, not helped by Tarzan, in trainers and tracksuit, jogging up and down the Wing with a school of three inmates in his wake, shouting at them and barging other inmates out of the way.

Jumbo Jackson decided he must intervene. 'Oi! Tarzan! What you doing?'

'Mr Jackson,' Tarzan called, 'I'll have these flabby unhealthy bastards fit if it's the last thing I do.'

'If you want to exercise, do it in the yard, not in here.'

Tarzan stopped and looked, then walked over. 'You stopping me?'

'Yes, I'm stopping you.'

Tarzan rammed his thumb up against his chest. 'I'm up for the Koestler Prize, I am.'

'That's got nothing to do with me, Tarzan. What you do on the Wing is to do with me. And you're getting up everybody's nose, charging around like this.'

'But it's exercise.'

'Then do it on exercise, not on association. Go on, get back to your cell.'

Tarzan eyeballed the officer, his lip quivering. He bunched his fists. Jackson stood his ground. 'Back to your cell, Tarzan, officer's direct order. Any more of this and I'll put you on report.'

The Koestler Prize hopeful relaxed his fists and took a

step back. Raising a finger, still glaring, he growled, 'Don't you threaten me.' And he spun on his heel and strolled towards cell number four.

Up on the threes, Samora lay curled up on his bunk, ignoring the attempt by Eric Haddock to cajole him down for a game of darts.

'You shouldn't stick in your pad like this, Brian. It's unhealthy. Pity you're not in the show. You will come to it, though, won't you? You got to come. You should hear those girls Carol and Meryl singing. Never mind the size of their knockers. I practised a song with one of them because I'm playing a woman, so I got to hold her . . . Let me show you.'

He posed himself with knees knocking and sang,

> 'So please you, sir, with much regret
> If we have failed in etiquette . . .'

'SHUT UP AND GET OUT!' Brian suddenly yelled. 'GET OUT! GET OUT!'

Roddy Marsh was passing and looked in to see what was causing the shouts. 'What's up with you, Brian? Oh, yeah! I know – missing your bosom buddy.'

At the mention of Buffy, Haddock sneered, 'Eugene Buffy thinks he's a big shot now, because he's in the SSU.'

Samora reached for a book on his table and hurled it at Haddock, hitting him on his bald head. Another missile had both Haddock and Marsh skipping out of the cell, just before Officer Jackson appeared, his bulk blocking the doorway. 'Brian, you all right, son? Not like you to stay in your pad like this?'

272

Samora returned to the foetal position. 'I'm all confused, Mr Jackson.' His voice was quavering. 'I've lost all me confidence.'

Jackson stepped towards Samora and at the same moment another voice called in from the doorway. Burt Threlfall was there, leaning in with a nasty leer on his face. 'How ya doing, Brian?'

Jackson saw the look of horror on Samora's face and turned to see who was there – but Thelfall had already gone on his way. He turned back to the fretting prisoner. 'Somebody been messing you about, Brian?'

'No. Nobody ever messes with me. They even try it and I beat them up!'

'Brian, if you need to talk to anybody you only got to say the word. Why don't you want to go down to education? I thought your education was your big thing. Is it Tarzan?'

Samora ignored the question and Jackson shook his head and began to walk out. 'When is Eugene coming back on the Wing, Mr Jackson?'

'I don't know, Brian. I really couldn't say.'

With Jackson gone, Samora started to weep again, as he had almost every time he'd been alone since he'd been raped by Burt Thelfall in Health Care. He pulled the sleeves of his sweater down over his hands and stuffed the loose wool into his mouth to repress the sound.

Jackson found Len Syons in the Wing office. Tarzan had been on his mind. The Goody-Two-Shoes effect was wearing off now and the big man's innate aggression was reasserting itself.

'Gov, I think Tarzan's getting a bit heavy. Unsettling a lot of the regulars.'

His boss expelled a tired sigh. 'Knew it was too bloody good to last. What do you suggest?'

'I don't know, but he's started to control the whole Wing. We'll have to do something.'

'I'll have a think about it. Let's get them out on exercise now.'

Tarzan was also the subject of conversation between Helen Hewitt and John Bunny. They happened to be walking near the A and C Wing exercise yard just as the inmates began to stream out into the open air, hugging themselves to keep warm.

Helen was saying, 'It was my decision to put Tarzan back on the Wing and he has really improved. I was told today that he's got through to the short-list of the Koestler Prize for inmates' writing.'

'Really? You wouldn't have thought he was the type. Is this his Wing?'

'Yes – this is the A and C Wing exercise yard.'

'Well, I'd like to congratulate him.'

Helen waved at Officer Chiswick. 'Mr Chiswick? Would you call Tarzan over, please?'

Chiswick scanned the inmates and saw Tarzan walking out at the head of a column of tracksuited followers. 'Tarzan!' he called. 'Over here, please. Tarzan!'

There was nothing sudden about Tarzan's response. He merely wheeled around and began walking towards Chiswick as Helen and Bunny advanced to meet him. It wasn't until the huge prisoner was twenty yards from them that they realized he was bearing down with a particularly ferocious look on his face, increasing the speed of his advance as he closed. When Tarzan was ten yards away, Bunny cleared his throat. 'Mr Tarzan? I am the Area Manager for Barfield Prison and I've just been told by Miss Hewitt that you've—'

He was interrupted by a glass-cracking scream from Tarzan as he thrust his massive face forward. One of his great hands grasped Bunny under the chin. The other went for a grip between his legs as Tarzan plucked the man off the ground with incredible ease. Then he hoisted him high over his head, a jungle roar coming from his mouth as his fellow inmates on their way out of the Wing stopped and gawped. Tarzan swung his easy burden around, bent his arms and pitched Bunny with all his phenomenal strength at the nearest mesh fence. Squealing, Bunny flew through the air and hit the mesh. His arms and legs were working like a swimmer without the water as he rebounded and thudded to the ground.

CHAPTER 23

IT WENT ROUND the prison like a flash fire that Tarzan had gone berserk, but they didn't hear about it in the SSU until officers' shift-change at five o'clock. Officer Kilroy was discussing it with glee during the inmates' late exercise period, sitting around with Officers Manison and Dougan, playing cards.

'Picked him up like he was a baby. Tossed him right up in the air, he did.'

The others murmured with approving laughter. Seeing an Area Manager lose his dignity was a considerable pleasure to them.

Someone slunk into the office and Kilroy tipped back his head to see who it was. Buffy.

'Don't you fancy some fresh air, Eugene?' He walked his fingers through the air. 'You know – exercise?'

'I want to make a phone call.' Buffy's voice was quiet, almost a murmur.

'Sorry, pal,' said Kilroy. The ebullience in his voice was still there from telling about John Bunny. 'You can't do that from in here.'

'I want to see the Governor.'

'Hey, hey. You know the rules. Put it on a request form.'

276

Buffy had started to shuffle out before he realized Terry Fowls was waiting in the door for him. He forced Buffy to turn sideways and squeeze past. Fowls spoke through the side of his mouth. 'I hope you do know the rules, Eugene.'

Buffy walked backwards a few steps, looking at Fowls, then turned and made his way towards his cell. Officer Collins was coming towards him. Buffy looked back to check where Fowls was and reckoned he was safe. 'If I write a note, Mr Collins, can you see it gets delivered?'

'Depends, Eugene. Who's it for?'

'It's for my pal Brian. C Wing.' He dropped his voice further and was now speaking in a whisper. 'I don't want to stay in here.'

They were interrupted by Salim Patel, who walked around covered in gold and Brut aftershave. He smiled, showing beautifully capped teeth. 'Come out into the yard, Eugene. We're having a game of handball.'

'Go on, son,' said Collins. 'Better do what the man says.'

Buffy went out hesitantly, his eyes flicking nervously between the three inmates as they slammed the hard handball against the wall.

Brian Samora had lain on his bed all day and the Wing was beginning to talk. It was so out of character, that was the thing. Samora was known as an uppity little sod who normally pogoed around the Wing giving out cheeky verbals left and right. Jumbo Jackson, with the lad very much on his mind after their earlier conversation, was sure that Tarzan had been at the root of the problem.

'Trolley's on the Wing, Brian,' he said, as he went

round rousting out the slow inmates. 'Aren't you hungry?'

'No.'

'If it makes you feel any better, we're moving Tarzan out.'

Samora brooded. He didn't even react to the news, he only said, 'I got to talk to Eugene.'

Jackson felt sorry for the lad. His heart went out to him.

'Mr Jackson! Mr Jackson!'

It was the voice of Len Syons on the walkie. 'Yes, Gov?'

'Mr Jackson! Hurry it up, will you? We want you down on the ones.'

He started to go out, then turned. He was such a softie, really. 'Give me a note, why don't you? I'll see Buffy gets it.'

Jackson tripped down the narrow stairs as nimbly as his bulk allowed, feeling he had done a small thing to make a miserable man a little better. The Wing Governor was waiting impatiently outside Tarzan's former cell. He jerked a thumb at the noticeboard.

'Curtis, did you see that Keith Smith's due in court tomorrow? I've got to go and organize the van to be at reception early, as he's got a long way to travel. Can you get started clearing Tarzan's pad? Then we can get him to sign for his belongings.' Syons nodded at the cell door. 'He had a lot of gear for his short stay with us. See if any of it's nicked from the rest of the Wing.'

Jackson entered the empty cell and looked around. He saw the possessions in a different way from Syons; from a more sensitive perceptive, he liked to think.

'Doesn't seem a lot for twenty-seven years, though, does it?'

There were two black bin bags to receive Tarzan's worldly goods. On the floor was a stack of books, a neat pile of cassette tapes and a mini ghetto-blaster. There was another tidy pile of A4 copy paper on the table: Tarzan's writings. With a sigh he crouched and went through the books, opening each to look for labels. 'Library . . . library . . . library . . .'

By the time he'd finished the books and started on the cassettes, Syons had come back with a clipboard under his arm.

'Right, Gov, most of the books aren't even his, filched from various nicks' libraries. These tapes are all jazz and blues and that kind of – Wait a minute. Look at this.'

He creaked to an upright position and handed a cassette to Syons, indicating the label. It read 'Eugene Buffy' . . .

'That's not a music tape!' said Jackson, in triumph. 'But I think I know what it is.'

It was late, almost nine o'clock. The prisoners were returning to their cells and to bed, Threlfall going up to the twos ahead of Keith Smith. He suddenly turned and blocked the stairs to speak to Smith. 'You going to court tomorrow, Keith? Eh, Smithy. I'm talking to you, you cunt.'

'Shut your face, Thelfall. Shut it or I'll—'

'Come on, Thelfall, up these stairs,' called Officer Brent from the landing. 'LOCK-UP! LOCK-UP!'

Eric Haddock and Roddy Marsh had gained the threes landing, passing Brian Samora's open cell and calling in their goodnights. Brent hurried along and posted himself outside the cell.

'Lock-up. Come on, stop messing about. Move along.'

Threlfall approached the officer, adopting a high-pitched whine.

'Mr Brent, if Buffy's not coming back on the Wing can I bunk up with my mate Brian, here? Jack Binton's got stinking feet.'

'Move on, Thelfall,' said Brent wearily. Then he looked into Samora's cell. The inmate was writing at his table.

'Lock-up, Brian. And remember, you're not getting out of showers tomorrow.' He banged him up then opened the flap. 'You know what we found in Tarzan's cell?' he hissed. 'The tape you gave him to hide. You little shit!'

Samora sat looking at his letter to Eugene Buffy. He knew the handwriting was primitive – and the spelling – but he had thought it a well-written letter. When he heard Brent's vindictive tones through the flap, he'd got to the bit where he had said,

I've not been getting out of the drum much because I've been ever so pissed off since they sent you down the SSU but I'm pulling myself together because I worked out I should go down to Tarzan's cell tomorrow, get that tape back. Then we can use it to get you out of that bloody hole.

There wasn't any point now, though, was there? Slowly he began to tear up the letter.

The story of Buffy's tape of Officer Hully had gone round the prison. Now that it had ended up, last as usual, in the SSU, the officers had started looking at him with almost as much hostility as the other inmates.

He was sitting miserably watching some crap television show when he heard Salim Patel stroll up to the table where the screws, as usual, were playing cards. Patel was carrying a tray with a toppling pile of half-eaten meals and a roasting tin. 'Any of you guys want some French-style roast chicken? We cooked up too much.'

Officer Kilroy waved a hand as he studied his cards. 'No thanks, I got my sandwiches.'

'You sure? No takers? It's good cooking, only going to waste. Oh, well . . .' Wandering back towards the trash bins, which stood near the kitchen door, he made a detour past Buffy. Without looking or speaking, he tossed a half-eaten chicken wing into his lap.

At the bins, Patel was whistling and scraping food off plates. Buffy picked up the piece of greasy chicken and went across to the bins. 'I don't want this.' He tried to throw it into the same bin that Patel was using. He could see the bags had just been changed. He could also see that, in between scraping plates, Patel was drawing out a length of nylon rope and tucking it up inside his sweat-shirt. Buffy backed off fast and returned to the television.

Micky Beck was taking a shower when Terry Fowls and Patel came in with towels around them.

'Micky?'

The shower door opened to reveal Beck, naked and soaking. Behind him a single tile had been removed and the wall hollowed out to make a compartment. Patel passed him the rope and he began to feed it inside the hiding place. Patel said, 'He saw the rope. Buffy did.'

'We got a problem needs sorting out?' said Beck.

'Yeah, you sort him out, Micky,' said Fowls. 'It's getting too close for cock-ups.'

'That's right!' said Patel, his eyes shining. 'Friday!'

CHAPTER 24

Thursday, 24 January

ITT WAS *Mikado* day and the C Wing inmates involved were taking special care over their morning showers.

'Don't hang about, Eric,' called Jumbo Jackson. 'You've been in front of that mirror ten minutes.'

'He's doing his barnet,' said Roddy Marsh, 'or should I say what's left of it. Getting all ponced up for Meryl and Carol, Mr Jackson.'

'Well, I notice you been doing a bit of Brylcreeming yourself, Roddy.'

Eric Haddock patted the sides of his head and moved away from the mirror. He came past Officer Jackson and sniffed. 'Same could be said of you, Mr Jackson. Old-Spiced-out, I'd say.'

'Get out of it, Eric. Right, we all set to go back on the Wing? Line up.'

He started counting, then looked at his list. 'No Samora, no Smith.'

'Keith Smith's gone to court today,' said Officer Brent. 'He left before breakfast.'

'Won't be smelling so good as this lot for his trial, then. What about Samora? He bunked off this again?'

'No, he came down,' said Brent, looking down the

line of cubicles. The furthest shower was still running. 'Brian! Come on, lad. Come out of it now.'

Jackson was already walking down to have a look; he didn't trust Brent not to be too hard on the lad. 'Better start moving them up,' he called back. 'I'll collect this one. We're running late as it is. Hey, Brian lad. We're all waiting to go back on the Wing.'

One more stride and he came opposite the stall.

The water was running, though it was not full on. It streamed down onto Samora's back.

'Brian?'

He was kneeling, facing the wall, like a naked man at prayer. But his position was strange, sagging forward, the face resting against the tiled wall, the nose pressed up against the mixer taps.

'Brian?'

Jackson looked closer. He blinked.

'Oh my God!'

The nylon cord was no thicker than a shoelace. Jackson followed it up with his eyes and saw it was secured to the shower rose.

'Oh! Sweet Jesus!'

Samora had hanged himself.

Helen sat in the probation office of the VP Wing, watching Oswald Snooper as he smoked, jiggled his foot and picked stray bits of tobacco off his lower lip. Between them, on the table, was a pad of paper. Gary Marshall stood at the door with his arms folded.

'We have a transfer arrangement for you, Mr Snooper, but we do want the names of the men you know are dealing drugs in Barfield. The barons, the runners and the prisoners who are being threatened.'

Snooper did not look at her. 'What protection do I get?' he muttered.

'Well,' said Marshall, 'you'll be out of here. But first we want the information so we can check it out.' He stepped forward and placed a pencil on top of the pad.

Snooper looked up and there was both fear and anger in his eyes. 'How you gonna do that, man? I give you names and you start duckin' and divin' around. Then they gonna know they gotta grass.'

Helen shrugged. 'You could also give us any name you pulled out of a hat,' she said. 'Or all the people you don't like.'

'No, man.' He shook his head. 'You in charge here, right? You don't get what you want from my information, you tellin' me you can't get me back? I wouldn't screw you, no way. Deal is a deal, on my kid's life – two kids' lives.'

He fiddled with the end of a dreadlock. 'I *got* to get off this Wing. These guys down here are doin' my nut in. One of them, all he can do is play Doris Day and wank. Things he shouts while he does it – well, it's disgustin'. If I hear Doris Day anytime the rest of my life I'm gonna flip, man. I make it plain enough for you, Miss Hewitt?'

Helen nodded. 'Yes, you do, Mr Snooper. I don't much care for Doris Day either.'

There was a tap on the door and Officer Wallis put his head round. 'Could I see you for a second, Governor? It's urgent.'

She rose and slipped from the room. Marshall glanced out through the internal window – Wallis's face was grave, and as soon as he started speaking, so was Helen's.

He wagged a finger at Snooper. 'You better not be messing us about, Snoopy.' He stepped forward to the

table and rapped the pad with his knuckles. 'Names –
barons, dealers, users. We'll check it out after you're
away.'

And he walked out slap into the news that Brian
Samora was dead.

Losing a prisoner by suicide was the worst kind of escape.
It meant you had failed in the most basic of your duties
– looking after the man, making him safe from others,
safe from himself. And there was no recapturing him.
But Helen had no time to brood on it. There were things
to be decided, people to tell. The first decision was
whether to cancel the dress rehearsal. Mavis already had
Hermione Ellison waiting in the ante-room. The others
would be on their way.

'What do you think, Gary?'

'Was Samora in the show?'

'No. A lot of C Wing are in it, but this one was out
on parole at the start. Or just about to go on parole.
Does the Wing know yet?'

Marshall shook his head slowly. Helen knew he felt
this as much as she did. 'They were out of the showers
area before Jackson found him. They'll be devastated on
the Wing, though. Samora could be a toerag but he was
well liked by the cons.'

'So we'd best let the show go on. They'll need
something to take their minds off this.'

Anywhere outside a nick it might have seemed a
callous decision. But to Helen, governing Barfield, it was
simply a practical one.

Marshall felt in his pocket and pulled out an envelope.
'Oh, and one of the SSU officers brought this over. It's
a note from Eugene Buffy – addressed to Brian Samora.'

Helen tore it open and read aloud: '"Dear Brian: I am being got at in here and they won't let me out. Write to the Home Office . . ."'

She sat down and finished it privately, then handed it to Marshall. 'Says he wants Brian to start a campaign as big as the Guildford Four.'

Marshall sighed as he read the brief note. He folded it and put it back in the envelope. 'Well, somebody better go over to the SSU and tell him before it gets on the grapevine that his campaign manager's dead.'

Helen stood up. 'I'll go. I need a walk.'

The walk across to the unit helped. The light was clear, the sky blue and the air she breathed was cold and refreshing. But when she was standing in the open area of the unit she suddenly felt coldly angry.

'What the hell is that doing still covering that window? I thought I gave instructions that it should be taken down.'

She pointed to the internal window, which gave a view into the hobbies room. Officer Kilroy told her, 'They said it was an invasion of their privacy, Miss Hewitt.'

'Did they? Well, it's a workshop not a sauna. Get it down – and by today. Ah, Mr Buffy. Come over here with me, will you, please?'

She led him into the television area, with Kilroy following. 'Turn off the TV will you? Thanks.'

Buffy spoke uncertainly, suspiciously. 'Am I going back on the Wing?'

Helen looked up. Two inmates had strolled across and were leaning on a wall within earshot. 'Could we have a little privacy, please?'

'Am I?'

The eavesdroppers moved a little way off and Officers Kilroy and Manison shifted positions so that they stood between the inmates and the Governor.

'I'm afraid I've got some bad news for you, Eugene,' Helen went on. 'And I wanted to come over and tell you myself.'

'I been expecting this,' Buffy said loudly. 'You're not going to do anything about that bent screw. You found the other tape. I knew it. You're all bent, the lot of you.'

Helen shook her head. 'Eugene, it's not about the tape. The officer in question will, I believe, be charged over it. But this is another matter, a very sad matter. I am sorry to be the one to tell you. There's no easy way to say it. Brian Samora committed suicide this morning.'

Buffy froze. He looked as if he'd been hit. His eyes stared. Then he sprang up. 'No! No!'

Helen looked up at Kilroy and Manison but they simply stood there.

'Would you like a cup of tea or . . . something?'

'No!'

'I'll ask the prison psychologist to see you, or, if you prefer, Dr Harris.'

'No!'

Buffy was looking around him, like a trapped animal. He took a step towards the corner of the room. It was the only direction he could walk without going near anyone. He walked towards it, right up to the corner, and pressed his face into the angle of the walls. Helen noticed he made no attempt to cover his face. His arms were held straight down, fingers clenched, at his sides.

'No! No! No!'

Helen got up and said to the officers, 'Keep an eye.

287

Call me if you need to. And *please* remove that blanket over the workshop window today.'

As she walked past the two grinning inmates, Beck said, 'He's a right nutter. Shouldn't be in here with us anyway.'

They would have had some corroboration for this view, had they been able to read Eugene Buffy's mind. They were all against Brian. They probably killed him too. We dared to challenge the system, thought Buffy. They'll come for me now. Got to get away. Got to get out.

Back in her office, Helen went at her paperwork with ferocious concentration, working through until three when she dropped her pen, rubbed her eyes and went and got her coat. Mavis was putting up a new poster of *The Mikado*.

'I'm going now, Mavis,' she called out, and mouthed, so that the rest of the office couldn't hear: *doctor*.

'Like the poster?' said Mavis. 'We might have to do more than one performance now, you know. It's full up.'

Gary Marshall came in with a memo for Mavis to type into e-mail.

'Miss Hewitt, Oswald Snooper's on his way and we got the list.'

'Good.'

'And Keith Smith's back. For twelve years.'

'I know. Twelve! Jury took less than ten minutes, so I'm told. Look, I'll see you later, Gary. I've got an appointment and then I must go and get tarted up for the VIPs. Can you take the Wing Governors for me?'

As she went down the stairs, she heard Gary asking Mavis, 'Where's she going?'

And dependable Mavis simply said, 'Will you take the flowers over to the chapel – for presentations at the end of the show? And put these posters up to replace the misspelt ones? Have you got tickets?'

'You kidding? The lads have booked three entire rows.'

When Eugene Buffy walked out into the SSU exercise yard, amid the handball game, all the players noticed the change in him, even though not all of them would have been able to articulate it. The hard ball was going to the wall and zipping back with rigorous efficiency and speed but he didn't flinch or seem particularly to notice. His step was not hesitant. The scared look had completely evaporated from behind his glasses. Fear had left him.

'You stopped talking to yourself, then?' jeered Terry Fowls, hurling the ball. It was neatly caught by Micky Beck.

'Yes,' he said firmly. 'And now I wanna talk to you.'

Fowls stood still and then approached with a threatening look.

'Just like that, eh? Get stuffed, then.'

Beck came up to help deal with this sad unwanted little prick. He should be got out of the SSU. They wanted to be among what they considered their own kind. They only wanted to know other hard men.

Buffy looked from one to the other, and then to Salim Patel, who also approached. 'I know what you're planning. I know you're planning to go over the wall.'

Beck growled, 'He's a fucking nutter. Doesn't know nothing.'

'Don't I? I know something you ought to know. I

289

know a night when all the cons and screws in this nick are busy thinking about something else. It's tonight!'

'What do you want, creep?' Beck showed him the ball. 'You want this down your throat?'

'No. I want to come with you. But it's got to be tonight. Tonight it's showtime!'

CHAPTER 25

BY FOUR O'CLOCK heavy thumps, laughter, singing and piano music had been emanating from the chapel for quite some time. Inmates who normally thought about little else except their release date had completely forgotten to tick off the days of their sentence. In the last few days they had been ticking off the days until the show. Now it had come it was a sell-out, and excitement and expectation were high.

Mavis was typing into the computer with Russell Morgan sitting opposite her. He looked strangely out of place in his civilian gear; he felt it, too.

'Bit of a panic all round today,' she said, rattling her keyboard furiously. 'We've got this musical. It's a nightmare with all the security guys double-checking everyone who's coming in for it. Not something we normally have to cope with, is it?'

The phone rang and Mavis picked it up. 'Yes, it is . . . Yes, I'll hold.' She beamed at Morgan. 'The gate.'

'I can always come back another time, Mavis.'

'No, no. And Gary Marshall will go bananas if he knew you'd been in and not seen him.'

'Well, we used to go to the pub a lot, you know. Saw

a lot of each other. But that was when we were both still married – at least, when his was alive and mine—'

'How is Nora?'

'It's been tough on her. Maybe even more than me. I've been trying to get out from under it, you might say. Applied for a job with a security firm.'

'Security? Well, that's where the jobs are nowadays, so they say.'

'Do they? Well, that's lucky. It's something I know a bit about, after fifteen years in prisons.'

'Yes, that's right,' said Mavis to the phone. 'Edward Streatham, photographer. He's to take photographs of the cast . . . I sent you his particulars down. Miss Hewitt should be back any time. OK. 'Bye.'

Morgan shifted on his seat. He didn't look comfortable. 'I'm in the way, Mavis. I just wanted to thank her for this Simon Lennox. He's very positive. A good chap. Reckons I might get some compensation so that added to the pay-off money and I might be OK.'

In the boardroom Gary Marshall was presiding over the Wing Governors' meeting. 'Miss Hewitt sends her apologies. She's gone to get ready for tonight so we'll have to get cracking without her.'

'This bloody show! I've not had time for lunch,' complained Len Syons.

'Thank you, Len. I'm sure we've all been struggling. Now . . .' He picked up a typed memo, stapled on top of a ruled sheet of A4 covered in handwriting. 'Oswald Snooper. We have a list of – you won't believe this – thirty-five known dealers, five barons and inmates under pressure to bring in heroin, cocaine and crack. We don't know how up to date this list is or if it's a load of bull.

But he was a heavy dealer on the Wing himself so if it *is* legit we have the opportunity for one hell of a major bust.'

The phone rang and the Deputy Governor paused while Len Syons took it. 'Len – want to share it with us?'

'Yeah, its Mavis. She says Russell Morgan's in with her. And she wants to know if the flowers are in water. She's worried about them.'

'Yes, they bloody are. So can we get back to this, because, seriously, if you look at this list, there's also eight prison officers here . . .'

Helen was sitting in the patients' car park, and she was weeping. She had a crumpled prescription in her hand and an appointment with the Ante-natal Department at the hospital for an ultrasound scan. How? How could she not have known, with something like this going on in her body? Her own body!

She wiped the tears and found a Kleenex. Then she started the car and took off. She had to see Simon. Nothing else mattered but telling Simon.

Gary Marshall spent only ten more minutes on the planned drugs bust. He knew there wasn't time to do the nuts and bolts now. He ran through the plan for getting the Wings into the chapel for the show this evening, then cut the meeting short. He went straight in to Mavis. 'She not back yet?'

'No. Can't think what's keeping her. But look who's here.'

'Hello, my son.' Russell Morgan stood up and Marshall pumped his hand.

'Hello, Gary.'

'Good to see you. Looking very sharp. How you doing?'

'May be working for a security company soon.'

'Security? Service would always have you back, wouldn't they?'

'No. Not with the medical record I got now. Down as a fruit-and-nut case, I am.'

Marshall looked at his watch.

'Look, you're busy,' said Morgan. 'Maybe have a drink sometime . . .'

'No, no, Russell. Come up to the lounge. Be some of the lads up there. You know, we're getting a big darts match on.'

The phone rang and Mavis answered smartly. 'No, she isn't here. What? Gary! Can you take this? It's Officer Horrocks.'

'What time *IS* she getting back? Hello. Marshall. Yes . . . yes . . . how long for? OK. I'll be right over.' He replaced the receiver and looked apologetically at Morgan. 'Sorry about this, Russell. You know how it is, only there's a problem with Tarzan.'

'I'm just off to change, Gary,' said Mavis.

'Right. I have to get down to the Block.'

'Tarzan?' said Morgan. 'Do I know—?'

'You don't remember? Oh, no, course not. In your day he used to be called Victor Braithwaite. Now he's called Tarzan and the Gov's the only one who can handle him. Anyway, he'll be out of here tomorrow and I for one will be happy if he never comes back among this happy throng. Anyway, he's making more noise than a hyena down on the Block. I better go down, might be able to stun him with the amazing news that he came second in a writing competition. We just heard.'

'See you, then, Gary.'

'Yeah. See you, Russell.'

Tarzan hadn't been mollified by news of his literary success. He'd simply reverted to what he had been when he came in – wolf-howls, tiger-growls, llama-spit. There was nothing for it but to send him on his travels again. Another failure to chalk up . . .

'How did you think Russell Morgan was?' asked Mavis, when Marshall returned from the Block to see if Helen had turned up.

'Not well, but he was pleased with her ladyship's bloke, Simon Lennox. By the way, you heard George Falla – now of fond memory to Barfield, thank God – will be charged with threatening to kill, malicious wounding and false imprisonment? Great news.'

He checked his watch. 'She's cutting it a bit fine, isn't she? We got to go up dead on time, you know.'

'She's had a doctor's appointment. She's not been well.'

Marshall snorted. 'That's no excuse. I've had a bad back for weeks. What's the matter with her?'

'I can't say.'

'Not serious, is it?'

'Depends.'

'Women's problems, is it?'

'I think she's – well, just that she's got all the symptoms of it.'

Marshall was looking through a memo about visit-room security. An SSU inmate wanted compensation for a hundred and fifty pounds' worth of frozen food which had defrosted during his transfer from Full Sutton. Dear oh dear. What were they coming to?

'Symptoms of what, Mavis?'

'I can't say.'

'Won't go any further, I swear. What she got?'

'Well, often you're the last to know, and having had two myself, I can't help feeling . . .'

'What? Blimey, Mavis, not up the spout is she?'

'I never said that.'

Helen was at the flat by five fifteen. Simon, of course, wasn't back from the office. She rang him. He had left. She paced around the flat, thinking furiously. Career woman with baby and nanny. Career woman with child-minding treasure. Career woman with house-husband called Simon. Ex-career woman. Nothing seemed right.

At last he arrived. She told him in the hall. Under normal circumstances she would have enjoyed watching his jaw drop, but not today.

'How many months?'

'Four. I just can't believe it. I mean, I thought it was food poisoning.'

They went through to the sitting room where Simon poured them drinks.

'I have to have it, Simon. I mean, it's over four months, and . . . I just feel so stupid. I should have known.'

'And now you do, we both do. So I'm going to try again.'

He helped himself to a vase of semi-dead flowers on the sideboard and went down on one knee. 'I now formally ask you – all one-and-almost-a-half of you – to marry me. I love you and if this is what it takes – a shotgun marriage no less – I'm your man.'

Helen stood above him for only a moment, then sank

down to the floor beside him. 'I thought . . . I was even scared you might not want it. Some men—'

'I'm not some men, Helen. I want you and I want our baby. So, third time lucky – will you marry me?'

Helen nodded, a tight smile on her face.

'Good. That's settled. And are you free for dinner tonight, Mrs Lennox-to-be?'

Dinner? There was something . . . She looked at her watch and remembered. 'Oh, my God, I've got to go. I forgot all about it!'

'All about what?'

'It's the show! *The Mikado*. It's tonight. I can't be late. But I'm going to be!'

'You want me to drive you?'

'No. It'll be over by eight, then I'll come home.'

They kissed.

'I love you,' he said.

'And I love you. I love you both,' said Helen.

CHAPTER 26

I N THE SSU Officer Collins was late clocking on.
'Buggers at the gate almost didn't let me in.
"Oi," I said, "I frigging work here." They got a full
house for Gilbert O'Sullivan.'

Three officers on general duties were sitting in the
television area, along with the inmates. They were watching an old re-run episode of *The New Avengers*.

'And,' said Officer Manison.

'And what?'

'Gilbert *and* Sullivan.'

'What do I care? Not seeing it, am I? Stuck in here.'

He strolled over to the window and looked out into
the darkness of the exercise yard. 'Floodlights on, yes?
Might rain, though.'

Terry Fowls got up and yawned, scratching one of his
scars. 'Why the fuck not? Must do me usual exercise
before beddy-byes. Anyone want a game of hardball?
This programme stiffs.'

Anyone listening with an ear for it would catch the
unnatural way he was speaking – tense, almost like
someone reciting lines. This was not registered by Manison, Kilroy and Becker, who were watching Purdey, with
men's pyjamas on and a gun in her hand, climbing to the

top of a construction-site crane. Collins called through to Dougan in Control to put on the yard lights, then went across to the TV and Joanna Lumley.

At the prisoners' end of the room, Eugene Buffy was whispering, 'Show doesn't start for fifteen minutes. Just wait – wait until it starts. There's a big opening number, very loud, good cover. OK?'

Fowls nodded. 'OK, but not a moment after. Our transport won't wait.'

They made a show of further relaxation. It would not have been convincing, had anyone been watching. No one was. The SSU control room were looking at pictures from the chapel, checking to see if the fun had begun.

'Saw the Area Manager coming in with me,' Collins was saying. 'Only wearing a neck brace, he was. Remember how Tarzan threw him across the yard?'

'He's being shipped out, Tarzan,' observed Becker, his eyes riveted to the screen as Purdey began inching along an exposed girder two hundred feet from the ground.

By five fifty the inmates were coming into the chapel and filing into their places, martialled by every officer available. The Deputy Governor had made the decision. They'd go curtain up at six with or without Helen. To keep this lot waiting was to invite catcalls, football songs, Mexican waves, if not a riot. And in front of the likes of Andrews and the Board of Visitors, no way! Right now the VIPs were in Hospitality, enjoying a glass of sherry. He would bring them down at five fifty-seven precisely.

He was pleased with the way it was going. Moving the prisoners out of the Wings was the nightmare part. Some stayed behind, sourpusses who didn't want to see the show or strops who weren't allowed to. The Block, of course, stayed where it was, so did the SSU. The rest of the Wings would have men milling around like Calcutta railway station, were it not for the systematic plan he'd worked out with the Wing Governors. The plan was kept to and it worked. The nightmare was unfolding like a dream.

At six o'clock he would go up and make a bloody speech – *her* job, that, but still, he'd manage. Then let the show begin.

The New Avengers finished at six. At the same moment, in the chapel, the opening chords of Miss Purvis's accompaniment struck up. The Gentlemen of Japan cleared their throats.

'Who's got the cards?' said Kilroy. As Dougan produced a new deck, Kilroy cleared newspapers off the officers' table, preparatory to their usual interminable game of Hearts.

Terry Fowls stood up and stretched. 'Well, come on, then. Never mind the rain. Just a quick game.'

The inmates rose, nearly as one man, dispersing casually to the four corners of the room. Each of the stations they took up had been carefully worked out and almost unnoticeably chalk-marked on the carpet. They were all in blind-spots of the surveillance cameras.

Fowls put his hand under his tracksuit, which covered the layer of black clothes beneath. Under them he was wearing woollen long-coms. He felt hot under three layers of clothes, but he knew the underwear was necessary. As likely as not, he'd be spending the night in a ditch. He glanced around to check they were all ready, then produced the gun and in one movement cocked it.

'THIS ISN'T A TOY!' he shouted. 'ONE MOVE FROM ANY OF YOU AND I SHOOT!'

One of the officers laughed before he looked up. Collins did a double-take. At first glance he did not register what was going on but at the second he realized that one of the biggest break-outs in recent prison history could be about to take place.

Fowls was speaking again. 'Hands up and flat on the table.'

It had started raining hard but fitfully. Helen was muttering to herself as she drove the Range Rover along the dual-carriageway to the limits of safety, splashing through the rapidly forming puddles. Why, why, *why* could she not be better organized? She came up behind two trucks, side by side and apparently going at exactly the same speed.

'Come on! Come on!'

She parped the horn and looked at the dashboard clock. It flicked over to 18:01.

The prisoners showed their four hostages to the SSU's control unit cameras and, while making sure they hit no alarm buttons, brought the surveillance officers out of there. The six crestfallen uniformed men were herded into a cell and banged up. Then the escapees stripped off their tracksuits and, except for Eugene Buffy, pulled on black balaclavas and gloves. Buffy, meanwhile, rapidly blacked-up his face and hands with boot polish. His dark blue jeans and black sweater would have to do. He bent to smear blacking onto his white training shoes. They didn't look all that black but it couldn't be helped – he felt good. He felt like Steve McQueen.

Paulso had a pair of bolt-cutters. He ran out ahead of the others into the exercise yard and cut a hole in the fence. It was not alarmed. They crawled through and now they were below the SSU wall. In the hobbies room they had designed and made a metal clamp, which fitted exactly over the plastic overhanging beak at the top of the wall. It was attached to the rope. The first time Howel threw it up, it fell back, failing to bite.

'Come on, come on!' he muttered.

'Eugene,' said Beck, through teeth chattering with tension and adrenaline. 'You know what to do? You're the big man.'

Buffy mimed a machine-gun blast, grinning. 'Yeah, I'm gonna kill the lot of them. That bitch she come near me, she's D – E – A – D.'

Howel threw again and this time was able to yank the rope hard. It held firm.

'Go on! Up! Up!'

The rope was knotted at metre intervals. Paulso with the bolt-cutters went up and over first. They heard the 'Oof!' as he hit the ground on the other side. Next Salim Patel climbed. Buffy was put up after him, still giggling about the mayhem he was going to cause with the shooter.

Standing at the bottom of the rope, Beck whispered to Howel, 'Soon as we get over we shoot that nutter.'

As soon as Paulso touched the high weld-mesh fence, topped by coils of razor wire, which ran round the inside of the massive perimeter wall, the alarm was triggered in Barfield central control. But with all eyes on the chapel monitors, Barfield's own TV show, there was little

302

urgency about the response. There had been incidents of animals, foxes usually, tripping the alarms. So the gate-house was called and an officer wandered out, lazily and protesting, to have a look.

Paulso cut with desperate strength, working like a man possessed. The others lay there panting and cursing him, but he could go no faster. At last he had three sides of a rectangle cut away. He pushed aside the flap and crawled through, beckoning for the wall-clamp and rope, which had been brought from the SSU wall by the last man over.

This time there was no pushing Buffy through ahead of anybody. He went last. First Beck, then Howel, Patel, and, last of all, Fowls followed Paulso through. Fowls got his clothing caught, hooking it up on a jagged piece of wire. As he struggled to get through, he put down the dark implement he was carrying.

Buffy picked it up: it was a sawn-off shotgun. 'Go on, move on. I'm covering you,' he yelled.

There was a shout from somewhere behind them, within the compound. The strolling gate officer had heard his voice.

'You pillock!' said Fowls, freeing himself and snaking through. He was on the right side of the mesh now, but the sawn-off was on the other side, with the pillock.

'Oi! Who's over there?'

The officer's voice echoed damply off the perimeter wall. He was a couple of hundred yards away. Had he seen them yet? And did he have a dog? Fowls didn't wait to find out. In a crouch he ran towards the wall, where the others had slung the rope ladder and were beginning to climb.

Buffy entered the jagged aperture in the mesh, hold-ing the shotgun by the stock. He crawled, but something was impeding him. His woollen sweater was snagged. He struggled. 'Wait for me, you bastards. Wait – for – me!'

He was grunting with effort as he yanked on the fence to free his sweater. At any moment he expected to feel the slimy teeth of a German shepherd burying themselves in his ankle.

Helen was on the last lap. She looked at the clock. Ten minutes late. God! Still, there was plenty of the show left. Entering the slip road which led to the main gate, she remembered she had cried, and thought, Make-up! She stopped the Range Rover and took out a compact, switching on the car's internal light. Out of the corner of her eye she saw, without registering, another vehicle passing along the road beside the perimeter wall. She inspected her face. Not bad, though the light was a little dim. It would have to do. She dabbed a little fresh powder and snapped the compact shut. Somehow she registered that the van had slowed and, oddly, changed direction. She looked. It had moved onto the grass verge underneath the prison wall, about two hundred yards away. She saw its lights go out.

Courting couple? Never been known, not here. Security checks were a possibility leading only to *coitus interruptus*. Helen reached for her mobile phone and, at the same time, slipped the car into reverse.

She suddenly swept the car round and headed along the road towards the parked van. Then her eye looked up and she saw activity on top of the wall: a silhouette, a rope snaking down. She couldn't see what was happening on this side of the wall but obviously men were coming down. She braked to a halt and pushed buttons on her mobile. She was shaking, appalled and unsure what to do. Only after fifteen seconds did she think of killing her headlights.

'Hello, hello, Barfield! This is Helen Hewitt. Sound the alarms. I am outside the north perimeter wall and there is an escape in progress. Sound the bloody alarms, will you? This is Helen Hewitt! The Governor!'

Now, suddenly, she realized the van was moving again, backwards and straight towards her. It picked up speed instantly, the engine screaming in reverse gear as the driver slammed his foot to the floor. On the edge of her vision she noticed yet another silhouette on the crest of the wall.

There had been no dog worrying his ankles when Eugene Buffy freed himself, just the sound of sirens attacking his eardrums. They began with a low croon and gradually built up in pitch and decibels until they peaked as a banshee wail savaging the cool silence of the night. He dragged himself through the hole and pulled the shooter behind him, then ran helter-skelter towards the wall. No one stood at the foot of the wall. One man was at the top. As Buffy ran, he watched the cut-out shadow disappear. Would he pull the ladder up behind? Bastard if he did. Buffy hadn't seen the rope ladder before. Home-made like everything else – rope uprights, wooden steps. It was a bloody miracle what these guys had done in there.

He reached the foot of the wall and the ladder was still there. The sawn-off was equipped with a crude rope sling and he put his head through, hanging the weapon down his back. Then he began to climb, panting like a dog, his sides heaving as he desperately sucked in oxygen.

305

Rung by rung he climbed up, swinging clear of the wall by three or four feet because the ladder was suspended from the overhanging beak. Half-way up he had to stop. He swung and gasped for a moment and then went on. At last he came to the smooth plastic overhang. He hauled himself up.

As he sat astride the wall, a gust of rain lashed his head – the first time he'd noticed it. He looked around, unslinging the shotgun. He was lord of what he surveyed. On the prison side, there were lights and sirens. On the other it was mostly darkness and the grinding of gears. There were two vehicles, a Transit van and another, neither of them showing lights. The van was careering backwards along a wobbling course towards the car, which looked like a Range Rover. He checked that the gun was ready. He said he'd cover them and he would.

The Transit, still on the grass and about twenty yards away from Helen, suddenly changed direction, swinging round through a hundred and eighty degrees until it faced her. She could see the windscreen glinting and heard the van's gearbox screaming furiously as the driver looked for first gear. The van rocked forward and then started moving again. She slammed the Range Rover into first and swung around to block what she assumed would be the escape route but, as it came on, she knew the van was not going to stop or veer, it was going to ram. She waited horror-stricken. She couldn't move. She waited, hearing only the searing screech of the van's engine cutting into her ears.

Then she bundled herself out of the driver's door and ran.

She was running towards the wall when she heard the

van collide with Simon's car: a metallic thump, broken glass. It was followed by the revving of the van's engine, wheels churning the mud, trying to return to the road. But she never turned back to see because now she had looked up towards the top of the wall. A lateral search-light had come on, illuminating the length of it from a gantry. The man on the wall was a black man and he had some kind of a stick in his hand. She ran on towards him. She made out his features. He wasn't as black as he looked, he was blacked-up. He was Eugene Buffy.

'Eugene! Eugene!' she screamed. What she meant by it she didn't know. Don't jump, don't run away. Trust me. Believe in me.

She stood below him now, looking up, dazzled by the lights. Then there was an even fiercer flash of light in front of her eyes. It came from the top of the wall. Something powerful suddenly hit her chest or shoulders. But it did not bring pain, although the ramming feeling was hot, hard and jolting – like an electrical shock. It brought instead the descent of an odd silence, a slow-motion sort of peace.

Somehow, sometime, she hit the ground. She rolled over and saw her own blood seeping onto the tarmac.

'Eugene! Eugene Buffy!'

When they reached her, she was still whispering. 'Eugene! Don't run. Trust me. Trust me. I'm the Governor.'

And when the ambulance came and she was put on a stretcher, her lips were still moving.

All Pan Books are available at your local bookshop or newsagent, or can be ordered direct from the publisher. Indicate the number of copies required and fill in the form below.

Send to: Macmillan General Books C.S.
             Book Service By Post
             PO Box 29, Douglas I-O-M
             IM99 1BQ

or phone: 01624 675137, quoting title, author and credit card number.

or fax: 01624 670923, quoting title, author, and credit card number.

or Internet: http://www.bookpost.co.uk

Please enclose a remittance* to the value of the cover price plus 75 pence per book for post and packing. Overseas customers please allow £1.00 per copy for post and packing.

*Payment may be made in sterling by UK personal cheque, Eurocheque, postal order, sterling draft or international money order, made payable to Book Service By Post.

Alternatively by Access/Visa/MasterCard

Card No.

Expiry Date

Signature _____

Applicable only in the UK and BFPO addresses.

While every effort is made to keep prices low, it is sometimes necessary to increase prices at short notice. Pan Books reserve the right to show on covers and charge new retail prices which may differ from those advertised in the text or elsewhere.

NAME AND ADDRESS IN BLOCK CAPITAL LETTERS PLEASE

Name _____

Address _____

_____

_____

_____

8/95

Please allow 28 days for delivery.
Please tick box if you do not wish to receive any additional information. ☐